branded

scarlett finn

Also by Scarlett Finn

NOTHING TO...
NOTHING TO HIDE
NOTHING TO LOSE
NOTHING IN BETWEEN: ONE
NOTHING TO DECLARE
NOTHING TO US
NOTHING IN BETWEEN: TWO
NOTHING TO SAY
NOTHING TO GAIN
NOTHING IN BETWEEN: THREE
NOTHING TO YOU
NOTHING TO THIS PREQUEL: ONE WILD NIGHT
NOTHING TO THIS
NOTHING IN BETWEEN: FOUR
NOTHING TO DO
NOTHING TO FEAR
NOTHING IN BETWEEN: FIVE
NOTHING TO DENY

GO NOVELS
GO WITH IT
GO IT ALONE
GO ALL OUT
GO ALL IN
GO FULL CIRCLE

KINDRED SERIES
RAVEN
SWALLOW
CUCKOO
SWIFT
FALCON
FINCH

EXILE
HIDE & SEEK
KISS CHASE

THE EXPLICIT SERIES
EXPLICIT INSTRUCTION
EXPLICIT DETAIL
EXPLICIT MEMORY

THE FORBIDDEN NOVELS
FORBIDDEN DESIRE
FORBIDDEN WANT
FORBIDDEN WISH
FORBIDDEN NEED
FORBIDDEN BOND

WRECK & RUIN
RUIN ME
RUIN HIM

MISTAKE DUET
MISTAKE ME NOT
SLEIGHT MISTAKE

THE BRANDED SERIES
BRANDED
SCARRED
MARKED

TO DIE FOR...
TO DIE FOR TRUTH
TO DIE FOR HONOR
TO DIE FOR VIRTUE
TO DIE FOR DUTY
TO DIE FOR LOVE

RISQUÉ & HARROW INTERTWINED
TAKE A RISK
FIGHTING FATE
RISK IT ALL
FIGHTING BACK
GAME OF RISK

FORBIDDEN PREQUEL DUET
ALL. ONLY.
ONLY YOURS

LOVE AGAINST THE ODDS STANDALONE COLLECTION
SWEET SEAS
HEIR'S AFFAIR
RESCUED
MAESTRO'S MUSE
GETTING TRICKY
THIRTEEN
REMEMBER WHEN...
RELUCTANT SUSPICION
XY FACTOR

LOST & FOUND
LOST
FOUND

ONE

AFTER A LONG NIGHT of shaking her ass in Sizzle, Nya Yorke was ready to go home. Her role as manager came with certain demands. Cashing out, locking takings in the safe, that sort of thing. Meant she had to keep her head on straight until the last second of her shift. Even when exhaustion had other ideas.

The muted blue lighting of the vast nightclub was perfect for shady dealings and intimate encounters. Drugs and loud music accompanied partiers in a place where nothing was off-limits. No one batted an eye at the amorous, the lines of white powder cut on the booth tables, or the concealed weapons, some licensed, some not.

The night was over. Strobes were off, music silent. She and Jamie were the only two bar staff left. Three security men did a last sweep. Once the place was confirmed secure, they'd lock up and get out of there.

"Anything else you need me to do?" Jamie asked, flopping her arms on the bar from the patrons' side.

The cute blonde with the pixie cut drew plenty of attention with her bubbly personality. Most people who worked, or frequented, Sizzle were jaded, cynical, in need of oblivion. Jamie was none of those things. The youth smiled with ease, she laughed, and could turn anything into a positive. Men loved her because she exuded corruptible innocence. Nya had nothing against her colleague, sure, her optimism could be grating, but she was a good worker. No argument about that.

If they were in a better neighborhood, she'd have sent Jamie home already. At three thirty in the morning, no one was safe on these streets. After herding customers out, the rest of the staff were sent home in couples and groups. Leaving alone would be asking for trouble.

Jamie stayed draped over the bar, awaiting instructions. Nya had none.

"No, I'm finished," she said. "Tell the guys we're done."

Jamie walked away, presumably to head for the breakroom accessible on the opposite wall by a door marked, 'Employees Only.' Containing a few couches and a stained beanbag, none of the lockers worked, but it gave the others a place to stash their things on shift. Not her. She didn't leave anything anywhere she couldn't see it.

Nya ducked to get her purse from a secret corner of the lowest shelf under the bar. She didn't have anything valuable in her long-strap, leather slouch bag, and there were no more than a few bucks in her wallet. Defending her privacy was the aim; her purse was sort of a symbol of how much that meant to her.

Instead of going to the breakroom, Jamie went toward the corridor that bottlenecked the entrance. To relay the message to the bouncers? To make her way out? Whatever her intention, before she got there, a shout and a scuffle reverberated from that passage, echoing in the cavernous club.

Nya surged to her feet in time to see five masked men burst in. The first grabbed a screaming Jamie and pulled her to his chest, trapping her wrists in his hand between her breasts. Shuffling forward, allowing his cohorts to swarm in behind him, the assailant raised the mass of a silenced gun barrel to Jamie's temple.

Her colleague's screaming drowned out the men's shouted conversation. The one holding Jamie clamped a hand over her mouth to stifle her panicked shrieks.

Being the only other one there, all spare guns were pointed at her. On instinct, Nya raised her hands in surrender. Her duties didn't extend to giving up her life to tweakers.

"In there, go!" the hostage-holder ordered Nya into the breakroom.

With weapons waving at her, she kept her hands up and emerged from the bar to do as directed. Sizzle wasn't worth dying for. She didn't benefit from the takings beyond her wage. If these guys wanted a windfall, she'd open the safe, but they'd regret it. The club owner wouldn't take kindly to being robbed by disorganized chancers like these guys.

Wearing ski masks and carrying guns, their frantic movements suggested they weren't honed professionals.

Swept into the circle of invaders, they squeezed through the breakroom door, two in front, three behind.

Before the door closed, one of them grabbed her. Struggling to get loose, she was rushed to the furthest wall and thrown against it, pinned by two men. The lump of her purse shielded her when the one in front tried to grind his hips closer. Oh, shit, that was a whole different ballgame. Would she fight for money? No. Her dignity? Damn, fucking, right. She'd rather die.

Trying to lash out, she pushed and kicked. These guys were bigger, her strength didn't match their capabilities. Long ago she'd learned her petite figure didn't physically match many people. Despite self-defense classes, her might was pathetic.

Jamie was screaming again, if she'd ever stopped. The gut-wrenching sound of terror was unsettling, but at least it betrayed the woman was still alive. Shaking her hair away from her face, Nya stopped fighting to look beyond her attackers. Their tight hands bruised her limbs, their body weight restricted her breathing, but ignoring them, she sought Jamie.

Checking her colleague was meant to be reassuring, to give her a focus. It did the opposite. Jamie was thrust onto the couch and felt up by two men. The last man was at her ankles, pulling them apart, rubbing his way up her legs, giving his friend access to wrench up Jamie's skirt.

"Hey! Leave her alone!" Nya exclaimed, forgetting her own problems.

The hip grinding was an unwelcome reminder. She tried to push away from the wall but was slammed back against it. Winded, she struggled for breath as one guy shook her with brutal force.

"You'll get yours once you tell me where he is," a grotesque molester snarled in her face.

Any lingering illusion this was a simple robbery was quickly erased. The hands on her breasts had to belong to the second man, because the first still grasped her shoulders. Switching into survival mode, she closed her mind to the assault. Just like old times.

"Who?" Nya asked. "Who are you talking about?"

Jamie kept screaming and kicked out at the man on top of her. Yes, fight. Fight with every fucking ounce of strength. She smiled, maybe that girl wasn't so innocent and harmless after all.

Payback came quickly. They wrestled her onto the floor. One man kneeled over Jamie, punching her face and chest while another grasped his groin, swearing in pain. Good girl, Jamie, she'd hurt the bastard. Judging by his watering eyes and red face, it was a damn good shot too.

The third wasn't amused or deterred, he scrambled up the floor between Jamie's legs and thrust his arm in a stabbing motion at the apex of Jamie's thighs. His fingers, at least, would be inside her; those manic movements would be agonizing for the kid.

The screaming stopped and the puncher climbed off Jamie to stand up and wipe sweat from his upper lip. He bent down to rip Jamie's top from her body, exposing her, to use the fabric as a cloth to wipe blood from his hands and face.

Concern iced Nya's gut, Jamie's head flopped one way, then the other. Please stay. Please don't give in. Was there still life in the woman? The groin-clutcher snatched his friend from between Jamie's thighs and tossed him aside. No loyalty between thieves. He kicked Jamie between her legs and yanked open his jeans, pulling his dick out before dropping to the floor to lie over the unconscious woman.

Each of his violent thrusts pushed bile from Nya's stomach. Ominous red bubbles foamed at Jamie's mouth. They could be breaths; please be breaths. There were no other signs of life. Jamie wasn't conscious or moving, she couldn't be, not after the assault of blows to the head rained upon her.

The other two men jeered as the third raped the lifeless woman on the floor.

She'd be next.

"Like the show?" A swift slap brought her focus to the thug restraining her. Propping an elbow on the wall over her shoulder, the guy clearly wanted to watch what was going on with Jamie. But he couldn't suspend the interrogation all night, so got in her face again. "Tell us where he is!"

"Who!" Nya screamed, tormented by the torture of her friend and the prospect of her own fate. "Who do you want!"

"Taggert!" he demanded, spittle and halitosis triggered her gag reflex. "You know! You know where he is! Tell me!"

The one answer she couldn't give. Wouldn't give. Jamie was enduring a second man on top of her. A whimper granted her a kick to the head, and the young woman went quiet again.

"I don't," Nya said, provoking their already hot anger. "I don't know where he is!"

Two more masked men burst in, drawing the concerned attention of everyone except the perp on top of Jamie still pumping hard and fast, grunting with each invasion.

"He's not here," one of the new men said without blinking an eye at the ongoing assault.

The man with a hold of her was in charge; the two new entrants awaited his instruction. While he was distracted, she assessed Jamie's chances. While being fucked by one man, the next guy waited his turn. The other, who'd been the first to take his shot on top, spat in Jamie's mouth then kneeled over her to force his dick between her lips.

Jamie wasn't moving, her face was a bloody mess, eyes swollen, but when he pushed in hard, his victim's body heaved and choked. She was still alive, for now, though after enduring this horror, she may wish she wasn't.

The one standing, waiting for a chance to have his fun, unbuckled his belt in anticipation. Sick. He was excited by the prospect of assaulting a defenseless woman only a fraction more responsive than a corpse.

Her attacker grabbed her chin, compelling her to look at him. "You'll get your fun, soon as you tell me where he is."

Hardly an incentive for honesty. Eagerness wasn't her reason for watching. If the point was to scare her with the spectacle, it was working. Not that she'd show him. Fear burned inside her, fueled by the heat of anger.

"When he finds you, he'll kill you," Nya snarled. "Do you have any idea who you're dealing with?"

"We know it and we want him. He doesn't scare us."

Either this guy was ignorant or had an army larger than the one present. If he wanted to take on Taggert, he'd need one.

"He should scare you," Nya said. "He'll torture you and your men for weeks. He'll make you suffer before he kills you. No one crosses Taggert."

"A lot of spunk for such a little thing," he said, pulling his gun from his waistband to step back and press the circle of the barrel to the center of her forehead, rendering her immobile.

Closing her eyes, she waited for the shot. Terror receded to an odd peace that shattered when someone ripped open her shirt. Flattening her palms on the wall at either side, she could do nothing but let this second guy fondle and grope. The weight of the gun heated as it dug deeper, trapping her head between it and the wall.

Opening her eyes, Nya burned her fury into the perverse smile of her jailer. Two men closed in behind him. After feeling her up, one crouched to drag up her skirt.

These were the two new men; the other three had to be with Jamie. The barrel bruised her forehead, fixing her in place, so she couldn't check.

"Pretty girl like you could show my boys a good time; would that persuade you?" the gun-bearer asked.

Narrowing her gaze in defiance of the invading hands

roaming her body, no way would she express how their violation curdled her blood. It would only spur them on.

"Tell us what we want to know and we'll leave you alone."

She didn't believe him but wouldn't answer even if she did. The door opened again. Holding her breath, she couldn't see through the mass of men. What had arrived? Salvation or sadism?

What was next? More men? More weapons?

"You fuck everything up, Jonno."

The hands left her body when the men whipped around. All of them. Clearly in shock. Even the gun at her head fell away as the man holding it turned to gape at the new voice.

Just inside was a dark-haired, scruffy-faced brute. Whoever he was, he didn't wear a mask like the others. His hands hung loose at his sides, carrying no weapons, no care in the world. The three men on Jamie hadn't been disturbed by anything. Until this. Until him. Now there was no movement in her peripheral vision; the noise of their jeering and grunting ceased too.

"Fuck off, Archer, we got this."

The gun was pushed into her ribs until the pressure became pain.

"That her?" the new guy, apparently called Archer, asked.

Archer swaggered up to them. One slow step followed another, like a guy sauntering to a bar for a drink, not one who'd walked in on this abomination of a crime. He kept on coming until he was hanging over Jonno, the one holding the gun.

The newest guy was much taller than the one threatening her. Maybe, what? Six four. Shit, had she thought her strength was pathetic before? His broad shoulders weren't bulky, but there was a strength in them, a tension that roiled her insides.

Tapered brown eyes met hers for half a second, then dropped to her exposed breasts. "Copping a feel more important than getting the job done, Jonno?"

Lunging past Jonno, Archer snatched her forearm to haul her through the gang. The pain of his locked grip yanked her a few feet until Jonno grabbed her other arm to tug her back. Or try to anyway. The other men approached.

"You're not taking her," Jonno snapped. "Not until we know."

Jonno and his buddies had manhandled her, dangled threats of violence and rape to scare her. They'd worked too, though she did her best to conceal the revulsion. Without physical strength, she'd learned to project confidence. Being fearless, facing adversity head on, was the only way to get through life intact.

The guy trying to steal her from the crime scene remained aloof; he didn't bat an eye at Jonno's fierce attitude.

"Has she told you yet?" Archer asked.

The two men growled at each other, sneering and snarling, this was the proverbial circling of the prey. Being right in the middle, if one chose to attack, she'd be caught in the crossfire.

Some of Jonno's bluster deflated. "We were getting there."

"Sure you were," Archer said. While fixated on Jonno, assessing his reaction to Archer's nonchalance, her nipple was flicked through her bra by the latter's rigid fingertip. Gasping, she jerked away, but neither man let go. "You had your chance, Jonno, now it's my turn."

He jolted her again, Jonno countered. Archer's chin hitched and his eyes ascended. Ha, this Jonno guy was testing his patience.

"She stays with us," Jonno asserted.

Archer crowded in close to Jonno, her the meat in their distressing sandwich. "You left those fucking bodies lying in the street," he growled. "Tick, tock, little man, how long you got 'til the cops show up?" As if on cue, sirens wailed in the distance, tensing the men. "This bitch is our one link, our one lead, who'll get what we need? You or me?"

That was enough of a prompt. For some reason, Archer's question clinched Jonno's decision. The men shared another brief glare, then Jonno released her and stepped back, hands up. The others retreated as the sirens got louder.

Without waiting, Archer hauled her toward the door. She dropped her weight, pulling back, desperate to delay him. If the cops arrived before he could get her out of there… She had to—if she could just… Fuck, nothing worked, he wasn't slowed down.

Picking her up with one swoop of his arm, he tossed her over his shoulder and clamped a hand on her ass. The other pinned her legs to his torso to prevent her kicking.

Resorting to using her core, she tried to buck away and punched at his back. But he didn't slow down, didn't flinch, just kept shrugging her up to the powerful shoulders she'd been right not to underestimate.

His athletic body had strength from the tips of his hair to the depth of his bones. He carried her out of Sizzle's front entrance, over the bodies of the security guards dead in the street just as he'd described.

"Stop! Please! Help!" she called at the top of her lungs.

"Hush," Archer said and paused.

Just when she thought he might put her down and give her the chance to run, she heard a click then was tossed on her ass. Bouncing in a hard landing, she hit the back of her head on something cold and solid. Blinking through a daze, it was… a car trunk, he'd dumped her in a—he covered her mouth with a length of tough duct tape.

Hooking his hands on the edge of the trunk, he leaned down. The sirens were blaring, but she saw no lights.

"Don't be naughty, Squirm. Obey and we'll get along great."

Chucking her chin with the swipe of a knuckle, he winked, stepped back, and slammed the lid on her.

TWO

THE CONFINED SPACE got hotter with every rotation of the wheels. Bumping along at what felt like an insane pace, she was shaken and tossed, left and right. Without knowing if she'd be thrust up, down, this way, or that, it was impossible to anticipate the direction of the next knock. Battered and beat whenever they turned corners and hit potholes, she banged up her arms and legs trying to brace.

Being enclosed threw off her sense of time. Claustrophobia distracted her awareness of speed and distance. How far were they from the club? If she got a chance, would she know which way to run?

Her joints were stiff, skin bruised, and her head pounded. No, forget injuries and self-pity. Staying alive would take everything. Keeping her wits would be tough but essential. Though… after witnessing what Jamie went through, did she want to make it out the other side?

Jamie. The girl was younger than her, not a lifetime younger, sure, but had so much life left. And what kind of life would that be? The light in the beauty's pure soul would dim after suffering through that night, and there would be no igniting it again.

Nya knew that too well.

Her body was hurled toward the front of the car in time with the screech of brakes. Dazed, she missed the engine turning off and the driver's door closing. The trunk lid popped and she was grabbed and tossed over his shoulder again.

Bouncing upside down in darkness, all she could see was asphalt, glowing under the artificial flare of an occasional streetlight. He turned sharply to the left, bounded up one stair and pushed through a communal door.

Urine, dirt, and body odor poisoned the air. Glimpses to each side showed graffiti and grime covering the water-stained walls. He ascended stairs, squeezing her ass to keep her secure as he cleared them two or three at a time.

Fuck, get with it. Wits. Right. Wits. If he got her in one of the apartments in this dilapidated block, she'd never come out again. Using his back, she rubbed the tape from her mouth, working it off into a tight flap. Breathing became easier, shouting was still aways off.

Her struggle provoked the span of his large hand to spread and close, squeezing her flesh. The molesting action enflamed hatred in her belly. How dare he touch her? How dare he use his strength against her, against any woman.

Just as she almost snatched the banister, he walked away from the stairs down a hallway.

One arm loosened and he dug a hand beneath her to pull keys from his pocket. A chance. When he let her go to put the key in the lock, she kicked out on the wall, using everything she had, forcing him to stumble. He didn't go far, his grip loosened just enough to let her flail.

Falling to the floor on her face, she landed on her hands and shoved up, scrambling in the direction of the stairs.

A strong arm hooked around her belly, hoisting her from the floor. Still fighting, despite the taste of futility, she opened her mouth in a desperate screeching howl. He flung her into a wall, smashing her into it so hard that light flashed across her vision. She choked for breath, unable to suck air into her aching, shocked lungs.

A heavy form crashed into hers; she clawed, fighting to free her smothered body. Metallic jangling sounded. The keys. He was unlocking the door.

After being shunted down the wall, she was propelled forward and fell into an apartment. A rug caught her foot. Before she could fall, he grabbed her again, half-carrying, half-dragging her to the back wall and down a short, dark corridor.

When he threw her into another room, she came up hard against a sink. The door was slammed; she whipped around. He was gone.

Alone, she searched for escape. No windows. Only a narrow vent not big enough for a cat. A bathtub ran the width of the wall opposite the door, fixed shower over it, and a mildew-stained shower curtain.

No sign of a weapon.

The door opened and there he was again, all bulk and menace. He hauled her forward, forcing her onto the floor, squashing her down into a tiny space.

Contorting her leg, he coiled a cold, hard chain around the narrowest part of her ankle and clamped a padlock in the links. Tugging, resisting, struggling did nothing, he hung over her to work, fastening her wrist to her ankle with a handcuff. With the sink to her left, bathtub to the right and the toilet opposite, there was no route to run.

After fastening the chain to the pipe running from behind the sink to under the bathtub, he stroked her from ankle to thigh as he rose to full height. Without pausing to examine or question her, he went to the door like… nothing.

"Wait," she called. Why would he bring her there and not attack or interrogate her? "What's happening? Where are you going?"

"Bed," he replied and came to press a new length of tape to her mouth. Reversing his course, he stepped out, slamming the door in his wake.

***

THE BATHTUB FAUCET dripped all night and he'd left the overhead light on. Sleep was impossible in the awkward corner. Listening to the plop, drip, splash, plop, drip, splash in its irregular rhythm all night drove her insane.

Nodding off in short bursts, she rested her head on

the edge of the tub only to be frequently awoken by the acidic scent of citrus. The sink pedestal was cold and the basin hung over her head. The floor around the toilet looked clean, but there was no way she'd put her head there.

Discovering anything about her keeper could give her a foothold in finding a way out. From looking around, all she could deduce was he brushed with whitening toothpaste and used bar soap. Magazines on the back of the toilet were related to weapons and survivalism. Okay, so she didn't recognize the titles, but it was a surprise to see something other than tittie mags or Anarchist Monthly.

Whoever this Archer was, he wasn't concerned about being caught holding her hostage. Carrying her over his shoulder in the street and through the hallway of the building showed confidence. He didn't blink at her protests and didn't exude any signs of anxiety about being spotted manhandling a woman.

Unless someone had done this before, it would be unlikely they'd have chains and padlocks lying around. Attaching her to the pipe seemed practiced. This was no rookie. He hadn't had to think about where to take her or how to restrain her, he'd done it on autopilot.

Who could he be? Motive, reason, what drove him? Why restrain her?

Time grew arduous. Or maybe the predicament dragged out the seconds. Hours passed that felt like days, maybe weeks, or months.

God, she was losing her mind.

When the door next opened, she was hanging off the edge of the tub. Startled, she gasped and plastered herself to the wall beneath the basin, tucking her head into her neck.

Her captor didn't look at her. Wearing only his boxers, she was stunned by the definition of his tanned physique. Athletic, muscular and ready, the sinews in his ribs moved when he raised an arm, adorned with a full-sleeve black tribal tattoo, to scratch the back of his head.

The ridges on his belly were next on his scratch list as he lumbered over, yawning, and lifted the lid and seat of the toilet. Her mouth fell open when he landed a hand on the wall and, with his back to her, peed like she wasn't there to witness it.

Closing her eyes wasn't enough. Why, oh, why couldn't she close her ears too? At least sound signaled when he was finished. Dropping the seat, but not the lid, he flushed, yawned again and padded out, slamming the door as he had the previous night.

THREE

STILL UNDER THE TORTUROUS light, her vision was blurring from lack of sleep or sustenance or something. Cold and uncomfortable, access to the toilet and water in the sink were the sum of her optimism. That was it. The beacons of hope. A piss pot and hydration. Wasn't life just dandy.

Throughout the day, she'd picked the duct tape from her mouth. Taking her time, so as not to cause pain, an angry red stamp across her face was unavoidable. She didn't care. Breathing freely again was some kind of progress.

Next time he came in, Archer pulled the cord to turn off the light and stayed in the doorway. Nothing but blackness shone behind him. It was night again, but in the bitter winter, the light faded early. It could be evening or the dead of night, there was no way to tell.

"What's the plan?"

She couldn't take the silence. Her voice was a deep, alien croak; probably because the last time she used it was to scream for her life.

A night of sleep hadn't softened his attitude. "I know how to make you cry. I can make you beg. I can cause you all kinds of pain." Maybe she shouldn't have asked. "But I don't wanna. Do yourself a favor, Squirm. Cut your losses. You put up a good fight. Just tell me where he is and I'll let you go. No hard feelings."

Tag. This Archer might find it simple enough to betray a friend, her outlook was different.

"No," she said. "I can't tell you what I don't know."

A deep nasal inhale suggested calm impatience. "Your call."

When he walked off, the door stayed open. Anticipating more from her captor, she squinted, crawling as close to the door as possible, listening for hints as to what he was doing. Metal rattled like a cutlery drawer was being rifled through. Wooden legs scraped on a hard floor. A few moments of nothing, then there was a flare of light and a zippo clicked shut. Light glowed from beyond.

A minute later, he returned. Stepping over her like she was a cast aside toy, he loosened the chain and dragged her away from the wall. She struggled, not that it made much difference with the chain attached to her. The handcuff locking one of her wrists to her ankle still hindered too, making it impossible to stand or run.

Her attempts to resist didn't slow him down. He picked her up under his arm and carried her into the body of the apartment. Open-plan kitchen and living room, the sparse furniture was hardly visible in the night. The windows were blacked out, barring entry to even a slither of light.

One candle flickered in the middle of an otherwise bare table. He dumped her in a chair then crouched to lock her chain onto a huge, thick eyebolt driven into the solid floor. Pulling and tugging didn't budge it an inch.

Archer spun the perpendicular chair on a leg, flipping it around to straddle it and wrap his arms around the back. With her ankle and wrist connected, she remained in a half-crouch. Her chin almost rested on the wood, not the most dignified position.

Already pissed she'd been forced to spend the night on his bathroom floor, she was in no mood to be intimidated. Anger wouldn't get her anywhere, and she couldn't relax. Everything this guy had done suggested he meant to do her harm. She'd protect Tag's life with hers, if necessary, although she'd rather not die at the mercy of an unforgiving stranger. Especially since Tag would probably face a similar fate when this Archer caught up with him.

This could be an opportunity for answers. How had she ended up there? What was motivating this guy? And the most pertinent question…

"What do you want with Tag?"

"You think I'm gonna kill him?" he asked, tipping his chair onto two legs to swipe a large roll of leather from the breakfast bar behind him.

Gasping in resented, panting breaths, fear had to be subdued. "Are you?"

Untying a strip from around the leather roll, he laid it out flat at the other end of the table. Inside the pouch, the glint of sharpened blades in all shapes and sizes shimmered in candlelight.

"Give me his location," Archer said, unnervingly calm.

"Tell me why you want it."

Carefully, he slid one wooden-handled blade from the sheath. Inhaling as each inch slid out, speculation about his plans flared her horror again.

Rising from his chair to reach her arm, he wrenched it over the table. She swore and pulled back, but his strength was too much, fuck, fuck—her muscles burned, and his grip only grew tighter until she gave in. Shit. The victor, his fingers remained locked around her wrist while his forearm pressed her hand flat on the surface.

Holding up the knife, he turned it above the flame, admiring the blade. "This is a spear point," he said, lowering the metal apex into the fire of the candle. "It's beautiful, isn't it? The tip's just perfect for piercing skin soft as butter like yours." Her heartbeat kicked up. "I sharpen them every day, keep them ready."

"Ready for what?"

Oh, why the fuck did she ask?

The wry almost-not smile that thinned his lips wasn't reassuring. Neither was his non-answer to her question. He wanted direct answers but avoided her questions without guilt.

This ice-cold, composed guy was definitely a pro.

"This was a gift from a very good friend."

Did a man like this have friends? Turning the tip in the candle, he heated an inch, rotating the handle to coat the end in heat until it almost glowed.

Transfixed by the metal in the fire, she didn't register him twisting her hand until his palm pressured hers. In a slick move, he pulled the blade from the flame and forced it flat against the tender flesh on the inside of her wrist.

Screaming at the searing agony until her lungs were empty did nothing to temper the pain. The sickening scent of her own skin cooking contorted her guts until she wretched.

Kicking and shouting, she fought to get away, but couldn't retreat.

He held her firm without breaking a sweat.

"Please! Stop! No!"

Her words didn't reach him. Her screeching and yanking failed to get through. When he did release the pressure, she whipped her hand away, holding it to her chest. The pain scorched through to her heart.

Tears soaked her cheeks. Cradling the injury, she turned her forehead to the table and sobbed.

"That's what I call the warmup," he whispered into the back of her bowed head.

She couldn't look up. Pain permeated, pulsing from her injured limb until it reached the other. Numbness collided with agony; heat bled from every fizzing, electrified pore. Was she dead? Dying? Whichever it was, she wanted the hurt to be over.

"Ready to talk?"

Taking half a dozen deliberate breaths, she rolled her head, keeping her cheek on the table. "Why not kill me?"

He wasn't at the table. At that moment, he leaned against the sink, one ankle crossed over the other, a glass of water at his lips. When he finished gulping, he put the glass by the sink and sauntered back.

"No result and no fun."

"Fun!" she wailed. "Do you think this is fun?"

Sinking astride his chair as he had before, he opened

his hand. "Give me your arm."

Yeah, right, like she was stupid enough to hand herself over. She wouldn't do it; she wouldn't make this torture easier for him. In defiance, she closed her lips tight. The pain was excruciating, but she'd endure it if it saved her friend even for a single day.

With a scowl, he lunged over to wrestle for control of her injured arm and slammed it onto the table.

"No. No!"

Jolting her forward, he squashed her breasts to the blunt angle of the table edge to get her arm as close to him as possible.

As she prepared for more hurt, he grazed a thumb over the wound in a tender gesture rather than a vicious one. What was he…? The perimeter of the pointed injury was an angry, bloody mess, suggesting the edges of the knife had pierced her but been cauterized by the heat.

Within the bowed triangle brand were two unaffected shapes and it was those shapes he traced with a fingertip. The intrigue and pride on his face appalled her. He wasn't examining it out of concern, he was admiring his handiwork, impressed by his own despicable act.

His grip was loose enough that she could snatch her arm away.

He let her take it. "It's clean," he said, resting his arms on the chair back again.

The inflamed flesh would bear his mark from then until forever. Peering closer, she tried to decipher the shapes on her skin that almost looked like connected letters, C and Λ.

She kept her wrist straight to avoid aggravating the wound. "What is this?"

"What's next, Squirm?" He relaxed as he selected a new blade from the flattened roll. "Do you like the smell of blood?"

His appetite for torture hadn't been satisfied by the flame?

"Wha…? What?"

Grabbing her hair, he jerked her head back, urging

the point of his new dagger under her jaw. "It's intoxicating," he growled. "Thick and rich, sexy when it coats the smooth steel."

Holding her breath, she waited for the cut… that didn't come. He trailed the metal down her shoulder, rising as he did, letting go of her hair, giving her command of holding herself away from the blade. It didn't hurt, it was strange, the threat, the almost—he yanked her chair out from under her, sending her to the floor with a thud.

Was he trying to humiliate her? Punish her? What the fuck did bruises matter? The pain in her wrist trumped everything else. Curling into the fetal position, she waited until his shadow blocked the candlelight before confessing the truth.

"Beat me." She coughed. "Cut me. Burn me. Rape me. It won't change a thing, Archer."

Use his name, remind him of his humanity. Her only hope was to change his mind, divert him, from hurting her. She wouldn't cave, that left one avenue: breaking through his tough, detached exterior.

"What did he do to earn your loyalty?"

Rocking until she could see him crouched beside her, knife still in his sure grip, the curiosity in his expression outweighed the anger. Her hysterical smile almost became a laugh, but she didn't have the energy to muster it.

"You'll never know," she said. "Even if you did, you'd never understand."

Archer, a mystery, and a thief, had plucked her from her life to demand she betray her oldest ally. It wouldn't happen. Never. He was under the illusion there was some kind of choice here, that it was within her power. It wasn't. There was no choice.

Expecting further interrogation and torture, she steeled herself when he grazed his knife against her cheek to move her hair away. She shivered against the cool metal, but there was no pain.

"We've got plenty of time, Squirm," he murmured. "You need to get used to wearing my mark."

Unfastening her from the bolt driven into the floor,

he seized her arm and hauled her back to the bathroom, attaching the chain to the pipe again.

"I'll leave off the tape," he said. "If you get any ideas about screaming, forget it, you'll piss me off. Around here, nobody gives a fuck."

As if on cue, a distant argument became a feminine scream. Archer shrugged as he turned and walked out, leaving her with the light and the dripping faucet.

Like she had to be told. She'd grown up in worse places. No one cared about domestic violence, crime, or any woman in need, anyone in need.

In the cramped internal room, she couldn't hear vehicles or foot traffic. How many floors had they ascended? Damnit, she hadn't counted. How far above street level were they? Muffled arguments and bangs were more distant than the barking dog that often became frantic about nothing.

Adrenaline and exhaustion weighed her body. She slid down the wall, her spine cooling as it pressed to the bathtub panel. In a final surrender, her head dropped to the floor. Citrus buzzed her senses, but it wasn't enough to wake her anymore, this time slumber stole her.

FOUR

PLOP, DRIP, SPLASH. Gazing up at the cracked ceiling, arm in her cleavage, the blistering wound ached and itched. Ignore it. Just ignore it. With few distractions, that wasn't an easy ask.

When the bathroom door opened again, she didn't flinch. If he wanted her, he'd grab her.

"Give me an address."

Licking her lips, she moved her tongue to moisten her mouth, delaying her answer. "One, two, three, Bite Me Street."

"Play your games, girl. You've got plenty more skin for me to burn." That wasn't an experience she wanted to repeat. "Give me an address."

She didn't have the energy to sass him. "I can't. Even if I could, Tag wouldn't let you in."

"I'll worry about that. Give me an address."

"No," she said, closing her eyes.

A loud thwack by her ear startled her adrenaline. A knife was embedded in the floor, an inch from where her head had been. Stuttering at the sight, she experienced something positive, for the first time since she got there: relief he was a bad aim.

Negativity returned fast when he came to hunker

down. Pulling the knife from the floor, he stuck it in a horizontal sheath on the back of his belt then put a long metal tin on the closed toilet lid.

Transfixed, her eyelids were frozen wide apart when he popped it open. Inside? An empty syringe and an unmarked glass bottle. Panic erased lethargy in a heartbeat.

"No!" she said. "What is that?"

He pulled the plastic cap off a needle with his teeth and spat it away as he upended the bottle to fill the syringe. "Just a little prick, Squirm."

Fuck, she resented his strength. Despite her desperate thudding need for survival, when he snatched her injured arm, as usual, her resistance didn't divert him.

"No! No. No! Please!"

The pinch of the needle made her wince, but there was no getting away from it. Anything could be in there, opioids, poison, a sedative. She could wake up naked under anyone and there wouldn't be a damn thing she could do to defend herself.

Too soon, heaviness held her; a moment later, she slumped.

***

COLD. Freezing cold. Under the stuttering urgency of shock, her mouth opened, freezing water cascaded into her choking lungs. Blinking webbed lashes, she couldn't focus, couldn't think—her arms burned, she spat and sputtered out the water flowing over her face. Her arms, her shoulders strained, blazed but—the sink, there, and the chain… She hadn't gone far.

Still in the bathroom, in Archer's bathroom… on her feet in the bathtub, teetering on the end of her toes, barely able to stand. All her weight hung from her bound wrists stretched far above, tethered to the solid steel shower curtain rail, more secure than any she'd known.

Freezing water from the showerhead surged through her hair; the intense, piercing pressure stung her scalp.

"Why?" she chittered, her whole body going into cold

shock. "Why are you doing this?"

When her vision cleared enough to pick out details, her captor came into view, sitting on the floor against the closed bathroom door, his long legs laid out toward her. With a knife in hand and a metal stick in the other, he slowly sharpened the blade.

"Your loyalty got me thinking," he said, deliberately dragging the blade in long, thorough strokes against the sharpener. If the scraping was meant to intimidate, it failed. She couldn't process anything beyond the throbbing headache akin to the worst brain freeze ever. "If you're this wild about him, he's gotta feel the same about you."

The chill slowed her thoughts. "Wha…? What?"

"Your boy owes me money. A lot of money. I've been chasing him down for months. Now I figure, why waste the time looking for him when his girl can work off the debt?"

Casting aside the knife and sharpener, he pounced to his feet and came to turn off the shower.

Spitting cold water and matted hair from her mouth, she couldn't see him properly, not until he picked up hunks of her sopping locks. Peeling them from her face, he draped them over her crown; they slid down in soaked slices to the back of her shoulder.

"You've got a pretty face. Those big doe eyes guys love to see tear up when they fuck you deep. If you cry, they'll pay extra. I know some real sick fucks who'll pay top dollar to break you. Beg 'em for mercy and you'll clear Tag's debt quick."

Since Jonno's buddy ripped the buttons from her shirt to fondle and violate her, it had never been fastened again. Bra saturated, her breasts ached and tingled, stimulated in the new temperature. Discomfort she could endure, including the constricting cling of her skirt, if the alternative meant parting with the clothes.

Shivering, the chattering of her teeth got worse. "I'm not a whore," she said, fumbling her words through purple lips.

He leaned in, resting a hand on her shoulder. Although repulsive, his touch was warm; her body craved the sensation awakened beneath his heated palm.

"You will be for me," he growled. "You will be until I have every cent your boy owes me."

Most men would take advantage of an enemy's woman before pimping them out… unless that was the way he made his money.

"Why not take it from my body yourself?"

The question didn't come out right.

It sure hadn't been an offer. Though the brute was attractive, she didn't want him touching her, didn't want to be anywhere near his bed. Far from it. Except experience taught her one maniac at a time was better than several.

Drawing back, his head tilted. For a second, she saw astonishment like he hadn't considered that an option. As he checked her out, she squirmed under his scrutiny. In this enclosed space, with her sopping clothes clinging to her skin, he'd be able to make out every detail of her figure.

It didn't take him long to reach a decision. "You wanna fuck? We do it for fun. You've got no worth to me unless I turn you out. You're a commodity to exploit. That's it."

She'd seen the kind of men he associated with and what they'd done to Jamie. In a flash of anger, she reared back and thrust forward, spitting out at him with everything she had. She wasn't a product, and the idea of sleeping with him for fun disgusted her.

Wiping the spittle from his face, he sneered at her breasts and leaned past her again. She shrieked when the cold water dribbled down her spine and braced for the same gush that assaulted her before. Instead of turning it up, he left it on that slow, dripping ooze.

Icy water hit her back, trickled into the valley of her spine and over the rise of her ass.

And he wasn't done. Tearing her cuff with one efficient tug, he ripped the shirt from her body to toss it away.

Grabbing the sides of her neck with both hands, he yanked her forward. "You're not a whore, but you'll fuck around on your guy?" he snarled. "You bitches are all the same."

His reaction suggested he'd been hurt before and had a hatred of women. Though he hadn't abused Jamie like the others, that was little reassurance given the sequence of events. By the time he'd got to Sizzle, the cops' arrival had been imminent. If he was any kind of smart, avoiding arrest would take precedence over getting his ya-yas with a comatose woman.

The cold water tickled as it tormented.

"I'm not Tag's woman," she said, drawing in a quivering breath. "We're not together, never have been."

Tightening both palms around her neck, he came closer. "Then why the fuck does everyone say you're the way to get to him?"

"Because. He's protected me since I was fourteen."

The trauma of physical injury, sleep deprivation, and a lack of nourishment were taking their toll. She never spoke of Tag, never to anyone. Privacy was her keystone, sharing went against the fiber that constructed her every cell. And there she was telling the truth.

Her relationship with Tag was more complicated than simple sex. Treasuring him came from within her; he'd saved her life. Since then, he'd guided her, always been around for her, and held her up.

"Why?" he asked.

Shaking her head, she vibrated, gooseflesh raised every hair.

"Sell me to your friends. I'll work until you have every penny owed, but he'll come for you. You think this is torture? Tag will let what's left of me watch as he takes you apart one inch at a time."

Bowing, he touched his mouth to the corner of hers. "I look forward to it, Squirm."

Leaving the water on her back, her arms elevated, and the light on, he stormed out, taking his weapon with him before slamming the door.

FIVE

AT SOME POINT in the night, he'd come and unhooked her from her hanging tether to put her on the floor again. She'd been somewhere between awake and asleep, between consciousness and oblivion. Details eluded her.

What had to be hours later, liquid dripped on her face, bringing her into reality. Blinking in response to the water blurring her vision, it took time to focus. The bathroom floor. Chained to the pipe in her original position. This was her life now. The drips dropped from the man standing over her, but she couldn't concentrate so closed her eyes.

Something nudged her a minute later. A foot; a toe prodded her.

"Are you dead?" he asked, giving her another jolt. "Where's all that action you gave me last night? Come on, little Squirmer. Time to wake up and fight with me."

Groggy, she could hear the words but couldn't figure out what they meant. Not until she tried to lift her head and found her cheek was numbed by the vinyl flooring beneath.

The foot in her shoulder was annoying, her pressure point ached, so the next time it shoved her, she tried to grab it to throw it away. And failed. The cuff connecting her wrist and ankle made it impossible. He stroked her cheek with his bare foot, rubbing it from her forehead down her temple to her jaw.

Grumbling, she rolled away, using her other hand to swipe it from her face. "Don't touch me," she croaked. "What the fuck did you do to me?"

She remembered the shower and his sinister mood. The ache in her arms still lingered from when they were tied above her head. She couldn't remember how or exactly when she'd passed out. The memory of the needle tensed her. He'd had access to her body and could've given her anything, done anything to her.

Pushing back into the corner, she got as far away as she could. "Did you rape me?"

His brows went up. "Rape? Yeah. I did. 'Cause that's what gets me off, a woman lying there like a sack of flour without moving or making a sound, real sexy."

She didn't appreciate his sarcasm. Nothing about the situation was funny.

"I deserve the truth. Did you?"

Now instead of being amused, he just looked angry. "Why would I rape a bitch like you, who's nothing but straight up trouble? Look at me. I could walk into any bar in town, pick a slut, and let her ride my cock like a rodeo cowgirl all night long."

"Nice," she said, reassured enough to relax. Her sore joints and muscles didn't appreciate the night spent curled on the floor in a cramped space. As far as she could tell, her clothes were no more disturbed now than they had been last night, and none of her orifices hurt. "Tell me what I'm doing here."

"Tell me where he is," Archer countered.

Steam plumed above the closed curtain, the drum of water behind betrayed the shower was on. Archer wore a towel around his hips giving her a glimpse of another tattoo. It started around his ankle and wound up round his calf to his thigh, black and tribal like the arm sleeve on the opposite side.

The thickness of his thigh muscles was impressive. Was his physique cultivated in a gym or was torturing exercise enough?

"So that's it? Tag. Is it your plan to keep me here until

I give him up?"

"Yep."

He could keep her there and drug her every night for the rest of eternity, she would never betray her friend.

"Won't happen," she said.

Resting a hip on the sink, he folded his arms. "I'll keep you until you give him up, but there will be a variation on the 'here.'"

"A variation?"

His confidence was bold. She'd done nothing to encourage him or let him think she might surrender information on Tag. Why wasn't he angrier or stressed about her defiance? Turning to the sink, he admired his jaw in the mirror and began to trim.

Sitting for a while, she watched him, wishing he would just leave. The steam from the shower was nice. It cleared her sinuses and helped her sore body; getting out of there would be nicer. Clearing her throat, she rotated until she could lift herself to rest her back on the side of the bathtub.

She needed to learn more about the room; she'd already learned something about the man. He would release her from the chains, even if it was just to torture her. The next time he did, she would be ready, strong and aware. She couldn't be drugged or tired.

The back of her head thumped against the tub, and she took a long breath. What a shitty end to a shitty week. Yeah, sometimes life sucked, didn't mean she wanted this to be the end of her shitty life.

When Archer was done, he turned his scowl to her. "I know a bunch of ways to encourage people into telling me what I need to know," he said, hunkering down to stroke a finger on the path his foot had followed. She tried to wriggle away but was already squashed in the corner, clinging to the bathtub to keep herself steady. "I'll let you think about that for a while."

"Go to hell," she said, refusing to let him scare her.

She was too tired and disorientated to fight.

"Right now, the shower is on, and it's your turn."

"Wha…? What?"

Running his fingers through his wet hair, he shook his head, showering her in water again. "Get in the shower, Squirm," he said, rubbing a hand over his more defined jaw now that he'd rid himself of the overgrown scruff.

She wanted to remind him of her confinement, but when she lifted her ankle, the padlock came loose. Pulling it off, she scrambled to her feet, untangling herself from the cuff that had linked her ankle and wrist for days.

Her strength was lacking, and her legs buckled. She expected to go down, but he caught her with one arm, using his body to anchor her. No, she didn't believe he was capable of kindness, and this act didn't challenge that belief. Something was going on, and it wouldn't be something good. Bending her back, he grabbed the shower curtain and rattled it aside to lift her up and dump her in the tub under the hot shower water.

"Strip, dump your clothes out, I've got something for you to wear in the bedroom."

In the bedroom. She didn't have a chance to ask what that meant because he whipped the curtain closed.

The water was comforting, soothing for her aching bones, but… Was it smart to take her clothes off in a room with a man she didn't trust? Did she have a choice? A towel appeared over the rail, farther down from where she'd been hung last night. At least that gave her a way to cover up when she was done… Unless that was a decoy he'd whip away when her clothes were gone.

What exactly was the alternative? Angering him to the point he may strip her himself? Yeah, no, not a good option. She did as told, taking time to steady herself before washing and grooming. She shut off the water, squeezed the moisture from her hair and drew down the vast towel. "It was far bigger than her small body needed and wrapped around her twice with plenty to spare.

The curtain was whipped aside, and he pulled her out, lifting her up to carry her from the room. Her legs were more secure, so she could have walked herself, but he didn't ask permission.

Blasting through the door opposite the bathroom,

they arrived in a modest bedroom with a large bed, two nightstands and a sliding closet door running the length of the right-hand wall.

What immediately struck her after he put her down was the neatness of the space. Bed was made, the blankets flat without a crease. The blinds on the facing wall were closed. Nightstands were clear and there wasn't a single speck of dust in sight.

"Put this on," he said, tossing a dress on her shoulder.

Opening it out, she hooked the spaghetti straps of the black micro-mini dress onto her fingers.

"This is a dress."

"Smart and pretty, your parents must be proud," he said, sliding the closet door on its track to seek something inside.

The snide bastard deserved a slap.

"Patronizing and arrogant, yours must just glow." Maybe he hadn't expected sass, but when he glared over his shoulder, she tried to smile. Keeping emotions in check? Yeah, she'd never been good at that. "I'd rather have jeans… and underwear."

From where she stood, there were no extras for the outfit.

"This ain't Macy's."

No kidding. Thanks for stating the obvious.

Carrying a small box, he sat on the edge of the bed. Holding the dress in one hand and the tucked-in part of the towel in the other, she stayed put. He popped the lid to produce supplies… medical supplies.

Ripping open a sachet with his teeth, he pulled a wipe from it then leaned forward to snag her towel in two fingers. If she wanted to keep her modesty, going to him was the only option. She went to the side of the bed, stopping between his parted knees.

A bedroom. They were in a bedroom, and she wasn't wearing much, what did he intend—

He grabbed her other arm, the one responsible for the dress, and turned it to see the angry red burn inside her wrist. He examined it for a second, touched the edge, then pushed the wipe into it.

She yelped at the horror of stinging pain and dropped the dress, but he held fast and kept on wiping, squeezing the alcohol into the wound. The pungent aroma of it smacked her senses. When he was done, he tossed the wipe away and kept her arm extended to apply some ointment. While it was soaking in, he retrieved a roll of bandages from the box and pressed gauze to the wound before wrapping it.

Quite a turnaround and one she couldn't explain. Was this treatment about regret for causing her pain? She didn't interrupt but didn't hold her breath either. Still, sympathy was preferable over torture.

"You have a client," he said.

Smack. That might as well have been a gut punch. Shock didn't begin to identify what seized her. Nothing could describe such instant terror.

"A what? I have a what?"

"He's a rough motherfucker," Archer said, securing the bandage with tape.

"If the point is to cause me pain, why are you bothering with this?" she asked, trying to tug her arm free.

As usual, her feeble attempt to liberate herself was fruitless.

"Because…" he said, opening the drawer of the nightstand to produce a leather cuff. "Unless he's careful when he ties your wrists, the rope will infect the wound. You're useless to me dead or disgusting."

Hence the shower and the crappy cheap dress.

"And you're some expert I suppose?"

She kept struggling because it was better than doing nothing.

"Got some experience," he said, slipping the cuff onto her wrist over the bandage and buckling it so tight her hand tingled.

"From where?"

"Had a girlfriend into that S&M shit."

Now she resorted to being snide. "Not your thing?"

He stood up, so close that her body swayed with the force of his ascent. "I don't like hitting women."

But he had no trouble burning, starving, and torturing them.

"Doubt that's true."

He paused. "Have I hit you?"

Manhandled and illegally imprisoned? Yes. Physically struck? No, he hadn't done that. This wasn't the time to allow him any concession, so she held her wrist up to his face.

"What's this?"

"That's abuse," he said, nodding at her offered limb without taking his eyes from hers. "Abuse I have no problem with." Stating the obvious. Again. "Put the dress on. We've gotta get out of here."

"He's not coming here?" she asked, picking up the dress when he slipped out from in front of her to return his first-aid box to the closet.

Archer exhaled. "You think I want a fucktard pervert screwing in my bed? Not a chance."

If she'd had a weapon, or anything, she'd have launched it at him. Without one, attack wouldn't work. So she put the dress over her head and wriggled it down in the wake of the towel she shimmied from her body without baring an inch more than necessary.

"You don't want him in your bed, but you expect me to welcome him into my body?"

"The more you fight, the more he pays," he said, tucking something onto his belt beneath his tee shirt. "You can't be with a guy like Taggert and not be used to getting fucked with."

"We're not together," she said, like she'd told him before. As far as that was concerned, he'd never catch her in a lie because it was the truth. "And if anyone touched me without consent, he'd cut off their hands."

Turning to her, his hands went to his hips. For a second, he seemed… normal, though maybe a little exasperated.

"That's where you lose me, Squirm. I know plenty of guys possessive of their women, but none who'd give a fuck about a random slut. He's in love with you or he's blood. Which is it?"

"Neither," she said, feeling slightly superior that her secrets perplexed him. "And it's damn clear you're not half the man he is, so I'm not surprised you don't understand loyalty."

"Oh, I understand it. Did you save his life?" She shook her head. "What's the connection?"

If he ever figured it out, she'd be useless to him, and he'd find a way to dispose of her. Though anything else was a pipedream, she wasn't ignorant to how this would end.

"Why does it matter? He owes you money, I won't give him up, so you'll pimp me until you recoup your losses. That is your plan, right?" Her legs became his focus, admiring focus, not malevolent. Oh no, she didn't want his interest, and didn't want to like him scrutinizing her as a woman, not a captive. Especially since his treatment of her wrist was already making it feel better. She didn't want to be indebted to him for anything, not even curing the ailment he caused. "Do you mark all your girls?"

Breaking his concentration, it went straight to anger. "I'm no pimp," he snapped, darting across the room.

Relating to him as an abductor, not a human being, was easier. "That's exactly what you are. If you transport me to a john's house for sex and take my earnings, a pimp is exactly what you are."

His scowl became more depraved. "Done this before, have you, Squirm? Am I poaching Taggert's turf, that it? He'll fuck me up if I lease one of his girls without giving him a cut?"

She recoiled in offense. "I would never!"

"Sure you would. Don't tell me you worked at Sizzle for tips."

Yeah, so maybe the club was in a red-light zone, but so was just about every other neighborhood she'd ever lived or worked.

"I have never sold sex."

One of his brows slunk up. "Never taken your clothes off for money?"

That she couldn't claim. "I stripped for like twenty minutes. Tag heard where I was and how I was supporting myself… He stormed in with a posse, shut the place down, and dragged me out. He set me up in Sizzle after that."

Sizzle was Tag's club. He'd ensconced her there to protect her. Well, kind of. She was smart enough to recognize being handled. After arguing against him monitoring her at all times, they'd come to a compromise. She'd manage the club, pull her weight, earn her money honestly, and not get herself into trouble.

Oops.

Lowering her miserable smile, resignation reigned. How frantic was Tag? Did he know what had gone down in Sizzle?

Archer interrupted her reflection when he grabbed her hair to yank her head back. "You enjoy being on his leash?"

So much for their momentary truce.

"I'd rather be on his than yours," she spat out.

"The quicker you do your work, the faster I get my money."

Spinning her around, he clutched a handful of her hair in one sure fist to compel her forward, through the living room and out the front door. Her feet were bare; apparently the budget didn't extend to shoes. The gritty floor was sticky in patches, she tried not to think about what caused either.

They went down two floors, past the graffiti, used condoms, and scattered drug paraphernalia, out to the grimy street into a mist of rain.

Not far from the door he threw her against a beat-up black Camaro, pinning her to it with his body as he unlocked the door. Thrusting her inside, he locked her in. She was still clawing at the door when he got into the driver's seat.

The engine roared and he sped away from the curb. Intent on his route, wherever they were going, he wanted to get there fast. She couldn't say she was so eager.

SIX

ARCHER DROVE FAST the whole way, he barely paused at stop signs, and screeched away from amber lights like they were green. Nothing would hinder their arrival.

To her surprise, they drove to a suburban area. Residential streets with tended yards had decks around pools. Hope grew that the man she was supposed to submit to might not be a lowlife scumbag after all. His identity wouldn't increase her willingness, but maybe he'd be gentler than Archer implied. A vanilla experience would be better than one which required a hospital visit.

"If you think the rich pay for boring sex, you're wrong," he mumbled like he'd read her thoughts. "They pay premium for a whore so they can do whatever the fuck they want to her without upsetting their respectable lives."

"I'm not a whore," she said. "You keep saying that word out loud like you're trying to convince yourself it's true. Delivering me here, forcing me to do this, it makes you as culpable as them. How many women have you raped?" His rage didn't deter her even as the car got faster. Sitting up straight, she got closer to him. "You're just like Jonno and his buddies at Sizzle. Did you see what they did to Jamie? That was her name, by the way, Jamie. Bet you didn't even know that. You just saw her bloody, battered body on that floor and got the boner of your life, didn't you? Were you sorry you didn't get your turn to violate her? Your poor little pea-dick probably forgot all about the cops when you saw your BFF fucking the life out of her."

Swinging a harsh turn, that forced her to grab for the door, Archer slammed the car into park and whirled on her. "You don't know what the fuck you're talking about! Your friend couldn't be helped, okay? She was collateral damage. Your lover-boy Taggert? He's the reason those fuckers were there! If he hadn't stiffed a bunch of people, your friend would still be sucking down Martini's and you'd be shaking those cans for your sugar daddies."

Good, he was angry, so was she. This bastard didn't have the right to use her. What he intended to force her into would change the course of her whole life. She'd never forgive him for doing this irreparable damage.

"I'm not what you think I am."

"You're what the fuck I say you are 'til you've paid your boyfriend's debt."

Grabbing her hair again, he opened his door and dragged her over the center console to pull her out his side. He had no regard for how he hurt her and made no apology for being so rough.

They were in a double garage. The door must've been left open so they could slip in unseen and avoid anyone noticing a shitheap car in the driveway of this reputable neighborhood. They knew what they were doing was wrong, all of them. Why hide something unless you're ashamed of it?

Yanking her past him, he opened an internal door and threw her into a dining kitchen. Laughter carried from another room.

Archer came in close behind her to growl. "Don't fuck this up," he hissed.

If given a chance, that's exactly what she'd do. Freedom. How could she…? Archer said the client wanted her to fight. If he fought back, injury was guaranteed.

Even if it might not be smart, she couldn't submit, just lay back and make Archer's life easier. It wasn't in her. It wasn't who she was. Doing as much injury as possible was one last vestige of hope for dignity.

She stumbled along when Archer took her arm to pull her through the kitchen and a set of double doors into a dark, dingy den.

Three men, no, she couldn't—she tried to retreat but came up against Archer's solid form. He walked forward, forcing her into the room. She struggled to twist, to resist, to get away, but he grabbed her shoulders and faced her forward.

The men's laughter drifted off as they looked her over, each with more hunger in their gaze than the last.

"I promised you boys a party and it just arrived," the man to the right said.

Three couches were arranged around a faux fireplace. Beyond the thick central rug, toys lay by the hearth. They transfixed her even after the speaker rose to come toward her.

Distinguished and tanned, his appearance bore no suggestion of sexual perversion. Rapists and sadists were like serial killers, they could look just like everyone else.

The host came up close, blocking her view of everything except him. "I wish I could tell you not to be afraid, or that I wasn't going to hurt you," he said in a kind voice that didn't match his snarling smile. Leaning in, he rubbed his mouth in her hair. "But that would be a lie."

Snatching her arm, he wrenched her across the room. She fought and screamed, not that it made a difference. His cohorts joined him to wrestle her onto the rug and her dress was pulled down, freeing her breasts for one of them to kiss. One nipple was sucked, the other was pinched, and the speaker came down on top of her, sticking his tongue into her wide, screaming mouth.

Seeing her chance, she bit down, and he reared away, but not before his blood spilled.

"Oh, boys," he said, clasping his mouth to check the blood. "She wants to play!"

His first slap sent her face to the right, the second sent it the other way. In a daze, she languished, vaguely aware of him unbuttoning his shirt to tug it off over his head.

"No! Stop!" she called when her dress was yanked

from her crotch to her waist.

The central man unbuckled his belt. "Beg, girl, that's what I want you to do, beg," he said, his speech slightly slurred probably, hopefully, as a result of her assault.

Though from the wild, frenzied way the trio manhandled her, and the craziness in their eyes, she'd guess they were high on some kind of substance. Worse news for her. Their inhibitions were low; they were goading each other on. It would be a long, horrific night.

"Shit," Archer muttered somewhere in the distant background, then his voice grew strong. "Get your fucking hands off her."

A vast shadow materialized behind the principal assaulter to lift him off her body. After some swearing, the other men let go to jump up. Scrambling to her feet, she clawed the straps of her dress to her shoulders and staggered for the door.

Someone grabbed her and hauled her back. One of her attackers threw her to the floor to run over and slam the door, blocking it with his body. Confused, dazed by adrenaline, and uncertain about what the hell Archer was doing, she couldn't… she…

"Change of plans," Archer said.

"You fucker!"

She wiped blood from her mouth.

The assaulter she'd bitten swung for Archer, he bowed back to avoid the punch and grabbed the guy's wrist, spinning him around to thrust him against the wall. Archer produced a knife from his belt and swung it around to the throat of the man he was restraining as he assessed the trio. One man he had against the wall, the other was at the door, and the third stood on the other side of the fireplace.

"Do we have a problem?" Archer asked the men.

"We had a fucking deal!"

Archer's glare snapped to the man under his knife, the same man who'd assaulted her. Sympathy didn't visit when the color drained from him.

"Get the bitch!" the man at the door called out to the one by the fireplace.

No. No one would touch her. She couldn't let it happen. They could be prepared for trouble and have stashed weapons.

The guy at the fireplace stuttered and faltered. Archer spun his victim around, pinning him to the wall with an arm pressed the width of his chest.

As the bastard struggled to draw breath, Archer scanned the room. "Any of you fuckers touch her and he dies," he said, insinuating the edge of his blade into the ringleader's throat until a thick red line formed against it. Nobody moved. "Get up and move."

Archer assessed the men like they were hungry hyenas capable of snapping any minute. Stunned, she couldn't think or… get up and move. He'd said—she was the only one on the floor and—shit, Archer was talking to her. She clambered onto her feet and staggered toward the door, pulling at her dress to straighten it.

For whatever reason, Archer hadn't followed through with his plan. She could be on that floor being screwed by these slobbering maniacs right now. Archer's change of heart was the only reason she wasn't.

"He's going to kill me anyway," said the man under Archer's blade. "And he'll kill you too, bitch!"

Archer didn't flinch. "Move!"

Leaving Archer was an appealing idea. Inching toward the door, she kept her distance from the man blocking it. When the prick cleared the way, she couldn't get out fast enough, and ran to the door to snatch it open.

Archer wasn't finished with the man at the wall. Thrusting a hand to the bastard's forehead, Archer forced his victim's head back to expose the soft flesh of his neck beneath his chin.

In a deft move, Archer used the tip of his blade to carve a continuous shape into the objecting man's skin. When he lowered the weapon, her breath caught in her throat, immobilizing her. Examining her cuff-covered wrist as though she could see her burn through it, the brand was similar to the shape Archer just sliced into that guy.

Getting in close, Archer ignored the whimpers of the

now disfigured man. "Think about coming after me or her, and you'll get yourself more than a flesh wound, Bryant."

Leaving Bryant to clutch his chin and whine, Archer shoved away, satisfied he'd taken care of business, and stormed over to grab hold of her.

Carting her along behind him, he dragged her through the kitchen into the garage to stuff her back into his car.

"Archer, I—"

"Don't say a word," he growled and gunned the engine. "Don't say a fucking word."

Good because she wouldn't know where to begin. Something had to be said. What the hell just happened? Questions wouldn't be wise when it was clear Archer was in no mood to fill in the blanks.

Throwing a hand to the back of her headrest, he reversed out and sped away from the house at far greater speed than he'd used to get there.

While watching Archer scar Bryant, an odd calm had come over her. But as her jailer seethed, the calm receded to panic about their speed. They drove for miles, out of the quaint respectable neighborhood, back onto the highway into the city.

Clutching her seatbelt, she pressed herself back. "Archer," she said. "Please slow down." Before tonight, she'd have assumed he wasn't a man to be reasoned with. Had her opinion changed much? Maybe not. But her survival instinct spoke up. "Please, Archer, I'm scared."

His scowl was so fierce it could crack the windscreen. Without warning, he slammed on the brakes, swinging a turn so tight, two wheels may have left the road. Still braced for the impact of a possible roll, the car jolted to a stop in a dark corner of a convenience store parking lot.

She didn't blink. Didn't breathe. She fixated on his profile and waited for her heart to slow… and for him to say something. The huff of his breathing intensified the humidity. Should she speak? Would that anger land on her? What was he thinking? What might come next? Was this the end or…? Not?

"Fuck!" he exclaimed, startling her. "Fuck! Fuck! Fuck!"

He kept swearing and smacking the steering wheel with his fists and palms.

Her impulse to flee was thwarted by a locked door. All she could do was sit there and wish for the past to return: the speeding was scary, but not as scary as this.

Tears tracked down her face. She didn't even know what they were for. Fear of this crazy, frantic, angry man? Relief she wasn't being violated by those letches anymore? Gratitude Archer stepped in when, quite clearly, doing so hadn't been in his best interest?

With that last possibility, she reached out to touch him. When she laid her hand on his arm he stilled. Immediately. Either the act of contact, or reminder of her presence, calmed him down. Which could just mean he didn't like to lose it in front of anyone. Until then he'd been a picture of composure around her. Always cool. Never provoked.

For the first time, she sensed anxiety, enough to rouse some sympathy for the guy who'd just cut her a break.

"How much money does Tag owe you?" she asked.

Her friend was no saint. She was under no illusions about what he did or who he associated with. Archer existed in the same gray area of legitimacy Tag did. Different men had different limits; she'd learned tonight where her abductor drew his line.

"Twenty grand."

Okay, so wow. A figure that high was unexpected. No wonder he'd chosen an upmarket orgy. Standing on a street corner, offering twenty bucks a blowjob, would've taken her years to earn that kind of money.

"Did you earn it? Win it? Lend it to him?"

"Does it matter?" he asked, resting his forearms on the steering wheel.

No, she didn't suppose it did. After what just happened, he had other things on his mind, so she didn't push.

"Thank you," she offered after a dozen quiet seconds. "For not making me—"

"Don't," he said, tensing in a disgusted recoil. "Don't

thank me.”

Too bad, she was grateful he'd fucked himself out of whatever dough she could've earned for him. For whatever reason, he hadn't wanted that man to touch her. On arriving at Bryant's, she was certain she'd leave his house a different woman. In a way, she had. Not broken, violated, and repulsed. Instead, clemency granted a reprieve and provided some relief. Archer had abused her, no doubt about that, but he was human and capable of compassion.

Quid pro quo might earn her freedom.

"Let me talk to him," she said and he laid his glare on her. "Let me talk to Tag, find out what's going on, why he hasn't paid you." His stony expression didn't flinch. Suspicion might be due, except, he had nothing to lose. "What's the worst that will happen? I tell him I'm with you and he storms over to fight with you? You want to see him anyway, don't you? If I'd given you his location, you'd have gone to see him."

"Tell me where he is," he said in the same deep drawl he used to intimidate her.

It didn't have the same effect as before, he'd become a different man. Yes, he'd put her in peril, but he'd also saved her life. His actions changed her perspective on almost every second they'd shared.

She shook her head. "I can't," she said and shrugged. "I honestly don't know. But I can get in touch with him."

"You're in love with the guy, but he won't tell you where he's living?"

What was the point in hanging onto her if she was so unimportant in Tag's life? That's what the look on his face suggested. If she were an obsessed stalker, she'd understand his doubt. The truth was the opposite. Tag had to know where she was. Always. If he'd discovered she hadn't been home for days, he'd be livid.

By now, Tag would be aware of what happened in Sizzle. At the very least, Tag would know his bouncers were dead and Jamie was… whatever she was. Unless the cops caught any of the assailants and interrogated the truth from them, no one would know Archer turned up to steal her out of there.

"I'm not in love with him, not like that."

Archer frowned again, the first sign he was about to ask a question. "For real? Thought you were feeding me bullshit to protect his ass."

A new honesty formed in their relationship. An equality.

"You have a lot to learn about me, Archer. I would never be ashamed of loving my guy. I'd shout his name with pride before I'd deny it."

"Who is your guy?"

Was he worried about an unseen threat he hadn't considered? Not that it mattered.

She shrugged. "Don't have one."

"Why not? You're hot and guys will fuck anything."

What a compliment.

"I haven't met a guy who's ready to declare me so honestly," she said. "I'd like my guy to have some integrity."

"Not many of those around," he muttered, scrutinizing the neon open light in the building down the lot. "No."

Giving him the time to sort his thoughts and make decisions, she said nothing. Her offer to talk to Tag was a win for him. If he chose to take it. She wasn't making promises or proposing to go out of her way to help him, but it wouldn't hurt to get some information. Now he'd proved his stomach for the abduction thing only went so far, his options were running out.

She didn't know where Tag was exactly, so couldn't hand over his location. Not that she would. Archer couldn't force her to turn tricks to earn him his money, that plan hadn't worked out so great. From her point of view, this was the only solution left.

It was that or Archer kept her on his bathroom floor until Tag eventually found her. Except if the cops hadn't figured out who'd attacked Sizzle, they could be waiting a while. Investigations, official or otherwise, took time, weeks or months, and this case wouldn't be a priority. How long was Archer willing to wait?

"Two minutes," he said, fixating on the payphone at

the boundary of the lot. "You call him and tell him if he hands over the money, I'll let you go."

That was a terrible idea and she'd never been shy with candor.

While squinting, she shook her head. "If you threaten him, he'll dig in. The two of you strike me as similar in that way."

Turning in his seat, he rested an elbow on the shoulder of his chair and his hand on her headrest. "What the fuck?"

Despite his surprise, she didn't retreat. "Sure! You're bull-headed and stubborn. I've seen it. You kept me chained to a pipe in your bathroom for days. That takes dedication. If someone you cared about was threatened and held for ransom, would you just hand over the money and say 'sayonara, no hard feelings'? I don't think so. The point is to end this, not to draw out the craziness."

He may not have been expecting her to be so forthcoming but humored her. "What do you suggest?"

Her immediate suggestion wouldn't be popular. She'd rather be vague about specifics until getting a measure of Tag's mood.

"Trust me." His brows rose. "Let me talk to him, this could be a misunderstanding. If it is, you don't want to start a fight with Tag." Archer didn't flinch, he wasn't impressed. "You don't, Archer. You'll lose. Against Tag? There's just no way. No one ever beats him. He prides himself on that."

"You've got a lot to learn about me too, Squirm."

"My name is Nya," she said because they'd never actually been introduced. "And you've gone about this the wrong way from the beginning. If you'd come to me, explained yourself, I would've helped you."

Maybe. Okay, maybe not.

He didn't appear convinced. "You give out your boyfriend's money to every guy who comes to the bar looking for him?"

That wasn't what she meant. But she was way more reasonable than Tag, and definitely fairer. If Archer's beef was legitimate, she might have brought up his name with Tag and maybe argued his case. Speculating about what-if was pointless. They were there now, in that moment. All she could do was react to current circumstances.

"If you trust me, and you're genuinely owed that money, I'll get it for you. I'm the only one who can."

Another truth. He didn't have to accept her and Tag's special relationship, or that she had influence with her friend. But Archer was obviously curious about the veracity of her last statement; he didn't shut her down or backtrack.

Trusting each other wasn't easy. Each had the ability to help the other achieve their goal—his money and her freedom. She could try to cut and run but didn't want Archer on Tag's tail. Tag was formidable, but Archer was capable. Would Archer relent some of his control and let her help him?

SEVEN

FROM THE VEHICLE'S ashtray, he tossed her a pack of gum before prodding around at the coins inside. Glad of the chance to dilute the taste of her attacker's bloody tongue, she squeezed out two gum nuggets.

Archer scooped up some change and left the car. When she tried to follow, her door still wouldn't open. She was stuck until Archer came around the hood to let her out.

"This door only opens from the outside," he said, hooking a finger through the metal loop on the leather cuff he'd buckled to her wrist.

The maneuver signaled her being on a leash and was a sign he wasn't in the mood for a chase.

Being she would rather he touched the accessory than her, and it was better than being carried or dragged, she didn't object. A more pressing question was why the car door was rigged. Didn't that imply he had to detain people, other than her, on a regular basis?

Leading her to the payphone, he picked up the receiver. "I'll be right here, don't get any ideas."

Right there was right. After he gave her the receiver and positioned her to face the phone, he pressed his weight into her spine, reminding her who was in charge. Looming over her, he fired coins into the slot.

Hiding the numbers with her body and hand, she took the receiver from her shoulder after dialing.

It rang. Too aware of Archer behind her, she couldn't focus on what to say. Wriggling her weight back, she tried to get him to give her some room, but he swayed forward in a gentle, but full, body push, communicating he wasn't going anywhere.

"Hello?" Tag snapped down the line.

She sprang to her tiptoes and gasped. "Taggy?"

"Oh my God, Yorkie, where have you been? What the fuck happened?"

Tag didn't usually do stress. Her being off the grid would've scared him given he didn't have the full picture of what went down.

"I need to see you," she said. "Can we meet?"

"Tell me where you are, I'll pick you up."

Having been her savior and support in the past, Tag would drop everything to be there for her. That said, a confrontation in a deserted parking lot wouldn't be smart. While emotions were running high, neither man would be reasonable. She also didn't want it to look like she'd set either of them up.

"I'd rather come to you. I need somewhere to lay low."

He didn't ask any more questions, just gave her an address. Triumphant relief put a smile on her face. She pumped an elbow back into Archer's ribs, not that it made any difference.

"What happened at the club?"

The question extinguished her satisfaction. "Jamie," she murmured. "Where is she? Is she recovering?"

"Jamie?" Tag said. "The waitress never made it, she's dead. I don't give a fuck about her. I give a fuck about you. The bouncers were dead, the cops show up, there's blood everywhere, and you're gone."

Jamie. Dead. No. She couldn't think about explaining herself with the shock of that rattling in her head, in her heart. Tactful wasn't in Tag's vocabulary, he cared about few things.

He and Jamie never met; he had no reason to care about her…
but she cared.

Tears weighed on her lashes, she croaked before she
spoke. "I'll… I'll tell you everything, Taggy. Soon, I'll come to
you soon. I… I have to go."

Slamming down the phone, she buried her face in
both hands, desperate to conceal her tears. She cursed this
place, cursed the loss, blamed the world and its spite. Jamie
was young, she'd done nothing wrong. It wasn't right she
should be snatched from her life by that evil.

Whirling around, she wanted to punch and kick and
spit, but when she lifted her eyes to Archer's, she couldn't
make herself hate while this numb.

"What happened to the kid?"

That was his first question. Not about his money. Not
about Tag's address. Jamie. His first question was about Jamie.
There was a heart in this man. One he kept well-hidden and
rarely used, but it was in there.

Releasing all her breath in a sob, she sank against his
chest and allowed every iota of pain to bleed from her eyes in
a torrent of tears. She wasn't a crier and prided herself on
keeping her shit together, especially in front of people.

When his arms closed around her, she should've
remembered who he was and backed off. She didn't. Tears of
exhaustion, stress and grief came out in a perpetual conveyer
she wasn't capable of slowing.

"I guess she didn't make it," he muttered.

Standing in the parking lot, forgetting about her
captivity, in the fresh air of the crisp night, she felt free. She
had something Jamie was denied: life. Her troubles faded in
the light of a new perspective.

"They killed her," she said. Acknowledging it aloud
stoked familiar anger and her tears began to dry. "Your
hideous, disgusting, depraved friends murdered an innocent
woman."

"They weren't my friends. Jonno's the only one of
them I know," he admitted. "Rape is fucked up. There's never
a need for it. It disgusts me… I found out just how much
tonight."

That was why he couldn't let Bryant and his buddies violate her. No, she wouldn't think about herself, this wasn't about what she'd been through. Focusing on Jamie, the injustice of her employee's death, gave her purpose.

"I'll make them pay," she said, determined. Helplessness infuriated her. A goal, direction, choice became resolute. No one else would avenge Jamie, she had no boyfriend, few friends, and none of them knew the true, detailed horror of what Jamie endured. Not like her. "I won't let the bastards get away with it. Those sick fucks don't deserve to jeer and pat each other on the back. They were proud. They enjoyed her agony. I can't let it happen. I'll find a way, I'll make them pay, I'll—"

"Calm it, Squirm," Archer said, opening a hand on the back of her head to gather her hair in a fist. Using the anchor point beneath her crown, he eased her chin up to look down at her. "You don't go after guys like that, not a woman like you."

"Why not?" she demanded. "Someone has to show them, has to—"

"It's revenge is what it is. And if you go into a situation full of rage like that, you'll never be thinking straight. They'll do to you what they did to her."

He could be right. Her anger turned itself inward. God, she was feeble, pathetic, a disappointment, unable to act because she wasn't physically strong enough.

"You didn't see it, Archer. What they did to her…" The pictures played in her mind every night and came back to her in a rush. She hadn't slept much while locked up in Archer's bathroom but wouldn't have found slumber in a five-star penthouse suite. What she'd seen those men do to Jamie in Sizzle was too horrific to forget. "It's like a movie playing on repeat and I—"

"I'll help you."

Her thoughts jarred to a halt and the mental image of Jamie paused then dissolved.

What was Archer saying? What did he…? "Wh…? What?"

Blinking into the face of a man who, a few hours ago,

she'd wanted to spit at, her own determination bled into his eyes.

"Tonight… at Bryant's…" he said. "What I saw those guys do to you… I don't kill in front of witnesses, never have. It's the dumbest thing anyone could do…."

His lips narrowed when he clenched his jaw. The anger he'd battered into the steering wheel returned to his expression.

There was more. "But…?"

"You didn't scream like that when I burned you." After skimming a hand up and down her arm, he locked his fist around the cuff on her wrist, squeezing, not to cause pain, but to console. "What I heard tonight wasn't pain, it was terror. You were fucking terrified. I wanted to gut every guy there, me included… I should never have put you in that, I… I thought I could do it… It made sense…"

Because he needed his money.

For the first time, she looked beyond the brute who showed up at Sizzle, intimidating, aloof, domineering with his size and attitude. Given a choice, she'd have run away from him fast. Except he'd actually done her a favor. Deliberate or not, stealing her from Sizzle when he did, saved her from Jonno and his buddies. Yes, dumping her in a trunk then locking her in his bathroom were both extremes she wouldn't forget in a hurry, but she'd lived through worse.

"Why did you burn me?" she asked because it was the worst thing he'd done to her yet.

His hand left her wrist to rest on her cheek. "Better than cutting off a finger or scarring that beautiful face."

Tilting her head into his palm, she appreciated the human connection. Learning of Jamie's fate hit hard. Those men, those murderers, got the focus of her fury. The trauma of what she'd witnessed was far worse than anything Archer put her through.

The burning was meant to scare her into giving up Tag's location. If losing fingers or facial disfigurement were the alternatives, she was glad branding won.

"You'll help me?" she asked, trusting he'd had a fright of his own.

Could be he was rethinking his capabilities. Hearing her scream scared him into getting her out of danger. He could've abandoned her, turned his back and walked away. Waiting in the car with the radio on loud was an option that would've seen him come away with his money. But he hadn't. He'd rescued her and she doubted he'd put himself, or any woman, in that situation again.

"You get me my money, don't screw me over with Taggert, and I'll make sure you get your payback."

A trade. Yes, she could go for that. A man like Archer, who could torture and slice through flesh, would be a formidable weapon to have on her side. All he was asking in return was what was rightfully his, and a guarantee she wouldn't let Tag kill him for what he'd done to her. Fair. Easy. Maybe Archer wasn't as invincible as he made out.

Before shaking on it, she had a caveat of her own. "You won't hurt Tag, will you? This isn't some ploy to—"

"I won't hurt him," he said and cupped her chin. "As long as I get my money."

This money was important enough for him to kidnap her and risk his life by confronting Tag.

Hmm…? "Why do you need this money so bad?"

If he was anything like her, and they did seem to come from the same economic level, twenty grand was a helluva lot of money. But when you'd lived your life with nothing, it was less hardship to live without. The haves missed more than the never hads.

Taking a step back, he gave her room to breathe while weighing his response.

"I have a sister, she's sick."

Medical bills could ruin a person. Folks like them didn't have medical insurance.

"What's wrong with her?" she asked, not that she'd be able to help.

He snagged the loop on her wrist strap to lead her back to the car. "None of your business."

Shoving her down into the passenger seat signaled an end to their first moment of bonding. Wasn't a surprise he'd put up barriers, if he cared about his sister, loved her, he wouldn't want to share her business. And could be talking about his sibling's illness upset him. Men like him didn't get upset in front of unfamiliar women in deserted parking lots… or probably in front of anyone.

The journey back to his apartment was quick, a testament to his speed rather than the distance.

Traipsing up the stairs, he kept the loop of her cuff tight inside his knuckle to tow her along. Nice he let her use her legs for the short ascent between the car and his apartment. As to what would happen when they got in there…?

With his finger still hooked in her cuff, she waited, then followed when he tugged. She was in the rear hall before it hit her.

"No!" she hollered and tried to pull back by dropping her weight.

Archer was prepared. Ducking, he looped his arm around her waist to pick her up under his arm.

She punched and kicked and struggled. Not that her assault stopped him chaining her to the pipe, didn't even slow him down. In a patronizing show, he ruffled her hair. She snapped out in an attempt at a bite, but he was already out the door, leaving her alone as his prisoner once again.

EIGHT

"ARCHER!"

She'd been calling out since he left. Sorry to say, the fear was gone. They'd connected in that parking lot, and he'd brought her home. No take backs now, buddy.

When she'd started calling for him, anger was the drive. Now she called out in a sing-song voice to annoy him into acknowledging her. He'd told her not to scream, that his neighbors wouldn't come to her aid, but it wasn't his neighbors' attention she wanted.

If they were going to deal, he'd need a few lessons on treating her as his equal.

"Archer!" she shouted again. "Arch—"

The door flew open, bounced off the closet door and sprang back only to be stopped by his solid arm.

She smiled. Goal achieved.

He had no idea what he was getting into if he thought his patience would outlast hers.

"Will you shut the fuck up?" he said. "If I wanna hear you scream my name, I'll fuck you senseless."

Not discouraged by this progress, she hooked her fingers onto the rim of the basin and hauled herself onto her knees.

"Maybe you can hold that thought 'til after."

He frowned. "After what?"

"I'm hungry."

***

AND THAT WAS HOW she got on the couch.

The couch faced the wall-mounted TV by the window. The central kitchen table, where he'd burned her, stood between the back of the couch and the breakfast bar.

Blackout blinds covered the window, but enough light shone from the floor lamp in the corner to give her a look at the place. Not that there was much to explore, a coffee table was the only other furniture. Like the bedroom, the living space was meticulously clean. Apparently, Archer was a minimalist. No knick-knacks or pictures on the walls, just the basics.

The TV was on, muted on some sports event she wasn't watching. Her head was swimming. Food better feature in her immediate future or, experience taught her, oblivion would follow. That was why she elected to lie flat on her back on the couch. Fainting spells weren't as frequent now as they used to be.

Opening her hands at her side, there was enough space left that she could fit another of herself on there if needed. Her head and feet didn't touch the arms of the massive piece of furniture.

"Vegetarian," he muttered from the kitchen. "Who the fuck is a vegetarian?"

When she'd come out of the bathroom, he'd put her on the couch. Before he even got as far as the kitchen, she'd told him she didn't eat meat.

"Me," she said. "I don't like red meat; it's not a political choice. I eat eggs, wear leather shoes and even tickle the beaver once in a while."

He said nothing to her quip, and she wasn't going to sit up to seek a reaction.

A fridge opened; a couple of cabinets slammed then he huffed.

"Soup."

"That'll do."

Noise and movement in the kitchen ended with the microwave starting up. A second later, he appeared at the back of the couch, not to look at her, but to get closer to the game on TV. Seeing him doing ordinary things like an ordinary man helped her relate to him. It seemed more like he was simply a desperate person doing desperate things, not someone inherently evil.

To fend off the weakness before it became debilitating, she needed her pills.

"I had my purse in Sizzle," she murmured. "Do you have it?"

She could've lost it in the street; her memory of the night had been blurred by the flood of adrenaline coursing through her at the time.

"It was in my trunk," he said, fixated on the game.

Thank goodness, without it she'd be screwed.

"Can I have it?"

"I don't think so."

Irritation trumped her patience to be polite. It might be understandable he wouldn't give her back her personal belongings when they were captor and captee. But they needed to form a truce if their promises in the parking lot were ever going to work out.

"There's no weapon in it," she said, though it held almost everything else a woman could possibly need.

"It weighs a ton, what the hell *is* in it?"

A burst of surprised energy opened her eyes. His concentration was still set on the TV like it was no big deal that he hadn't gone through her purse. For a woman who valued privacy so much, it meant a lot to learn he'd respected it. Archer wanted Tag; he didn't want *her*, so he hadn't violated her privacy. That was her logic anyway.

"Everything I need to split in a hurry," she said.

"Get yourself into a lot of trouble?"

"I tend to… get involved."

Friends, boyfriends, employers, colleagues, it didn't help that most of the people she knew were criminals or poor souls with addiction issues. Being from the street, those who crossed her path tended to be too. They fought hard, fought dirty, and they never gave up. Battling through each day hardened them; taught them to accept and deal with whatever shit life threw at them.

In the past, Tag told her she couldn't leave well enough alone. That she thought she was steel and could fix anything… She hadn't been able to fix Jamie.

The microwave beeped, signaling it was done. Archer disappeared from behind the couch. A minute later he came back and put a bowl on the table.

"That shit's hot, you get any on me and you'll be back in the bathroom."

The idea of injuring him had its appeal. Except, the way she figured it, their "arrangement" could benefit from a reinforcement of trust, not a betrayal of it. They were partners now. Maybe he suspected her of manipulating him to gain her freedom. If that was the case, he had no idea the value of his offer to take down Jamie's murderers.

She needed him. But that would come later, right now, something else was more pressing.

"I really do need my purse," she said, slithering onto the floor.

He sat on the couch beside where she was on the hardwood. "No chance, Squirm. Girls like you carry Tasers or some shit."

Curling toward him, she put a hand on his knee. "I need my pills, Archer."

His scowl grew curious. "Pills?"

To prove she had nothing to hide and was willing to trust him, she said, "You can get them, they're in a bottle in the pouch at the back."

Getting up again, he went to the kitchen. A cabinet opened and she heard him raking in her purse, then he came back reading the bottle.

"Your last name is Yorke?" he asked, tossing her the bottle.

Tipping the medication into her hand, she swallowed it down without water and sagged against the front of the couch.

Her head fell to the seat. "Thank you."

"Why do you take them?"

"I get anemic. My blood pressure drops and sometimes I faint… I guess that's why I've been fading out."

"Eat," he said, touching the edge of her bowl.

Crossing her legs, she leaned over the bowl to scoop the smooth liquid onto her tongue. "I thought it might've been whatever you injected me with that floored me."

"It wasn't."

Access to food gave her a singular objective, it took another six spoonfuls before she asked, "How'd you know? What was in the needle?"

"Antibiotics, to stop your wound getting infected."

What? No way. The whole time she'd worried he was trying to poison her, he'd been treating her instead. The spoon clattered when it hit the bowl.

"But you… you let me believe it was going to hurt me."

Fixated on the television, Archer didn't notice her shock. "You made an assumption, Squirm," he said, rising half out of his chair only to flop back when his team didn't score. Exhaling frustration, he addressed her. "Thought you might've been allergic when you passed out so fast."

So he hung her on the shower rail and dowsed her with cold water to wake her senses? You know, to check he hadn't just committed murder.

"Just the anemia, no allergies."

"I'll remember for the next time I stick you."

That better have been a joke. From the lack of menace in his voice, she erred on giving him the benefit of the doubt.

"No more sticking," she said, punching his knee then returning to her food.

She didn't know he was still examining her until she glanced back and caught him peering.

"You're not afraid of me anymore, are you?"

Her shouting-out stunt in the bathroom should've proved his ability to intimidate her had dwindled.

"You showed me your limit tonight," she said, slurping from her spoon. "Not only do I know for a fact you won't rape me, but you'll rescue me from any other man who tries it."

"That's what you fear?"

Watching the light reflected in the red soup, thoughts of her past replaced her hunger. "More than anything."

"I hurt you; might do it again."

"The burn was terrifying," she said, turning her hand until she felt the bite of pain that came when she rotated her wrist a certain way. "I've been hurt by men before. I've had boyfriends kick the shit out of me."

"Men who hit you?"

She shrugged and finished her soup. It was never nice to be hit, but she was no stranger to it. Her father beat her until he was gone, her brother took over after that. Not all men were the same; she'd known good, decent men too. Like Tag, he'd never laid a hand on her.

It would be useful to know which category Archer fell into.

"You've never hit a woman?" she asked. "Never in your life?"

Being a strong, physical man who had no trouble watching another in pain, it was difficult to believe he always restrained himself.

"I don't like doing it."

"You told me about your S&M girlfriend," she said, running her finger around her empty bowl to catch the smudges of leftover soup. "Your bathroom is a great cell though, if you're going for discomfort. The floor is hard, the space cramped, with the light on and that damn dripping faucet—"

"I know," he said with a discreet smile. "I've done this before."

"Kidnapped and tortured innocent women?"

He didn't hesitate or apologize. "You're Tag's girl, you're not innocent, and my captives are usually guys."

Which explained why he had chains, padlocks, and reinforced pipes lying around.

How was she still fighting his assumption she belonged to Tag in a romantic way? That belief could cost her something further down the line, she had to rid him of it. Pronto.

Pulling his leg out of the way, she crawled around it to kneel between his feet. Without making eye contact, she rose, easing his face downward to push her mouth onto his.

The kiss was supposed to prove a point, not be… electric.

The power… The instant… need.

Oh, God, what was this? Tension coiled around her body in a new gravity that urged her to him. Gripping her face to take control, he forced her higher to welcome his dominant tongue. And, damn, she wanted to give into that power. Fizzing awareness zapped and tickled as she swelled in readiness. Desire was really that instant. Moisture thickened between her folds, warming her in preparation for the thing she shouldn't want from him. Not from this guy.

But, shit, it was too much to resist. Her throat narrowed as desperation to cry out called. Invigoration teased the flesh of her pussy that she'd never considered offering him… until now. When he slid his hips closer, he grasped her waist to steady her, encouraging her to press herself into him.

One of his hands slid to her spine, pressuring it as he closed his knees to clamp her in place.

"Archer," she breathed, bowing her shoulders to separate from him by an inch.

"What the fuck did you kiss me for?"

The reason seemed ridiculous while they were both still dazed by the impact of what they'd shared. She hadn't expected a one-two punch, a girl needed a minute.

"If I was Tag's girl, I would never have done that."

"You don't cheat?"

"I don't cheat," she said. "The guy I end up with will demand loyalty and guarantee it in return. He'd brand me deep to protect me against any other guy moving in on his turf. He'd protect our relationship with his life and so would I."

Fidelity was a passion, as if he couldn't tell.

His gaze drifted to her cuff. "Brand you," he

murmured. That was exactly what he'd done. Fuck, she didn't mean… "You're already wearing my mark and that baby isn't going anywhere."

With her point about Tag made, this should be the moment of retreat. Archer's arm still curved around her, his legs flanked her body. Resting her forearms on his thighs, she exhaled. Why was she always attracted to men who were bad for her?

"Loyalty is a rare quality."

It was. Fidelity was as rare as integrity.

"I told you, I'm not a whore."

"I'm starting to believe you," he said and leaned in for another kiss.

She was saved from spurning or accepting the kiss by a knock on the front door. Archer pushed her back to get up, lifting a leg over her head. He went to the door and answered it. Without checking who was there first. Huh, she'd have put money on him being vigilant. Then again, this guy was laid back right up until the moment he sprang into action. So far, he'd handled every threat thrown at him. Kinda seemed to suggest he knew what he was doing.

"What the fuck do you want?" Archer asked, laying a forearm on the doorframe and another on the back of the door.

"Came to find out what the fuck happened."

Ice.

Caution.

Dread.

That voice. She knew that voice. Just as she reached the point of seeing past Archer's barbarity, a worse example showed up. That voice belonged to the man who'd pinned her to the wall and threatened her in Sizzle.

"Get the fuck away from my door, Jonno."

Archer attempted to close it, but from the thud, she'd guess Jonno stopped it with a foot.

She couldn't see their faces. Archer had his back to her and was in the open door space, blocking Jonno's view. The tone of his voice said it all. He was pissed. The fucking nerve. Trying to be silent, she shuffled backwards on her hands and knees.

Crawling to the end of the couch, she stayed low, hiding behind the arm. Peeking over it, she listened close. Behind her was the hallway to the bedroom and bathroom. There was no escape back there, she'd trap herself in a dead end if she went that way. What choice did she have?

"Did you find him? Did the bitch give him up?" Jonno asked. "I let you have her. I deserve to know where the fuck that prick is."

"She didn't tell me. I don't know the answer."

"Bullshit! You get answers, you never fuck up. Why'd you think I let you take her?"

"You let me take her 'cause you didn't have a choice," Archer said. "And she was mine the minute I walked out with her. I don't owe you a damn thing."

"You came to Sizzle 'cause of me, I gave you the tip she was the way in. We had a deal."

"A deal?" Archer snarled. "Here's a fucking deal for you, Jonno, get the fuck away from my door before I slice you open, balls to throat. You don't come to my place shouting the fucking odds. I let you live once, I don't gotta do that again."

Tension remained, but Jonno's attitude swung a one eighty. "Hey, now, Archer, come on, don't be like that. I'm sorry, okay? I didn't mean no disrespect. I'm not used to you taking so long to do your job, you know? I've got the guys breathing down my neck; we've been chasing Taggert a long time."

Archer relaxed. "Now you wanna make friends? Did you forget who you were dealing with?"

"I just wanna see her," Jonno said. "You still have her, right?"

"Might."

She inched backwards again. If Jonno saw her in Archer's living room eating soup, he might get the idea they were allies, which they sort of were. Jonno didn't have Archer's limits. Jamie died while Jonno was in charge. That told her all she needed to know.

Avoiding unwelcome hands on her body was an

engrained ambition. In this situation, one simple act could protect her, should protect her, even if it wasn't the most appetizing choice. In reverse, still on her hands and knees, she edged into the bathroom, turned on the light and went back to her tether.

Oh, God, why did she…?

How well did Jonno know Archer's methods? Archer confessed to having prisoners there on a regular basis. Just in case Jonno was familiar with his routine, she copied what had been done and wrapped the chain around her ankle. Holding the padlock in place, she didn't lock it and wouldn't unless it became unavoidable.

Craning, she heard them move into the apartment. The front door closed, and their voices carried in tones rather than specifics. Would they come to the bathroom?

Curling on the floor, she held her fingers on the padlock, hesitant to snap it into place until the last second. That moment came a breath later when the bathroom door handle rattled. Archer never rattled it before; usually he just came stomping in. That was a warning. She snapped the padlock into place and closed her eyes to give the illusion of sleep.

When the door opened, her eyes stayed shut. What reason was there to talk? If the need arose, she'd take her prompts from Archer—he wasn't going to trust her until she trusted him.

"There," Archer said. "Now get the fuck out."

"Wait a minute," Jonno said. "We're here, she's giving you shit. Let's have fun with her. Teach her a lesson."

"You wanna watch me cut her?"

That deadpan tone was alarming, blunt and cold like he might follow through. The taste of his kiss still hung on her lips. Corners of her body trembled, enlivened by awakened curiosity. Yet he stood there implying he was ready to hurt her again.

"You and those fucking blades. Any other guy gets a babe like this locked up in his place and the bitch would be chained to the bed, not the toilet. We'd get off on sticking our dicks in her." Jonno had a laugh in his voice. "You'd rather stick her with your blade!"

"Who said I haven't stuck my dick in her?" Archer asked, still without emotion. "Why would I want you to watch me fuck her? I never understood that about you and your crew. You love waving your junk in each other's faces."

That almost made her laugh, though Archer's intonation wasn't humorous.

"If we work in tandem," Jonno said, ignoring the jibe. "She'll give Taggert up."

"You want me to cut her while you fuck her? Don't think so, Jonno."

"What's the problem?"

"You come here to get laid?" Archer lost some of his patience, which was impressive given it had already been almost indecipherable. "Go look for your kinky shit elsewhere."

One guy shoved the other and something soft hit her face before the door closed. She waited a few seconds before peeking. The men were gone and the light was off.

Taking the soft, fresh fabric from her face—the towel that usually hung in a loop by the door. Folding it, she stuffed it under her head to use as a pillow. While listening to movement and voices in the living room, she fell asleep.

NINE

MMM, COFFEE. The smell of it warmed her nose before she even opened her eyes. When she did on a yawn, there was a mug on the floor right in front of her face. The shower was running and from the noise of the water she guessed Archer was using it.

Sitting to pick up the cup wait… she was closer to the center of the room; there was only one way that could be possible. Whipping around, she grinned. The chain wasn't attached to her ankle. In fact, it was gone from the room altogether.

Getting to her feet, she drank the delicious java she'd missed so much, with delight. Coffee was her life blood. Gulping it down, she'd finished most of it by the time she put it on the ledge over the sink that served as a vanity below the vast inset mirror. Then, turning on the faucet, she bent to wash her face.

"Fuck, Squirm!" Archer called from the shower.

She quickly turned off the water. "Shit, sorry," she called back, unsure whether to cringe or laugh.

The latter came more naturally.

Opening a panel of the mirror, she found floss and used his toothbrush to clean her teeth. There was no comb or brush. Not a surprise. Archer's hair was short enough that finger-combing it would probably do.

She got a towel from the closet just as Archer's disappeared from the shower curtain rail. He didn't turn the water off, so she hopped onto the toilet lid to hang her towel over the rail. Without the boost in height, she'd never have been able to reach.

The curtain went back and he stepped out with a towel around his hips. Examining her position on top of the toilet, he ran his hands through his hair.

"Do what you've gotta, then we're straightening this out."

She didn't ask what; she knew what he meant. He went past the sink, out of the room and she was left to bathe alone, unsupervised, and untethered. Such simple bliss.

***

IT SEEMED POINTLESS to get washed only to put on last night's dirty dress. Instead she elected to keep her towel on and left the bathroom to find out if Archer had anything else she could wear.

When she opened the bathroom door, the bedroom door was open opposite. Archer was sitting on the edge of the bed, tying his boots as she stepped out of the steam.

"What do you need?" he asked without raising his head.

Daylight shone through the blinds on the window beyond his bed. Natural light, an odd treat. Who'd think something so basic could be so appreciated?

"Something to wear."

Sitting up, he took in her appearance. "I can give you a tee shirt. Not got many women's clothes lying around."

She'd guess not, Archer didn't strike her as the cross-dressing type. "Wearing a tee shirt is better than wearing nothing," she said. When one of his brows slunk up, she laughed. "If I'm naked when we show up at Tag's, he'll get the wrong idea."

"That you want to screw around with him or that

you're screwing around with me?"

His black tee shirt strained across his shoulders when he leaned forward to rest his elbows on his wideset knees and link his hands.

Holding on to her towel, she crossed the hall to enter his bedroom. "If I was screwing around with you, would you let me walk naked into a room full of men?" she asked, trying to get more of a measure of this enigmatic man.

Thrilling lust inflamed her again. What the hell was wrong with her? The confusion of yearning for this terrible, merciful conundrum of a man, only intensified her craving. She'd never had such an instant reaction between her thighs as she was having right then. The closer she got, the harder she yearned.

There was something about his large, formidable hands. They'd been used to inflict such pain and proved their deft capability. Those hands had hurt her, yet she hungered to have them apologize by committing themselves to her pleasure.

"No, I wouldn't," he said, sitting straight to curl his fingers around her narrow waist when she stopped between his feet. "But I don't screw around."

"You're not a whore?"

Smiling, she rested her hands on his shoulders and squeezed. He was so solid. Simmering sensation stirred in her breasts.

"No," he said. "Whores don't interest me; I like my girls to stick around."

A daring, irrational part of her wanted to drop her towel and climb onto his lap. But if he wanted relationships, not one-night stands, she had to figure out if she wanted to stick around first. Which, unfortunately, meant restraining herself.

As of that minute, there was no great love, just complicated desire. He was attractive and wrong for her, a dangerous bad boy who would break her heart if she didn't keep her wits about her. His pick-up lines probably enticed plenty of women. For years, men had been feeding her bullshit in attempts to get into her panties. If this guy was for real, she might entertain messing around with him. If it was an act, she'd be happy to drop him on the curb, mysterious stud or not.

"What time did Jonno leave?" she asked, tousling her fingers through his hair.

"Late," he said. "The bastard drank all my beer."

She pouted and got even closer, forcing him to tip his head back. "I had to take my cuff off," she said, showing him her wrist. After scrutinizing it for a minute, he brought it to his lips, stunning her with his affection. This seemed like the right minute to get the awkward formality of expressing her gratitude out of the way. "Thank you, for not letting Jonno…"

Was she doomed to thank him for protecting her virtue on a daily basis?

"I've never branded a woman before," he said, kissing her wrist again then setting her back to go get his first aid kit from his in-built closet.

The deep second-degree burn would scar, it still had to fully heal, but she could make out the edges now. The outer triangle was surprisingly even. Inside the shape, the non-injured parts were like an insignia.

The tail of the C led into the beginning of the uppercase A. The crossbar of the A was diagonal, coming from the lower right tip of the A crossing over the other side of the A and coming to a stop in a curved flourish in the middle of the C.

"Only men?" she asked when he sat and pulled her down beside him.

"Figured you'd prefer that to other types of torture I use."

Which was sort of how he'd explained it in the parking lot. Being alone in the bedroom, she had a chance to delve deeper into what this bad boy was about.

"You use torture?"

"It's more effective than you think," he said. "Lowlifes don't protect kin and country, they protect themselves. I don't have to exert much pressure to find out what I need to know."

"Is that why you have all those knives?"

He cleaned her wound with a wipe, then blew on it to dry it. She shivered.

"We'll leave it uncovered today," he said, putting some ointment on after bringing her limb to his lap. "Where will I find Taggert?"

The question made her draw back. "Tag?"

She recoiled. Was this a change in tactics? Torturing her didn't work, so he tried seducing her instead?

"I'm not telling you that. Haven't you been listening to me?"

"You said you couldn't give me what you didn't have, you've got it now, right? He gave you his address on the phone."

Turning her hand to curl her fingers on his thigh, she inched closer. "I meant what I said about him digging in if he thinks you're threatening me. You can't go to his alone, he's expecting me and if you tell him I gave you his address—"

"He'll hurt you?"

Suppressing her instinct to roll her eyes, she shook her head instead. "He'll hurt *you* because he'll assume you've hurt me." Which he had, not like Archer could deny it. "And, let's be honest, you have hurt me. This only got easier because last night I saw something in the way you protected me. And you've promised to help me punish Jamie's killers too. I need you and we'll be allied as long as we have to be."

Could be a while depending on how long it took to track down the men responsible for killing Jamie.

"What you trying to say, Squirm?"

"I'll take you to Tag. I'll talk to him for you. We'll get your money. You have to trust me and stop thinking of me as your prisoner. I'm here by choice; I want to help you, so you'll help me. This for that. You've gotta give up the tough guy act, Archer. You don't have to threaten or hurt me. You'll get what's rightfully yours. Relax, and show me you trust me."

"I loosened your chain and fed you, didn't I?"

Proof of trust? Taking a deep breath, there couldn't be any misunderstanding between them.

"Why did you take me from Sizzle and hurt me?"

"Taggert has enemies. More than I think you know."

She'd seen the men in Sizzle. Those not preoccupied with Jamie were focused on one thing: locating Tag.

"That doesn't answer my question."

"Jonno told me you were the link to finding your boy Tag. I don't know how Jonno figured it out."

As she'd told him before, Tag had set her up in Sizzle when he found out she was stripping. He'd stormed the place to pull her out. Plenty of staff and patrons had seen them together, both in that strip joint and in Sizzle. Their association went back years. It didn't surprise her they'd been connected.

"So you sauntered in to corner me?"

He didn't bullshit her with evasive answers, which granted him points in his favor. "I didn't know Jonno was gonna leave dead bodies in the street. He's an idiot. We should've had all the time we needed in the club. It was closed, and there was no one in the street. He should've got the bouncers inside, cornered them and Jamie, and used them to manipulate you into giving Tag up."

Wow, okay, this guy did have experience.

That night would've gone differently if Archer had been driving the ship.

"How would you have done that?" she asked because forewarned was forearmed.

He ran a fingertip down her arm, then got up to go to the dresser on the wall by the door. "I'd have hurt them," he said, without guilt.

Startled, it took a second to absorb his honesty.

"What is it that you do?" she asked. "To get by?"

Experience in delivering pain and extracting details didn't tell her how he made a living.

"I deal in information," he said, closing a drawer and turning around to hold up a tee shirt.

"White?" she asked and shook her head. "Not when I don't have underwear. Anything darker?" He went back to the drawers. "How does someone deal in information?"

Pushing back on her hands, she slid herself to the middle of the bed. Mmm, it was the most comfortable mattress she'd ever been on… though, compared to Archer's floor, anything would be heaven. She relaxed to lay down. Closing her eyes on her view of the ceiling, she stretched out her toes to discover she fitted the width of the bed.

"Sometimes I find out what people want to know and track that information down for them. Other times I hear something of value and hock it to the highest bidder."

"So you're an investigator?"

He scoffed and the bed shifted. "Not even close," he said. Opening her eyes, she found him lying on his side next to her, head propped on a fist. "I'm direct. Very direct."

"I noticed," she said, glancing at her wrist.

He didn't relinquish the gray tee shirt bunched in his hand. He dropped it onto his hip and curled his thumb inside the tucked part of her towel.

"What are you doing?" she asked when he pulled it out.

"Wanna see if those bastards hurt you."

Opportunistic pig. It was a thought. Not enough to upset her. Actually, she was loose and relaxed. He'd seen her chest last night and modesty was the first thing a stripper had to cast off. With meticulous care, he peeled her towel away and reached over to lay it flat on the bed.

Allowing his open palm to trace the high peak of the breast he'd exposed, he rose to lay the other side flat under him.

Naked, lying on the open towel in the middle of the bed, she scrutinized him as he did the same to her.

In his jeans, the thickening of his cock was obvious. Mmm, satisfied, she was proud of provoking that reaction. So proud that she arched her waist to better present her body for his hungry gaze.

"Are you playing with me, Squirm?"

"Are you playing with me?"

If she'd considered their flirtation could be manipulation, his keen mind would've considered the possibility for sure.

"Women and games don't go together. I get bored of bullshit," he said. "I'm a straight shooter."

"But a bad aim," she said. His fingertips touched the

inside of her knee but paused when his questioning frown emerged. "In the bathroom, you threw that knife at my head and missed."

"I never miss," he said. "If I'd meant to hit you, you'd be dead already."

And with what she'd seen of him in action, she could buy that.

"I've never been very good at games," she said. "I can have a temper. My poker face sucks."

"You're stubborn and emotional. I noticed."

Not much of a surprise. Those fingertips of his skimmed upward until she clamped her thighs together to block him.

"I don't think there are any bruises up there... he didn't get that far."

Looking over her again, he pulled his hand from between her thighs. "I don't know which bruises were him and which were me."

There were various blotches and bruises on her body, she'd checked them out in the shower, and couldn't identify the source of them either.

"Would you feel better if I said all was forgiven," she said. Startled, it was clear he hadn't expected her to say that. "We're allies now. Equals. If you help me like you said you would, all this, the bruises, the scars, it's meaningless."

"So if I slice every man who touched your friend, you'll forgive my sins?"

"Yep," she said because she needed his strength. "After."

Lunging down, he touched her ear with his lips. "Fuck your forgiveness," he breathed. "I like my sins."

Shoving off the bed, he tossed the tee shirt onto her body and left the room.

Were they making friends? If so, she didn't expect him to be antagonistic. Maybe it was just his way. After yanking the tee shirt on over her head, she dashed out of the room.

"The only way Tag lets you go without hurting you is if I'm on your side," she said when she entered the kitchen to see him cleaning the coffee machine.

"Your buddy can't hurt me, Squirm."

The confidence amazed her. "He won't be alone; he'll have guys with him."

He always did. Tag's charisma attracted an entourage; he was loyal to the men who were loyal to him. That core group would go to any lengths to protect each other. Archer was one man; Tag could have anywhere from three to thirty men with him.

"What you gonna tell him about us?" Archer asked, wiping his hands on a kitchen towel.

Sparks bounced between them, sure, but one kiss hardly constituted an 'us.'

"Us?"

"We rock up there together and your boy will think I'm fucking your pussy or fucking you over. We're not friends. I'm not there to protect your ass. Why else would we go there together?"

He had a point. Tag knew her friends and she didn't need anyone to protect her around him.

"Let me go in there alone," she said. "I'll go to him, find out about your money."

The slant of his mouth was almost a smile. "Don't think so, Squirm."

"You don't trust me?"

"I don't trust you," he said. Okay, she couldn't be offended by his honesty; their alliance was still in its infancy. "We're going to your boy's tonight, you and me, we're getting my money."

Tag would be suspicious of Archer. He'd never been known for cutting anyone a break, especially someone who might be considered an adversary. Reasoning with her oldest friend would be difficult. But if anyone could persuade him to make peace with Archer, it was her.

Protecting Archer felt right, he'd protected her. The only reason she survived in Sizzle was because he'd pulled her out. He'd protected her from Bryant and his friends. And he hadn't let Jonno get his hands on her last night.

She'd play mediator. "I will help you, Archer. I'll do

everything I can to make sure Tag doesn't hurt you, but… I need assurance that you won't hurt him."

The new set of his brow didn't inspire confidence about his intentions.

"If he comes for me, I won't hesitate to take him down."

She wouldn't ask him not to defend himself; she wouldn't ask that of anyone. If she asked Tag not to hurt Archer, he wouldn't, so she didn't have to worry about that.

"Is it your plan to go in there and…?"

"Kill him? How would I get my money if he was dead? I guess I could extort it out of you… You're so close to him, you must be in his will, right?"

Humor or an example of his information extraction skills?

"I don't know," she answered. "We've never talked about it."

His eyes traveled to her legs. "We've got a few hours until we go over there," he said, though she didn't know the relevance of delaying the trip until later. "I could do you a favor."

That sounded suspiciously like a line.

Cocking a hip, she rested her palm on it. "Meaning?" she asked, expecting a lewd answer.

"I'll take you to your apartment, you can pack whatever shit you need. Women are weird about needing their own crap, right? And I ain't having you walk into a room full of guys dressed like that neither… Wearing my shirt isn't better than wearing nothing, 'cause all I've thought about since I seen you in it is sex."

TEN

WEARING HER OWN clean and undamaged clothes was a treat. She'd never considered herself someone who placed much premium on material possessions. Oh, but it was nice to be comfortable.

In her studio apartment, Archer's form became an immovable feature. He'd gone around opening drawers and doors like he wanted to learn more about her and had every right in the world. Except she didn't like his prying, so went around after him, closing them in his wake. He'd respected her privacy to this point, now they were becoming associates, it seemed that chapter was over.

So they squabbled about his nosiness, and she found out he hadn't explored her purse because he had an aversion to the mystery of women's things, whatever that meant. He didn't like purses and medicine cabinets but had no problem sitting on her bed and checking out her underwear. He even switched on her vibrator.

They'd eaten at hers and stayed until he declared they were leaving. Much as she'd assumed it would be, Archer confirmed their destination was Tag's place when he asked for directions as soon as they got into his car.

Leading him to Tag might be a mistake, but it was the

only way to progress. It was this or live the rest of her life on Archer's bathroom floor. The men would come face to face eventually, either when Tag came looking for her or when Archer tracked Tag down. This just sped things along.

Okay, yes, Archer could be playing her; he was dangerous and could be ruthless. But he was a guy on his own and Tag was tenacious. Her friend would take Archer on while surrounded by his guys if he had to protect himself or her. In the opposite respect, she was confident of talking Tag out of hurting Archer. Meaning all being well, this situation should be defused soon.

During their journey to Tag's new apartment, she checked the map on her phone several times. The address wasn't in an area typical of her friend. Instead of the usual affluent districts he liked, this was in a student haunt.

The building they parked outside was twenty stories high. She checked it out while waiting for Archer to come around to let her out. When they were on the sidewalk, he curled a finger around the metal loop on the cuff she'd chosen to wear over her brand. Archer had advised her to let the wound breath for a day but turning up at Tag's wearing evidence of Archer's abuse wouldn't be a good kick-off point.

"Before we go in, I have to tell you," she said, pausing outside the revolving door to the lobby. "Once you get your money from Tag, just leave."

"Leave?"

Damn, why didn't she say this in the car? She'd been too busy thinking about why Tag might be staying in this weird area.

"You won't need me after you've been paid, right?" she said. "Take the money and walk."

With one sharp tug on her cuff, he got her tumbling against him. "We walk in together, we walk out together."

She shook her head. "I've stayed with Tag a bunch of times. Maybe I'll walk out tonight, maybe we'll have a drink and a meal… I don't need a chaperone with my oldest friend."

"And your other friend at Sizzle, what about her?"

This instruction didn't free him from their deal.

"I haven't forgotten our agreement. When I want to

call it in, I'll find you."

With that decided, they shared a final look before he turned her body and patted her ass, urging her into the revolving door. He wasn't gentleman enough to give her space in her own segment, he crowded in behind her, entering the lobby with his grip tight on her shoulders.

"What apartment is it?" he asked when they got into the elevator.

"Twenty-two," she said.

The placement of the apartment inside the building was another surprise. Tag liked to live on higher levels as those with better views tended to be more expensive. But this apartment was on the second floor. They could've taken the stairs but were already in the elevator, so traveled the short journey up the single floor.

The apartment door was in view when they stepped out. On their walk to it, Archer hooked her cuff again and she didn't object. Technically, this was her territory, she could walk in and demand Tag skin Archer alive. It made sense for her newest ally to be nervous.

Except one glimpse of his profile didn't reveal any hint of anxiety. In fact, after she knocked, Archer actually yawned before he put her between him and the door and rested his forearm on the frame.

The door opened and—Gio, yes, one of Tag's closest associates.

"Nya!" Gio said, welcoming her with a hug. "Where have you been?"

When she withdrew from his arms, Gio's glare was focused behind her. Archer shoved her forward into the apartment. Her body acted like a shield as he granted himself permission to enter.

Gio, Tag, none of the people there would appreciate a stranger in their ranks. She'd have to talk fast to explain who Archer was and why she'd brought him. It would just—

"Archer," Gio said. What in the…? "Going after Nya? Risky."

"It worked," Archer said while she stood gaping. "You and Tag have been dancing in the shadows too long.

Time to pay your debts."

"You two know each other?" she asked, sidestepping to quarter-turn and bring both men into view.

"Sure," Gio said. She didn't trust that flat smile; wasn't like Gio to go on the defensive. "There isn't a guy on the planet Archer doesn't know… Though not many can say they know him."

Archer kind of nodded but was no more relaxed than Gio. Alone in the square hallway, she wouldn't have a chance of separating these guys if a fight broke out. The hostility crackling between them suggested that might be an imminent possibility. She had to get them out of these close quarters.

"Where's Tag?" she asked.

There were two doors on either side of the empty hall with one at the head, and it was the central one Gio headed for. The living space they entered was wider than it was long. A kitchen/dining area to the right was occupied by three men she recognized as working for Tag, but she didn't know them as friends.

Tag was sitting in the middle of a couch on the far left wall with a colleague in each of the flanking armchairs and he immediately lit up when he saw her.

"Yorkie!" Tag rose to walk toward her but slowed as his smile slid away. He'd noticed Archer. Her friend stopped three meters away; this was new. By now, she should be in his welcoming embrace. "Did he hurt you?"

Archer was right about Tag's assumption and that posed a problem. Denying Archer brought her there against her will would lead Tag to believe they were sleeping together. But if she confessed the truth as to how she and Archer met, Tag would have his men take Archer down. She'd promised he wouldn't be threatened.

"I brought him here by choice," she said, not answering the question. "You have unfinished business."

"Do we?" Tag asked, observing her then Archer. Raising a hand, he swept his finger around and everyone else in the room cleared out. Once the door closed, Tag circled, keeping his distance as he repositioned himself to put his back to the windows. "Are you fucking him?"

Men must all think alike, she glanced at Archer who gave her an "I told you so" brow bob and she sighed.

"You told me you always paid your debts, Taggy," she said, not acknowledging the insulting question. "Do you owe Archer money?"

"No."

She hadn't expected such a flat, abrupt denial, or for Archer to move so quickly in an attempt to get past her.

Tag reversed in panic, but she opened her arms and put herself in front of Archer's stampeding form, body blocking him. He collided with her back, she strained not to stumble, but Archer grabbed her upper arms to steady either her or himself. Whichever it was, it kept them both on their feet.

"Move, Squirm," Archer demanded.

"No, just calm it, Arch."

His grip tightened, but he stopped trying to wrestle her aside.

"I don't know what he's told you," Tag said. "You shouldn't have brought him here, Yorkie."

The situation was more of a clusterfuck than she'd expected. Tag wasn't usually afraid of anyone, but when Archer got mad, fear brimmed in Tag's expression. Her friend didn't typically renege on deals either. Something serious was going on and she planned to get to the bottom of it.

"I brought him because if you owe him money, you should pay him. Are you telling me he's never done work for you?"

This time, Tag took longer to respond. "Yeah, he did… He killed three of my men… Bet he didn't tell you that."

No, he didn't. Archer must have felt her muscles tighten because the bite of his grip on her shoulders increased.

"I didn't kill those pricks," Archer said. "You wanted to know where the drugs were coming in and I told you."

"You sent my guys into a trap."

"You talk shit, Taggert. If I wanted your guys dead, I'd have taken care of them myself. I wasn't there, no one saw what happened. Your guys fucked up. You know it. You're too embarrassed to admit how shit your operation is. Luck is all that gets you through, Taggert!"

Her friend seethed; Tag didn't like anyone questioning his ability. Few men took kindly to being labelled incapable. Being honest, she was kinda offended too. Taggert was smart, thoughtful, and thorough. If he trusted the men he'd sent in to do a job, then she would've trusted them too.

The argument wasn't over and Tag didn't need her to defend him.

"You were offered two keys for your trouble, Archer," her friend said. "More than you deserved."

"What the fuck would I do with your drugs? Green is what we agreed on. You're a con man, Taggert, the worst kind."

Word could hurt, sure, but not as much as fists. That was why she kept her body in front of Archer's.

"And what about you? Feeding clients bullshit information. We would never—"

"You owe me, Taggert. And as your man Gio said, I know everyone. Want me to spread word that you renege on deals? No one will work with you once I'm through."

She'd asked him not to cause physical harm to Tag but neglected to include other kinds of damage.

Twisting, she glared at Archer. "Don't threaten him."

"Mouth shut, Squirm."

So much for this being a tense but quick meeting.

"If he says he doesn't owe you—"

"He does and he knows it," Archer said, monitoring Tag. "Why else would I be here?"

An excellent question. He'd been sure about his need to be there. With a sick sister, it made sense he'd be sensitive about collecting money owed to him. It was vital to his sister's survival that he could pay for her treatment.

Tag had acknowledged that Archer did work for him by providing valuable information. Based on that info, his men went in and got dead. Trap or not, they must have had a deal for payment.

"You've got balls showing up here," Tag said. "Doesn't matter if I owe you or not, I can't let you leave."

Archer had come to Sizzle looking for Tag after

Jonno and a bunch of others showed up. Those others wanted something from her friend too, something different to what Archer wanted. She hadn't found out what.

"What's going on?" she asked. Concern for Tag drove her to slip free of Archer's grasp. "It's not like you to hide."

"He's a coward," Archer said.

She chose to ignore him.

"Tell me what's going on, Taggy?" she asked, sliding her palms onto his. Linking their fingers, she got closer. "Are you in trouble?"

"It's my job to look out for you, Yorkie. Don't worry about the crap going on in my life. You'll be safe here… I never should've left you out there alone. We're too easily connected, anyone who asks will find out you're my girl." Something she'd asserted to Archer she wasn't, several times. This wasn't a time to say it again. "You don't mind hanging here for a bit, do you?"

"Course not," she said, he'd never steered her wrong. If he needed support, she'd stick around. "Give Archer his money, let him get out of here and—"

"He's not going anywhere," Tag said. "If he walks out of here, he'll send a squad of his buddies to—"

"I don't need backup," Archer snarled. "I can take you down any time I want."

Tag's machismo was showing too. "Oh yeah? Come on then, what's stopping you?"

Tired of the pissing contest, she growled at them both. "If it will hurry this up, I'll get a ruler and measure both your cocks right here. The posturing thing isn't attractive; can we skip it? Please?" Someone needed to cut through the bullshit. "You have to let him go, Tag. You can't keep a guy like him tied up in a little apartment like this. What are you going to do? Kill him?" She didn't like the shade that gathered behind her friend's gaze. "Tag, I won't let you. I can't—"

"You're protecting him?"

Retreating from abrupt, she loosened. "I'm asking you not to hurt him. Forget Archer. Get him out of here, so we can focus on figuring this out."

Whatever *this* was.

"I'm going nowhere without my money."

Given Tag's mood, Archer would be lucky to get out of there at all. But Archer was desperate. Tag's whole hand slipped onto her face to caress her cheek, from experience the action calmed him.

"Pay him the money, Tag, please," she said. "Anything for an easy life, just get rid of him."

Tag's other hand moved to her waist. "Why do you give a fuck about—"

"He needs it, Taggy, his sister is sick."

Tag's smile was slow. Outrage filled her, could her oldest friend be happy that another human being was in pain?

"Poor, Yorkie, always fighting battles," he said. "You've been taken this time."

Honesty should've enticed Tag to be fair. Except her friend was wearing a look of amused satisfaction that didn't make her feel good. Until now, there had been no reason to doubt Archer's story. And, if she was reading this right, Tag was accusing her of being naïve.

"What do you mean 'taken'?" she asked.

"He bullshitted you. Archer doesn't have a sister."

Turning away from her friend to pin Archer in her sights, she didn't have to ask if that was true. Although his expression hadn't changed, there was guilt written all over Archer's face. If that had been a lie, there was a chance everything else was too, including his pledge to help her.

"You don't have a sister?"

Bold, Archer didn't offer any apologies. "He owes me. What I do with the money is my business."

"You're a real prick," she said. So much for being street smart. Tag was right, she'd been taken for a fool, wanting to see good in the soul of the man who'd made a shitty first impression. She should've known better and was probably more pissed at herself than him. "Get your ass out of here."

As Archer drew his sneer away, she felt herself sliding down in his estimation. The guy was a lying jerk, it shouldn't bother her. But it did. Archer lied to her. He'd been the dishonest bastard. It wasn't right he should be dismissive like she deserved no respect.

With disgust, Archer focused on Tag. "This is your last chance to end this," he said. "If you make me take what's mine, I'll make sure it hurts you."

"I'll take my chances," Tag said, sliding an arm around her.

From Archer's point of view, it probably looked like she'd never intended to help him. Things weren't so clear anymore. She wanted to talk to Tag alone before doing anything else. Good thing Tag had the upper hand. Archer could start a fight, sure, but he couldn't fight everyone.

Finding out he was a liar put their agreement in jeopardy. She wouldn't go out of her way to get him money until Tag explained exactly why he'd withheld the payment.

Leaving with Archer wasn't an option, she wanted to support her friend, and wasn't sure Archer would support her. So when he looked at her like he expected her to speak up, she pushed her shoulders back and sealed her lips, sending him a signal about her intention.

"Just like I said," Archer said to her. "You're his girl. Watch your back, Squirm, he doesn't know the meaning of loyalty. You and me had a deal and I'm a guy of my word, but if I don't hear from you in forty-eight hours, we're through."

Archer glared at each of them in turn before pivoting to storm out, slamming this door and the front one a second after. Alone with Tag, she was ready to hear what he had to say.

ELEVEN

TAG TOOK HER SHOULDERS to bring her around to face him. "You need a drink, then you need to tell me how in the fuck you ended up with him."

Breathing in and out, she found her balance. Tag went into the kitchen to produce a bottle of wine from the fridge. He carried it and two glasses to the couch he'd been on when she arrived. When he held up a full glass to her, she unglued her feet from the floor and went to sit down beside him.

"Tell me everything," he said, filling his own glass as she settled back to drink her wine. "Start at the beginning."

Before all that, she needed some blanks filled in. In the past, her friend had never disappointed her. She wasn't ready to let herself believe he might now.

"I told him you'd pay him. That you paid your debts."

"Was that after he made up a dying sister?" he asked, smirking in a way she didn't like. He settled in the corner of the couch, facing her. "I'm surprised, Yorkie, you usually recognize men's bullshit from a hundred paces."

Yeah, accepting a lie was unlike her, but this wasn't an ordinary lie designed to get a guy laid. This was a genuine lie; one Archer sold with sincerity.

"What do you know about him?" she asked.

If Tag could be so certain about Archer's lack of female siblings, he had to know the guy to some degree.

"Not a whole lot. Everyone says he's the guy to go to if you need to know something," he said. "That's how I ended up hiring him, he's discreet, and can find out anything. Literally anything; that's what I was told. But he can also be paid to keep any secret."

Working with people who could keep quiet was vital to what Tag did, though she didn't understand the specifics.

"Why did he screw you over?" she asked. "Why would he send your guys into a trap?"

Tag shrugged. "Don't know. But they showed up and three got killed, the other three barely made it out with the cargo."

"With the cargo?" she asked, surprised he'd had his guys complete the mission. "If it was a trap, why didn't you pull your guys out?"

"There was a lot of money in that warehouse."

Money. His men were in danger and he got them to do the job despite knowing it could cost their lives?

"Did Archer know the men you were stealing from?"

It could be an old-fashioned double-cross.

"Stealing?" Tag said, bending to put his glass on the coffee table. "It's not stealing, they owed me."

"And you owe Archer, don't you?"

Tag didn't like the question, his tension betrayed it, yet he didn't argue.

"Are you tired or hungry?" He stood up. "I'll send one of the guys out to get us some food. Gio will want to catch up with you too. Stay here. I'll be back in a minute."

Cagey Tag. Hmm. Changing the subject was one of his standard modes of operation. She'd always believed he did it to protect her, which had been his default for a long time. Sometimes she resented his need to keep her at a distance from his work, because she wasn't as delicate as he made her out to be. But his business was just that. His. Given he dealt with drug dealers and lowlifes, she didn't mind being kept in the dark about most of it.

After Tag left the room, she slipped off her shoes and curled her legs underneath her. Archer lied to her, for some reason, she couldn't stop thinking about that. Did he lie to manipulate? Was the truth worse than the lie? He needed his money, or maybe he just wanted it. Whatever. He'd thought lying was the only way to get it.

Archer had threatened Tag and she didn't want the men to clash. Both of them were pigheaded. Averting a war would fall to her. If Archer did as he said and badmouthed Tag, he might have the reach to ruin Tag's business. And if Archer had done a job for Tag, and hadn't set him up, he deserved to be paid and she'd have to play Tag's conscience. She had some prying to do.

***

TAG DID HIS BEST to avoid the topic of Archer for the rest of the night. He brought in the men she knew, including Gio, and they ended up having an impromptu party. Because sleeping space was limited, she crashed in bed with Tag, as she had dozens of times before. Instead of breakfast, they ended up having brunch because they slept so late.

At the table, Tag whispered some instructions to Gio, causing him to take everyone else out of the room, leaving her alone with Tag for the first time since Archer left.

"What are you doing here, Tag?" she asked before he'd even turned away from the just-closed door. "This isn't a neighborhood you'd ever choose for yourself. Holing yourself up with a bunch of your guys? That's not your style either. Not unless you're scared of someone coming for you."

"Scared?" he repeated, whipping around. "You know me, Yorkie. I don't get scared."

"So what are you doing here with your whole crew in one small apartment?"

Sauntering to the table, he sank into his chair to pick up his espresso. "We've got a big job on, don't worry about it, Yorkie."

"I'm worried about you, Taggy," she said, pushing her own plate aside to get closer. "If you don't want to tell me why you're here, that's fine, whatever." She was worried about him but couldn't force him to reveal his secrets. "But you should pay Archer his money."

The movement in his lower lip betrayed he wasn't impressed. "You've got a real hard-on for this guy, why do you care if I pay him or not?" Because she needed him, she needed Archer and his skills to identify each of the men who'd hurt Jamie so she could hurt them too. "I don't want him coming after you."

That was true as well, but not the whole truth. Tag would never support, or understand, her need to retaliate against the Sizzle attackers. Her friend was caught up enough in his bravado not to doubt what she'd said.

"I'm not afraid of Archer," he said again. "You never told me how you hooked up with him."

Just as Tag never told her a bunch of things. Double standards were his specialty in a lot of areas. Still, she'd have to tell him the truth eventually and given it was a day after Archer left, Tag had cooled down.

"He was in Sizzle, the night that… that Jamie was killed."

Tag's nonchalance dissipated. "That fucker hurt you?" As he sat up straight, he gained mass. "He was one of the guys who killed my men?"

"No," she said, reaching over the table to catch his hand so he couldn't stand and storm off. "He came in after Jamie was… after they'd hurt her and threatened me. Archer took me out of there."

"He saved you?"

She hadn't thought that at the time, and it probably hadn't been his intention, but she nodded anyway.

"He asked about you and I wouldn't tell him, but… when he told me you owed him money, I thought… I didn't think it was a big deal to bring him so you could settle up. You always say you pay your debts."

He touched her face. "He told you his sister was sick and you believed him. I'm sorry he was a prick." Not sorry about being a prick himself though, was he? "Stick with me, kid. We have some shit going on around here; we'll figure it out. As long as you're close, you're safe."

Tag could be infuriating, he wasn't providing any valid explanation for scamming Archer. The more he gave her the brush off, the surer she became Archer was owed the twenty grand.

But as long as he wasn't talking about that, she'd get information on her next cause. "What's happening with Sizzle? Did the cops get any evidence?"

"They're not telling me much, the bastards."

And Tag was on their radar, his men had come close to getting themselves into trouble with the authorities. More than once. More than twice. And so on…

It wouldn't surprise her if Tag was doing his own investigation rather than relying on the official one.

What she didn't want was to forget the most important person.

"Jamie." Her hand loosened as her eyes fell to the brunch plates. "How long did she hold on?"

To his credit, his voice softened. "Never made it to the hospital." Clutching her, he rubbed a thumb across the back of her hand. "They hit her hard."

Yes, they did, she'd seen the blows. "How did she die? Did they at least…? Did they put her out of her misery?"

He shook his head. "They beat on her, she never regained consciousness."

After what they'd done that might've been a blessing.

"She didn't deserve to die that way," she whispered. "You should've seen it, Tag, what they did to her… No one deserves that."

"It can't have been easy for you… to see that. It must have brought back memories about—"

"No," she said, snatching her hand away. "This is not about me. It's about Jamie and the evil bastards who hurt her… I want to hurt them."

Letting her anger show, she waited for his reaction. Tag preferred to manipulate her life so it fitted what he thought it should be, as opposed to supporting her in what she wanted. Yes, he made concessions for her, and he protected her, but she never asked him to fight her battles.

"No," he said, getting stern and rising to stand while keeping his fists on the table. He adopted the air of a disapproving father, though he was only a few years older than her. "I've seen that look in you, and I'm telling you to forget about the girl."

She had no intention of forgetting that night. "How can I do that? You didn't see what I saw. You weren't there."

"And you're going to forget that you were," he demanded. "Yorkie, I know what's best for you. Haven't I always looked out for you?" She wouldn't deny that. "Going after those guys, it won't make you feel better. Revenge never does. Talking to the cops won't mean shit either. Even if they found anyone and got you into a court, they'd just fuck you over, they always do."

Frustrating though it was, his reaction wasn't a surprise.

"So I'm just supposed to sit here drinking my coffee and forget Jamie? She died because of us. Those guys who busted into Sizzle, they were looking for you!"

"This is my fault?" he asked, striding away from the table. She leaped up to follow. "Do you think I wanted them in there fucking up my club? I don't need eyes on what I do, Yorkie. I don't need the cops tearing the place apart looking for motive. They want to know why those guys were there, and the first place they look is me!"

The cops weren't the only ones interested in why so many people were pissed off with her oldest friend.

"I wouldn't give you up," she said. "The guys outside were already dead. I saw what they were doing to Jamie and… I wouldn't give you up."

His shoulders sagged and understanding overcame him as he approached to caress her face.

"I wouldn't have given you up either. People don't understand our bond, where it comes from, but it's real, Yorkie. You know that. I'm sorry your friend had to be hurt, but… you did the right thing."

Protecting herself and protecting him was the right thing even though it cost Jamie her life? It didn't feel like the right thing. Reliving the sounds and sights from that night was nauseating.

"I have to sit down."

Tag took her arm and led her over to the table to put her back in her chair. Archer would've carried her 'cause for some reason, he picked her up like a ragdoll any time it pleased him. Why was she thinking about him?

Tag pulled his chair up beside hers and stroked her forearm. "You'll be safe here. I'll look after you."

"What about Sizzle? I should get back to work and—"

"Work will be there when you're ready," he said. "You don't have to worry about anything. I'll take care of everything."

Take care of everything. Except Archer.

"Why would Archer set you up?" she asked, returning to the subject he'd avoided. "He gave you the information you asked for. Do you really think he double dipped? That someone paid him more than you did to set you up?"

He stopped touching her when he slouched against his backrest, then shook his head.

"No… But I wasn't paying twenty-five grand and losing three guys."

"Twenty-five?" she asked. Archer told her twenty. One of the men was wrong or Archer was taking a pay-cut.

"I lost three guys that day. I had to pay their families, had to clean up the mess, that's not cheap."

"So you do owe Archer the money?" she asked, guessing it might be his default to argue with another alpha; deferring might be the end of the world. Fighting for the sake of fighting made no sense. Tag didn't answer the question, which she interpreted as confirmation. "You can't screw him out of his money. He did a job. He deserves to get paid. Don't make an enemy of him. If he knows as many people as he says he does…"

Funny that she'd said something similar to Archer about never winning against Tag. It wasn't that she thought Archer would win, but he'd piss off Tag enough that her friend would fight back. They'd keep lashing out at each other and end up in a stalemate that benefited no one.

"Archer won't start shit, he's smarter than that."

Being too cocky could be dangerous. "And you're smarter than ripping someone off. Pay him and get him off our backs." Tag stood to bow over the table and retrieve the coffee pot. Ignoring her. Again. Man, he was frustrating. "Pay him or I will."

He wasn't affected by her claim. "Where are you gonna get that kinda money?" he asked, filling their empty mugs.

His arrogance was contagious. "You have that kind of money and if you have it, I can find it."

Tag snorted. "You wouldn't steal from me."

"It's not stealing if it's rightfully owed," she said because she really would take the money to Archer, now that she knew it was due to him. "Please, Tag, just pay him, and get him out of our lives."

Getting him out of their lives wasn't her motivation. As she'd said to Archer, if she got him his money, she intended to call in his promise. Maybe not right this minute, Tag had something going on that she wanted to help out with, but eventually.

If she got Tag to give Archer his money, Archer would owe her one. It would be good to have him in her back pocket for when the time was right.

TWELVE

SHE KNOCKED ON the door before she could chicken out. All the way over she'd been thinking up excuses why she should delay showing up at his apartment. She didn't have to be there after all; she could take the money acquired from her oldest friend's safe and run with it. Keep it as danger money. Compensation for what she'd endured.

Not that she ever would.

This mission wasn't about her, and it wasn't about Archer, not entirely. She held her breath when the door opened. Archer appeared, tongue exploring the back corner of his mouth, contorting his face like he was trying to locate a stuck piece of food.

When he saw her, he froze, then lost all affect. Okay, so it wasn't like she'd expected him to be pleased to see her; he wouldn't be impressed with the way things went down at Tag's for sure. She wasn't impressed by that herself.

After brunch yesterday, Tag did some business, and they ate dinner in the apartment. Tag liked to spend money and he liked to eat out. The fact they spent so much time inside proved something was going on. Not that he'd revealed what.

Impatient and in need of freedom from Tag's place,

she'd set her mind to solving the Archer problem that Tag continued to dismiss. That was how she'd ended up there carrying twenty thousand dollars in her purse.

"What do you want, Squirm?" he asked, tightening his grip on the door and moving deeper into the space between it and the frame, restricting her access and view of his apartment behind him.

Digging a hand into her purse, she pulled out the bundles of cash and presented them.

"What's that for?" he asked without touching the money.

Glancing this way and that, holding such a wad of cash was conspicuous in and of itself. Added to the shady hallway only illuminated by the splinters of afternoon light breaking through the dirty window at the end of the corridor, yeah, this was trouble central.

"It's your money," she said. "Twenty grand."

His stoic expression was impossible to read. "And what do you want for delivering that?"

"Nothing more than you've already agreed to," she said, shaking the money at him. "Leave Tag alone and…"

"And?"

"Help me get the bastards who killed Jamie."

In her panic about coming, it never occurred to her he might refuse the money. God knew what state her relationship with Tag would be when he found out she'd followed through on her word about taking the money Archer was owed.

Going back to Tag to return his money and admit he was right would be difficult. But it wouldn't be half as difficult as coming to terms with letting Jamie's attackers go unpunished. Alone, she'd be no match for seven hooligans. She couldn't even fight off the two who'd pinned her to the wall.

Instead of shooing her away, Archer snagged her shoulder to yank her inside. Giving her a nudge toward the dining table, he closed the door, bolted and chained it. As she turned, he came up behind her to reach around and steal the cash from her hands.

"Take a seat," he said with a knowing, but subtle, amusement.

That was the table with the eyebolt in the floor beneath it. The one she'd been locked to while he burned his mark into her wrist.

"Thanks," she said, wiping her moist hands together. "I'll stand."

"Suit yourself," he said and sauntered to the kitchen, counting his money. "Your boyfriend just let you walk out the door with this? What'd you have to do to persuade him to part with twenty grand?"

He tossed the money on the kitchen counter. The bundles scattered haphazardly. How could he be so casual with money he'd claimed to desperately need?

"Why did you lie to me?" she asked, moving across to fold her arms and lean on the breakfast bar, opposite where he was filling the coffee machine.

Inside the kitchen, to the right, was a door beside the fridge. As it was the wall shared by the bathroom, she guessed it led to a closet, and the sink was beside that door. The coffee machine was next to the stove. Another counter to the left with a hutch over it, cabinets beneath, enclosed the kitchen space.

"Does it matter?" he asked. "I lied to you. No big deal. I bet plenty of guys feed you bullshit all the time."

"When they're trying to get into my underwear, sure. But this wasn't that type of lie. Creating a fake, sick sister, why would you do that?"

"For sympathy," he said. The coffee began to percolate, and he pulled out mugs and sweetener from an overhead cabinet. "Got your attention."

True. It had. Her perspective on his need changed when he'd revealed his purpose for the money. Considering what an intense night that had been, their whole relationship shifted and emotions ran high. She hadn't thought to question him, not after what they'd endured together.

"So what do you really need it for?" she asked. "Drugs? Hookers?"

His half-smile told her she was way off base.

"I know enough about the scum in this town that I could blackmail my way into any score or any woman's bed. I don't need money for that kinda crap." He pulled an unopened packet from the cabinet and held it up. "Cookie?"

She shrugged. "Are they vegetarian friendly?"

Dropping his gaze to the packet for half a beat, he didn't make any attempt to read it. "Knock yourself out," he said, tossing the pack to her as he went about prepping the coffee.

Reading the packet gave her something to do, but she hadn't missed what he'd said before distracting her with cookies.

"Any woman's bed?" she muttered. Glimpsing the symbol she needed to see, she proceeded to open the packet. "You can't blackmail your way into any woman's bed."

"Sure I could, if I put my mind to it."

Carefully taking a cookie from the open packet, she held it between her thumb and forefinger, pointing her pinkie and making smug eye contact.

"You couldn't blackmail your way into mine."

Satisfaction spread on his face as he came over to fold his own arms on the opposite side of the counter. "Why would I need to when you're obviously hot for it?"

Her triumph withered and her cookie hand fell to the counter without her taking a bite from the crumbly sweetness.

"You're insane, Archer, if you think—"

"But if you needed an excuse, and wanted to convince yourself I'd made you fuck me against your will, blackmailing you would be easy."

"There's no fucking way—"

Rising, he got closer to lower his volume. "Don't want anyone to know where your boyfriend is, do you?"

Man, he was good and she hated him for it. Shit. She'd taken him to Tag. Far as she knew, Archer had kept quiet about Tag's location. That silence didn't have to last.

"You can't tell anyone."

Plenty of Archer's associates wanted to know.

"And I won't," he said, his gaze sinking to her

cleavage. "If you sit your smokin' ass on that table and open your legs wide for me."

Did he mean it or was this a game? What she didn't understand was the zing that accompanied every beat of her heart. The flutter in her chest was matched by a pulsing awareness between her thighs and a lightness in her belly. Excitement and arousal dulled her senses and heightened her need to explore the sensations zipping beneath the outer layer of her skin.

"Archer—"

"Go on," he said, nodding behind her. "Sit, Squirm. Sit like a good little girlfriend."

Was she supposed to be his girlfriend or Tag's? He did like to refer to Tag as her boyfriend, a fact that couldn't be farther from the truth. But Tag wasn't the man on her mind. No, her thoughts were reserved for the man assessing her now. She'd contemplated it, considered it… giving herself to him. Any assertion otherwise, even just to herself, would be a lie.

During their early days together, she hadn't known what to make of him; he'd hurt her and shown no concern for her well-being. But he was powerful, a man intent on getting the job done, and there was something intoxicating about his focus.

"If I don't…" she murmured, pressing her breasts together when she rested her forearms on the counter to lean toward him. "You'll tell everyone where he is?"

Slanting his upper body an inch closer, she met the light press of his kiss. "Willing to take the risk I won't?"

This wasn't about Tag. This was an excuse, just like he'd said. They were playing a game that allowed them to take the final step they'd resisted so far. Being with him on the table with its negative associations may turn that fortune around.

Easing her weight to her feet, she swayed, letting him wonder. Would she? Wouldn't she? Backing away, a single step at a time, she angled her route until coming up against it.

Using her hips to shunt his chair aside, she hooked her hands over the edge and eased herself onto the tabletop.

Deliberately, she lowered her chin and parted her

thighs as wide as they'd go.

Slowly, he straightened up. The fire in him inspired the smolder in her. When he rounded the breakfast bar, she swung her legs, waiting for him to take his position between them.

"Hair down. Tits out," he commanded.

When she hesitated, he stopped walking. Either he had no intention of touching her until she complied, or he took her hesitation as a refusal. Just the hint of reluctance was enough to stop him in his tracks. Oh, man… That integrity curled her fingers until her nails dug into the underside of the table.

This guy had saved her from rape. Twice. Much as they were implying coercion, his willingness to give her room proved he had no intention of forcing her into anything.

With a smile, she loosened the clip from her hair and shook her locks free. His jaw clicked in appreciation. And fuck that pulled her deeper. Whether it was her obedience or his secret fascination for long dark hair, either reason worked for her. He wanted her and man, that got her hot.

THIRTEEN

NOT SO LONG AGO she'd lived as his prisoner. Now he was standing four feet away, fixated on her hands as they ran through her hair, down her body, over her breasts to the hem of her top. Breathing in, she raised the fabric, arching her body to reveal it slow.

Who had the power now? Mmm, it warmed her from deep inside.

She tossed the top to his face, he cast it aside with a swipe and got moving as she unhooked her bra. Before her arms were free, he'd snagged her knees with a yank, wrapped her legs around his hips, and slanted her body back 'til only his arms held her up.

"You'd do anything for him, wouldn't you?" he asked, breathing in her exhale.

Right then? Tag who?

So much for friendship. This was all for her.

"Use my body, Archer. I'll do whatever you want."

"You like that, Squirm? Like to give me anything I want?" On the cusp of her nod, he snatched her ass to haul it forward, crushing her pussy against the erection pulsing behind his fly. "Only one thing you gotta know before giving yourself to me… If I have you, I keep you."

Maybe this wasn't a game after all. "You want to…" *be together*. "You want to…" *commit to each other*. "You want to…" *have a relationship?*

It was all so fast. She didn't know how to say the words without risking the mood. She wanted to do this, needed to do this. Do him.

Clasping his shoulders, his support came in the form of a kiss. "Yes, Squirm, I do fucking want to."

If the table was his base of operations, it must've taken a beating through the years. It was obvious that the pipes in the bathroom were reinforced. He'd probably done the same to the table. Right? As his power descended, she braced, fearing it may collapse under their combined weight.

"Will this hold?" she asked when he rose to free her bra from between them.

Driving his fingers into her hair, he groaned and sank his lips onto hers. His answers didn't come in the form of words. Urgency answered for him. Maybe he didn't care whether the table held up. Maybe he knew it would. Maybe he had experience. Maybe he'd done this before. Right then, she didn't care. She wouldn't think about his other women, his other experiences. This was their moment. Their first moment of giving in to what had been building between them since that night in the parking lot.

For a split second, she worried he was too much, that he would overwhelm her; he'd be too overbearing, too powerful. He knew what he wanted. Told her what he wanted. Demanded what he wanted.

She couldn't give it to him. Maybe she could. Right now, with the weight of him on top of her, and his hands skimming down her arms, up her waist, through her hair, all over her body, she wanted to be it. She wanted to give it to him. She wanted to give in to his demands, to be with a man so strong and potent.

Already he was between her thighs, but it wasn't enough, she wanted more. Being topless beneath his clothed form frustrated her craving for skin-on-skin contact.

When she tried to wheedle her hands beneath his tee shirt, he caught her wrists, pinning them to the top edge of the table. His strong grip tightened, pressing her fine, fragile bones into the harsh rim of the tabletop. Whimpering at the sensation of his crushing force, for a moment, she wanted him to stop, to tell him he was hurting her. Then, in a snap, the texture of his rough palm stimulated the brand he'd scorched into her.

The trauma of that night ebbed. The pain they'd shared at this table was worth it. Yes, he'd scared her. He'd hurt her. He'd pinned her down, heated his knife and scorched her flesh. Terrifying. She hadn't known what was coming next. Hadn't known if he planned to use that knife to slice her, to hurt her, maybe to kill her. The agony of the burn seared her memory, forever, just like the scar on her wrist.

His mouth, his skilled, soft, hot mouth skimmed over her jaw, down her neck; his hands loosened to slide down her vulnerable arms. She could feel every groove, every ridge of his fingerprints. She was so sensitive to him that every hair on her body reacted to the heat of his breath flowing over her nipple.

In a constant current, her body rippled, she couldn't stay still. Even with him there, holding her down with his own body weight, she managed to writhe. Responding to every move, countering it with her own, ensuring they never parted contact. This didn't make sense and yet it did. It made so much sense.

It was physical. Nothing but physical. The attraction of her body to his, the magnetism, the sheer chemical reaction of proximity was undeniable now they were on equal footing.

She needed him. He'd promised to help. That's why she'd come back. That's why she'd given him the money Tag owed him. She had to hold up her end of the deal so Archer would uphold his.

Jamie suffered in such a horrific way. It wasn't right. She couldn't…

Her arms, still stretched above her head, no, they… Without thinking, she touched him, splayed her fingers in his hair to draw his mouth away from her breasts.

He grumbled, groaned, and growled out loud, pissed off she was spoiling his feast. Her head rose from the table to meet his eye as he wrenched her digits from his hair to slam her hands down again.

This time, maybe 'cause of the eye contact, he let her speak.

"Archer," she said. "I want this. I've never wanted anything more than I want this."

"Good," he said, his primal rumble vibrating from deep within him.

His hips pushed into hers, teasing her with a sample of what was to come.

Looking into his dark eyes with their deep honey flecks, she knew this wouldn't be enough. One joining on this table wouldn't be enough. If they gave in to this, she wanted to learn everything there was to know about this man who held himself so far away from everybody else.

Gio said it. Archer knew everyone, absolutely everyone. But nobody knew him. She wanted to know. She wanted to know him physically, wanted to know what he did to keep in shape. Wanted to know what he tasted like, if he snored, what he ate for breakfast, how many beers he drank every night.

His head fell forward, but it was surrender, not passion that got his hair tickling her chest.

"We're gonna do this," he said. "Try to cut me off, whatever, it won't matter. I'll have you." He kissed each breast and her chin before shifting to drag his tee shirt off. "We're gonna do this; we're not waiting. I know you're fucked up. I'm fucked up. This whole situation is fucked up. We shouldn't be here. We shouldn't want each other. This shouldn't feel like this."

His panted words almost pained him, like they hurt or annoyed him or something else not so great. Whatever it was, she wanted to know but wouldn't ask. Not now. Not yet. They'd get there.

She'd seen his body, getting in and out of the shower. He had no shame or reason to be shy. Every toned muscle was defined, moving in chorus beneath his skin. Transfixed, she almost didn't notice he was undoing his belt, sliding it from the loops until he popped the buttons on his jeans.

"It's fucked up," he said again. Peering at her, his eyes narrowed when his palms landed on the table, caging her beneath him. "But tell me it doesn't make some kind of fucking sense."

And he was right, it did. It felt right. Unhooking the hip buttons on her skirt, she shimmied out of it, then coiled her legs around his.

She interlinked her fingers at the nape of his neck. "We have a deal," she said. "This changes nothing about that, right?"

"No," he said, scooping a hand under her chin. "I'll hold up my end."

She smiled. "Good." Taking a breath, she boosted up to rub her lips on his. "Because I do need you, Archer. But I'm not a whore. This is no kind of payment. I am not doing this out of gratitude or for any other reason. I sleep with men I want to be with. I sleep with men I trust."

And despite everything, she did trust him. Maybe she didn't trust him a hundred percent. Like, she didn't trust him not to walk away and not to break her heart. But when it counted… He'd heard her scream in pain, and he'd heard her scream in terror.

The first, he tolerated, but thinking about it, he'd never repeated it. God, how hadn't she…? That one night was it. The needle, the shower… No, he'd never caused her pain again. Not himself.

The second scream, the terror, he hadn't endured. On hearing her fear, he'd acted. He'd put himself at risk to pull her out. To save her life. Or more importantly, to save her sanity.

Rolling over to finagle her way off the table, her butt pressed to his groin, ringing a satisfied, almost savage, growl from him.

She laughed. "Not here. Not our first time," she said, not doubting he had ideas of taking her like that, bent over the table.

So she gathered his hands to wrap his arms around her forward-facing body and walked them toward the bedroom at the back of the apartment. He kept one arm around her, opened the door with the other hand, and shoved her in with a force so strong, she stumbled the few feet to land on the edge of the bed.

"That's better," he said, slamming the door behind him.

Why did he always do that? Slam this door and that? Shit, she didn't care, the show of strength worked for her.

Left in nothing but heels and panties, not much was left concealed. Archer was still wearing his open jeans, something she had to remedy fast.

Flipping to her back, she grabbed his waistband and hauled his jeans down with his boxer-briefs.

Mmm, and there was that wild sound of pleasure again.

"I like that," he said, stroking a large hand from the top of her head down the side of her face to her shoulder. "Open wide, Squirm."

Before she could even blink, that same hand planted itself on the back of her skull to guide the head of his cock between her lips. Sucking on instinct, the mass of him was a surprise. As was how quickly he filled her, stunning, she hadn't even taken half of him.

This had never been her forte, but she was willing to learn. She'd done it plenty of times, confidence could go a long way.

She sucked and bobbed her head, using her hands and her tongue to stimulate as much of him as she could. Rolling her eyes up to his, it pleased her to see his concentration on the circle of her lips around his shaft.

"Yeah," he groaned out, dragging out every syllable of his approval. "I like that all right."

He got closer, until the hairs on his legs tickled her smooth ones to push her knees apart, bringing her even nearer the edge of the bed. Withdrawing from her lips, Archer came down on the bed over her.

Hauling her toward the center of the pillows, he gave her a close-up view of the bulge of his muscles as they tensed to maneuver her. Then he relaxed on top of her, provoking that squirm to a new height as she struggled for every breath.

Damn, he was hot. This was…

Feeble, consumed by his mass, she gave him the power to dictate her breath, her range of motion, every part of her. Testing their trust fired her hormones. If she survived the encounter, it would be because he let her live, and if he did, their trust would be invincible.

He could kill. Torture. Torment. But in choosing to pleasure her, his despicable hands became benevolent for her and only her.

"You move, girl, feel it. Everything you want, baby, right here."

And she knew it, he loved exerting power over her, loved to be dominant. She wanted to test those limits, to see how comfortable she'd be living under his instruction, his rules, his authority.

There would be time to delve deeper into these new unleashed sensations. They'd be in each other's lives for a while, at least until their deal was fulfilled. So she satisfied herself imagining the possibilities, by stroking his body and welcoming his mouth on hers.

His dick was long, larger than she'd had. Still unsure if he believed that, no matter how many times she said it, she wasn't a whore. And yeah, she wasn't a virgin either. Though… it had been a while since she'd done this.

So when his hand snaked down between them and his hips rose from hers, she worried if he tried to plunge in, all gung-ho, he just wouldn't fit. But he didn't. With surprising finesse, his fingers went first, two pushed in deep, their mass elicited a whine from her throat.

Instead of being disappointed, he smiled. "Oh," he exhaled. "I like that a lot."

Since they'd entered the bedroom, he'd claimed to like a lot of things.

"Yeah?"

"Yeah," he responded. "We're gonna stretch you out nice, right now. Gotta get you slicked up first. Tell me what feels good, Squirm."

His fingers went farther, then came out, he slid them up through her juices, stroked her clit, circled it, learned each of her creases and folds.

"That," she moaned. "Oh, Arch, that feels good."

Again, his digits dipped into her and withdrew, then delved back in. On their next retreat, the tip of his cock met them at her opening. Instead of going inside, he smeared the juice he'd wrung from inside her over and around the bulging head of his cock.

"You feel good to me," he said, rocking his head against her in a series of intimate kisses.

"Archer," she murmured. Her heart raced. Her skin roused. Her mind wanted more, but her heavy body felt slaked and desperate at the same time. "Put it in. All the way in now, hard, fast…"

The words exploded. If he pushed too hard, was too rough, he'd hurt her. Yet she wanted it, him, all of him, now, there, inside her. She wanted this first joining to be complete, to know what it was like to be his absolute focus. Not in torture, or fear, or imprisonment, but in passion, in bliss, in desire consuming them both.

"Not yet," he said.

Pushing in and easing back, advance, retreat, he was taking his time. Maybe it was a tease. Maybe he was worried she couldn't accommodate him, whichever it was, this was driving her insane.

Balling her hands into fists in the blanket beneath, she arched up and called out. Her juices flowed, her core swelled, soft, wet, eager and ready to accept him. Oh, she couldn't take it, couldn't wait. What was with the gradual rocking? Why was he schooling her on his cock a tantalizing millimeter at a time?

Torture didn't have to be pain. This took it to a new level.

Her clit throbbed. It stung and buzzed, zapping ecstasy from every angle. Each nerve signal came and went from that sole, central, hypersensitive point. The girth of his first three inches broadened her entrance, then he flicked his fingertips over her clit and that was it. Orgasm ripped through her in a drowning tsunami that left her unable to draw breath.

Her already tight core clenched, and he swore, but she couldn't let go. She should, but she couldn't. Fuck. Fuck!

Grabbing his waist, clawing at him, she squeezed her eyes closed as all moisture left her mouth. Her breasts ached, her feet tingled, even her scalp quivered.

"Oh," she said aloud. "Oh. Oh…"

The moans, the whispers, the whimpers, his name, maybe hers, maybe she cursed, maybe she praised. Who the hell cared what came out of her mouth? And, bam, the full impact of him slamming into her brought her back. He hit so deep she cried out. The pain morphed to instant pleasure, sating her being.

Another… oh, her body may not be ready for round two.

Except it was.

This joining felt like she'd been created for this man. Created for this moment, for this cock. This was the meaning of her life. To have this moment, to share this moment. Noise quaked from her tingling lips. Pleasure, bliss, desire, her form moved up and down, left and right, every which way. Undulating her hips in circles and figure-eights, feeling him every way she could, this was her heaven. All the while Archer drove in, out, faster, harder, faster.

The commands were coming from her. She was saying them aloud. More. Now. She needed him. Needed something and everything. She wanted the world and he was delivering.

"Archer!"

Unable to stop saying his name, she was sure he said hers in response. Her ears rang. Her sight blurred. Her body was a liquid soup of hormones, responding to her plugged center with orgasm after orgasm.

Their bodies, joined together in union, moved in opposition; together, apart, together, apart. Each more intense, faster in and slower out. Time lost meaning, but their need narrowed. Everything became about that one moment when they clashed to their most intimate meeting before withdrawing again.

When he grabbed for her shoulders, her eyes popped open to meet his. This was it. Archer was galloping to his climax; her legs locked tighter around his hips. Her stimulated passage clamped around his thick, pulsing shaft and she said his name like it was both a dirty word and a blessing. Because for some reason, it was, *he* was.

Responding in kind, his tense expression contorted. He bared his teeth, clenched his jaw, then relaxed in one long rush of breath.

He rolled away, landed on his back and said her name aloud. "Fuck," was his next word. "What the fuck was that?"

"I have no idea," she said, rolling over to climb on top of him. "But it's not the last time we're doing it."

FOURTEEN

SLIDING A HAND around the bedroom door frame as she came out, she yawned and moseyed up the hallway. Archer was in the kitchen with his back to her, wearing only his boxer-briefs.

Going to him, she stroked a hand down his forearm and pressed a kiss to each side of his spine as she went by into the corner where the counters met.

"You let me sleep," she said, raising herself on her hands to sit atop the counter.

"Wasn't gonna kick you out of bed soon as you gave it up," he muttered, spreading mustard onto his ham sandwich. He put the bread lid on, then tidied things away, taking the foodstuffs back to the fridge. "You dropped out fast."

"I haven't slept well the past couple of nights," she said, neglecting to mention the few before that on Archer's bathroom floor. "Tag's bed isn't that comfortable and he hogs the blankets."

Her smile died when he slammed the fridge and whipped around to glare. "You're screwing both of us? What the fuck are you—"

"I'm not having sex with Tag, I slept with him.

There's not much space in that apartment. We've shared a bed a bunch of times. It's no big deal."

"It stops now," he said, returning to his sandwich.

"Are you telling me you've never slept in a bed with a woman without having sex with her?"

Gathering up his sandwich, he took a large bite. "Just my mom and that's only to make sure other dudes don't slide in there."

Interesting, his mom, so he did come from somewhere and was protective of the woman who'd birthed him.

"See much of her?"

"She floats in and out," he said, swallowing his food. "I don't want you sleeping with Taggert again."

Overbearing and possessive. Sleeping with Archer was either the start of her great love affair or the end of life as she knew it, could be both.

"Tag is a good friend," she said, bending to stroke his bare shoulder as far as she could reach. "But he's no threat to us. No one decides who I share my body with except me."

Not so long ago, to recoup Tag's debt, Archer threatened to make those decisions for her. He might've been thinking the same thing. He discarded his sandwich as though he intended to close the space between them. A knock on his door stopped him dead.

Both of them looked at it. Had Jonno returned with his buddies? Archer went toward the gap at the end of the breakfast bar. Their clothes were in separate piles there and he grabbed his tee shirt.

Without looking, he tossed it back toward her. "You shouldn't walk around naked," he said. "It can get busy in here."

That wasn't promising.

Sliding off the counter, she threw his tee shirt back at him. "I don't want to…"

"What?" he asked, stalling despite the knock coming again. Resting his hand on the breakfast bar, his scowl cut to her. "Be seen here?"

No, she wasn't embarrassed to be with him. Archer

was quick to jump on the defensive; she'd have to remember that as she reminded him of something else.

"Your friends and I don't get along." She approached to curl a hand around his oblique. "Did you forget?"

Before she could back away, he grabbed her chin and hauled her close. The intensity in his gaze softened her fear. She didn't need to hear it, his eyes spoke for him. He'd saved her from injury before and wouldn't let anyone hurt her. No one but him.

"Stay in the bedroom," he commanded. "No matter what you hear out here."

Laying an arm over her clothes and purse on the counter beside them, she scooped it all up and reversed until he freed her chin. With a third knock, she picked up speed and slipped into his bedroom again.

Dumping her stuff on the bed, she left the door open a crack to hear what was going on. If it was Jonno, he might expect her to be there as a prisoner or might want Archer to reveal Tag's location. This would be the test. Would Archer keep her confidence or confess what he knew?

For the last two days, she'd been at her friend's apartment. Archer could've set in motion his slander campaign, how was she supposed to know? Huh, probably should've checked before sleeping with him.

"Gio!" Archer declared. She sank to her haunches by the door to cover her mouth with her fingers. She'd been so caught up worrying that the guest may be one of Archer's criminal friends, she hadn't stopped to consider that it might be one of hers. "And a nameless goon, can I call you 'Goon' are you cool with that?" He didn't wait for an answer. "This is a nice surprise."

She smiled. Archer used condescension to put people in their place. It would be annoying as hell to be on the receiving end. But it was kind of funny when she wasn't. She guessed it would piss Gio off no end. It served him right for chasing after her like she was a teenage runaway—if that was why they were there.

"Step aside," Gio responded.

From the distance of his voice, she'd assume they

were still on the outside of the door.

"I'd invite you in, but the place is a mess," Archer said.

She could picture him sliding his hand up the doorframe to narrow Gio's view inside, just as he'd done with Jonno. The lie wasn't meant to be sincere, and the apartment wasn't untidy. Thinking about it… she'd never seen anything out of place for long.

"It's about Nya."

About her? Archer must've hesitated and she was guilty of craning even closer to the gap, shifting silently onto her hands and knees, tipping her head. Except it wasn't voices she heard, it was movement. The men came inside, and Archer closed the door. Did he invite them in because he assumed she'd go with them? Except he didn't call out for her, so… should she stay there or join them?

"I don't got all day," Archer said with a curious edge in his voice.

"We think she'll be coming here," Gio said. "Sometime soon."

"Why would she come here?" Archer asked.

Yes, good question, why would she? She'd told Tag she'd take the money owed to Archer. Soon as it came up missing, he must've known the identity of the perpetrator. That didn't explain why he hadn't called to ask about it.

"She's bringing you money she took from Tag without his permission."

"Ah, you mean my money?" Archer asked. "She's a good girl; I knew I liked her."

Being unable to see what they were doing was infuriating. Sitting on the carpet, she leaned against the wall and let the sound carry to her ear through the space between the door and the frame.

"Tell her to go to hell."

"With my money?" Archer asked almost sounding amused.

She could understand why, given how he felt about being paid what was owed.

"Refuse the money and tell her to get lost."

"Her? She doesn't have a name?"

Gio took a breath loud enough that she heard it. "Taggert thinks you've got your eye on her and we won't let you screw with her."

"Let me get this straight, you're telling me not to take thousands of dollars owed me? And I'm supposed to tell a woman who's hot for me to take a hike because your master asked so nicely?" It did seem extreme to ask for a favor when they hadn't accommodated him at all. Suggesting she was hot for him was extreme too. Except, well, she had come over and fallen into bed with him. "Thanks for the offer, boys, but I'll pass."

Gio got more aggressive. "Don't play with her, Archer. Taggert has no sense of humor when it comes to Nya. He's protective of her."

"You mean he's hot for her," Archer said. "I figured that out on my own. And I don't think your boy has a sense of humor, full stop."

With a hand flat on the wall behind her, she pushed up. Archer was misinterpreting this. Gio probably had orders to hurt him if he refused Tag's requests. She couldn't let this become a fight, not over her and a few bucks. Hiding was supposed to protect her from Archer's crazy friends. Except it was *her* crazy friends out there and she didn't have to hide from them.

Grabbing her underwear from the bed, she tugged it on and paused to make sure the men weren't fighting.

"If you take that money, we'll come get it back," Gio said. "And if you touch Nya, being broke will be the least of your problems."

"If you get the money and the girl, what do I get?" Archer asked. "That's no kinda fair deal. If I give you one, can I have the other?"

Quiet… more quiet. What was going on out there?

Sliding her hand onto the dresser, she got closer. Would they agree to that? She wasn't property to be bartered, but was she worth twenty grand to either side of the equation?

"Taggert said you'd say something like that," Gio said. Tag did like to try getting in people's heads. "You keep your mouth shut about this to everyone and… you can keep the money. But you can't see Nya again."

So she and silence were worth twenty grand to Tag. Somehow, she'd known that. She'd never steal from a friend under any normal circumstances, not one she held as dear as Tag. But Archer had been owed that money and he'd become a friend, maybe more than that. Stealing wasn't the right word anyway; she'd relocated the funds to settle an invoice, nothing more sinister than that.

"No deal."

Well, wow, that surprised her. She reassessed after that refusal. Returning her focus to the dresser, she opened a drawer and grabbed a tee shirt. Pulling it over her head, she scooped her long locks from the back when Gio spoke.

"You'll return the money if Taggert lets you screw around with Nya?"

Was that a proposition or incredulity?

"I haven't known her long, but Nya's pretty adamant she's no one's whore. I don't think she'd appreciate you selling her to me for twenty Gs."

"That's what you're suggesting," Gio said. "You're saying you'll return the money if we let you have Nya."

"I'm not returning any money and what I do with my cock is my call. It wasn't a fair question; I wanted to see what you'd say."

Gio got forceful again. "You don't want to get between Taggert and Nya, their relationship is complicated. It's deep and way more important to both of them than you'll ever be."

Her relationship with Tag was deep, but it wasn't complicated, not in her eyes. She knew exactly who he was to her and how they'd reached this point. It wasn't Gio's business to explain anything about her life to anyone.

"Then you got nothing to worry about, huh?" Archer said.

She closed the drawer harder than intended; the noise must've carried up the hall.

"What was that?" Gio asked.

"Pussy," Archer said in flat syllables.

"You have a cat back there?" Gio asked, skeptical.

"Pussy," Archer said. "Subtle, but important, difference."

"Quit playing," Gio snapped. "You don't have a girl in there. It's the middle of the afternoon, and you're eating a fucking sandwich."

"Believe what you want," Archer said. "You asked." Something must've happened that she didn't see, because there was more menace in Archer's voice when he spoke again. "If you want to fight and win, goon, you came to the wrong apartment. If you want to lose, this is the place for you. Think about that before you make your first move 'cause it'll be your last too."

Were they threatening Archer? She couldn't stay put and do nothing if they were getting physical out there. Grabbing the bedroom door, she went out to head for the kitchen. Except Archer was blocking the mouth of the hallway. With Gio and the goon beside the table a few feet away, she only saw them by peeking around Archer's broad arm.

Gio blinked in surprise; she'd never seen him so immediately dumbstruck. The goon was unknown, and less interested in her identity than he was in her bare legs.

"What's going on out here?" she asked, like she hadn't been listening this whole time.

"I got this, Squirm. Go back to bed," Archer said, turning his head while keeping his focus on the men.

"Back to—" Gio's horror flashed to her. An odd spike of shame flashed the thought of retreat. "You're not fucking him. You told Tag—"

"If Tag wants to fight with me about the money, tell him to call me," Nya said, head held high. "We both know the only reason he didn't do that already is because he's not gonna ask me for it back. He knows he's supposed to pay it. You came here to scare Archer into returning it."

"We didn't think you'd be here yet," Gio said.

She didn't like his scowl; it didn't fit his face. Gio was relaxed, usually her friend, now he was dark and pissed. Quashing her shame, she swerved around Archer.

Frustration stoked her anger toward Gio's judgment and Tag's too.

"Every time Tag tries to tell me what to do with my body, we end up fighting. It's been that way for fifteen years, he has to learn to butt out."

Archer caught her wrist and pulled her back before she could get too close to Gio. Though unexpected, she didn't mind. He didn't touch or coddle her, just held her wrist to keep her near.

"I told him he was crazy," Gio argued. "I said you'd never go near this trash. Why the fuck would you—"

"Don't come into his house and talk about him like that," she said and tried to walk, but, with another tug, she bungeed back to Archer.

"I got this, Squirm."

She was on a roll. "This is none of your business, Gio. Tag can have a problem if he wants, I'll tell him to mind his business and—"

Archer snapped his fingers right next to her ear so loud that she ducked to avoid the sound. Her train of thought lost, she turned to meet his eye. The intensity of his long gaze was expectant, not that she should say something specific, but that she should say nothing at all.

Ironic he'd brought her there in the first place to talk, now all he wanted her to do was shut up. This was his house; he didn't need her to defend him from anyone.

His gentle pressure on her arm guided her to where he wanted her to be, behind him, then he stepped up to talk to his guests.

"You come to my place uninvited, make fucked up demands, insult me, now you disrespect my lady," Archer said to Gio. "How do you think this is gonna end for you?"

"If she's your lady, you won't hurt us," Gio said. "She won't let you."

Although he was being so cocky that she wanted to slap him, he was right. Gio might be talking out of line, but she wouldn't want to see him hurt for being an idiot. Especially because he was being an idiot under Tag's orders.

"Archer," she whispered, curling a hand around his

wrist as she linked her other fingers between his.

She didn't know his first name. Shit, kind of an obvious question, why had she never asked?

Archer relented but didn't stand down. "You're right, I won't. But know I've got a long memory, boys. Your friend fucked me over and only got away with it 'cause this girl saved your asses. Next time, he won't get a pass. And next time, she won't be here to bail you out either. Take your fucking insults back to your leader. Get the fuck out of my house."

Nothing happened for a second, not until Archer picked up a foot as if to move. That got the two men spinning around to dash for the door and get out.

Breathing into silence in sync with Archer, should she speak or let him take the lead?

"If you want to go with them, you better run."

"I don't want to go with them," she murmured.

The moment her hands slid away, his body grew rigid. If he put money on her retreating, he'd lose every cent. She slunk around his incredible form to put herself in front of him. His height made it difficult to look into his eyes.

"What's your first name?" His chin dropped to meet her gaze, but he didn't answer. "You called me your lady. No one's ever called me a lady before. If you meant it, we've got a lot of getting to know each other to do."

"Chase," he responded. "No one calls me it except my mom."

She liked it, not that it mattered.

Wrapping her hands around his biceps, she rose to her tiptoes. "When they offered you the money or me…"

"You thought I'd take the money?"

She nodded and he curled a hand around her chin. "I wouldn't have blamed you. We hardly know each other and—"

"You could've hid in that room. Denied we fucked. You could've told them I was holding you against your will. But you came out. You stood beside me."

And that meant something to him; she could see it in the way he peered into her.

"I can only be with a man who has integrity," she said.

"And loyalty—"

"I remember. I demand it from you and guarantee it in return." She nodded. If they were going to start this, whatever it was, they had to get the rules clear up front. "And I'm supposed to protect you from other guys."

"You've already done that," she said, skimming her hands over his pecs. "You protected me by taking me away from Jonno and the others in Sizzle. Protected me from Bryant and his buddies. I know what kind of man you are, even when you hide from me."

"Get dressed," he said, stooping to rasp his teeth over her cheekbone in a primal kiss.

"Why?" she asked, hoping he didn't plan to kick her out.

"Because you need some meat on those bones and I don't have anything in the apartment you can eat... Vegetarian, are you sure?"

Even now, he made her smile. "Yes."

Maneuvering their bodies so he could pick her up and carry her to the bedroom, his lips warmed her ear. "You had my meat in your mouth."

Kicking into the bedroom, he tossed her onto the bed. It was so far away that she braced to bounce and whooped when she landed, but he went to the dresser to pull out clean clothes, showing no concern because he'd judged the throw perfectly.

"Your meat tastes good," she said, lying down on his bed again.

She should be getting changed, her clothes were right there beside her, but it had been so long since she'd been able to just stop and relax for half a minute that it felt good just to chill.

The drawer slammed and he pulled on a tee shirt as he turned around. "Do you swallow?"

"Excuse me?" she asked, peeping open one eye.

"It's a shot of protein; you probably don't get enough of that in your diet."

Like he'd be doing her a favor by letting her blow him on a regular basis. Just to ensure she was getting optimum nutrition, of course.

"I don't need a supplement. I get plenty of protein in my diet," she said, sitting up to cross her legs at the edge of the bed. Reaching with both arms, she gestured him over and he complied. "But I'll swallow for you. No animals were harmed in the making of your product." With a sultry gaze, her eyes wandered upward. The burn of his desire opened her hand on his groin. "I might need some more practice with this monster before I get it right."

"You did just fine before, but practice as much as you need."

So selfless. Just to return his tease, she rubbed him through his boxer-briefs, and it didn't take long to get him to attention. Bowing forward, she pressed a kiss to his shaft through the cotton of his underwear then leaned back. "Too bad you offered to take me out. It will have to wait until another time." Leaping off the bed, she grinned and kissed his arm because she couldn't reach his face. "You don't mind if I take a quick shower, do you? I know how everything works."

FIFTEEN

HE DIDN'T STOP her, and he didn't join her, which worked out 'cause if he had, they'd probably have ended up in bed together again.

Going into the bathroom, by choice, was an odd experience. Deliberately leaving the door open, she kept the water warm, and piqued at every noise. Part of her was eager to have him sneak in with her, the other part feared who might come visit the apartment while she was naked and vulnerable.

Turned out she was worried about nothing. They got ready, into Archer's car, and into a back alley Italian place called "*Louie's*" somewhere close to her apartment, though she hadn't known it existed.

Archer really did know everything and everyone. He was offered the best table in the house by the server, though he refused it in favor of a corner booth shrouded in shadow. The restaurant was so busy, it was standing room only. In the entryway people waited to be seated while others were turned away.

Not Archer. He walked in and got service straight away. That meant one of two things: Archer had helped these people, or he'd hurt them.

"Why did you pick this table?" she asked after the

server took their order and delivered their drinks.

"I like to watch." His honesty made immediate sense. "You never know what you'll see if you pay attention."

Her side had its back to the room, whereas he had an excellent view. Being seated in the middle of the opposite bench meant he could remain in the darkness, hidden, but still observe everything going on in the vast room.

"A girl likes to be the focus of her date's attention," she teased, hoping to catch his eye. Instead, he swooped a hand across the table to scoop hers up. Squeezing it in both of his, he kissed the back of her fingers, all the while watching the room. "Archer."

"Mm?"

"I like it when you kiss me here," she said, bending back her hand to present her branded wrist.

That got his attention. His eyes met hers, then lowered to the wound he grazed with his thumb. "Because you like reminding me I hurt you?"

"Because there's something hot about wearing your mark," she admitted. "I know it makes no sense and it hurt like hell, don't think it didn't."

His head moved in a slow shake. "I didn't want to hurt you. You were... supposed to be like any other interrogation. There are so many techniques I use and... I couldn't make myself use them on you."

"Like what?"

"You don't want to know."

Maybe in another situation she wouldn't. But how could she think about sharing her bed with this man again if she couldn't face up to what he did?

"I do want to hear about it. This won't go anywhere if you don't trust me, Chase."

"Don't use my first name," he muttered.

It didn't appear to make him uncomfortable; maybe he was just unaccustomed to hearing it.

"Calling you Archer all the time feels detached and I don't want that. What should I call you?"

"Just not that."

"Okay, Fella," she said, for lack of something better.

"What techniques do you use?"

Squinting at her, he was reluctant. "Are you sure you want to hear about this? We can be a thing without you ever being involved in that part of my life."

She wouldn't take part in what he did. Definitely not. For one thing, she wouldn't have the stomach for it. For another, she'd embarrass Archer with her incompetence. But this guy wasn't the type who'd let her have secrets, he had to know everything. Not only was it his job, but they were on a date and his focus kept flitting from her to the other patrons. His need for knowledge was strong. And if she didn't know what he was doing, she might take his distraction as disinterest.

"So I won't be allowed to stay over while you're working?" she asked. "What if I have to pee when you have a guy chained to your floor?"

For a second, he considered it. "There are ways of working around prisoners."

Like he worked around her? She didn't relish the idea of peeing or showering in front of a stranger begging for mercy.

"The first step to me getting used to it is you being honest about what I might see, about what you do. Tell me about the techniques you use. Do you water board people?"

His mouth opened over the base of her thumb in a long kiss before he responded, his lips still against her.

"Have done. A good start is stress positions," he said, sitting back, letting their hands fall to the table. One moved away from hers briefly to straighten his beer bottle. "Forced nakedness is another."

The cuff that connected her ankle to her wrist was a sort of stress position, she guessed. But he hadn't forced her to be nude.

"You didn't strip me," she said. "You could've."

"'Cause I'm not sure who that would've tortured more, you or me."

Appreciating his half smile, his gaze never quite met hers.

"What else?"

"Some of it is obvious. Sensory deprivation or bombardment work. Sleep deprivation is easy, keep the lights on, the floor is hard, cold—"

"Yeah, I've been there," she said with a smile and tightened her fingers around his.

Something as simple as holding hands had never had such an impact. His strong, capable hands wrapped around hers and he'd forgotten about the rest of the room.

"Starvation works, dehydration too if things get strained."

"In a room with a water supply, how do you enforce dehydration? I helped myself when I needed to drink or pee."

Putting his elbows on the table again, he brought her hand to his mouth once more. "The chain's adjustable."

Growling, she imagined how torturous that would be. "With the faucet dripping constantly, and not being able to access water…"

"I don't like doing that," he said, kissing her brand then her palm. "And restricting access to the toilet just leaves mess to clean up. Pain and humiliation usually work best. Like I said before, I'm not breaking trained vets. I'm dealing with street scum and the occasional socialite; they're not built to handle stress like that… You put up a fight though. Where did you learn that?"

She shrugged. "I couldn't give up Tag, I just couldn't and I never would. You should know that. I won't ever betray him."

Brushing his lips back and forth on her knuckles, he seemed to enjoy the texture of her skin.

He frowned. "What is the deal with you two? If you're not with the guy…"

Sighing, tired of the accusation, she almost rolled her eyes. "I'm not with the guy," she said. Eager to rid the question mark hanging over their heads. "It might sound dumb, and don't think I'm getting ideas about us, but… I like being monogamous. I like being with just one guy. There's an intensity that comes with exclusivity."

"Good," he said. "Because I don't screw around either. So long as we're sharing a bed with each other, we share it with no one else."

He probably used that line to tell other women not to have sex with other men all the time. For her, he meant she wasn't to sleep with Tag.

"I will be going back to Tag's," she said. "I'll have to talk to him about what happened at your place today and about the money. I have to explain."

"You stole it for me, what is there to explain?"

"It wasn't as simple as that. I did tell him in advance I was going to do it, it wasn't like a smash and grab."

The curl of his lips was hidden by her wrist, but she felt it. He kept turning her hand, exploring her palm, sampling her skin with his lips, rubbing it on his face. Seeing him so curious about something so simple intrigued and flattered her.

"Most people wouldn't get away with stealing that kind of money, even from a friend."

"My relationship with Tag isn't typical," she said. He lowered her hand to the table on top of his. Flattening his other above, he sandwiched her hand between his two and waited. "I've never been a very… open person. It's not easy for me to tell strangers about my history."

His eyes widened and his lips quirked. "You were sliding your tongue all over my cock a few hours ago. I think we're past strangers."

It didn't matter that his point was valid, she was still dubious. "How do I know you're not just doing this to manipulate me?" she asked, voicing her concern. "You lied to me about having a sister. Maybe this whole thing is a lie."

"Maybe it is," he said. "But why bother? I have my money. I have no reason to manipulate you. I could make one up… if it would make you feel better about what we're doing."

Just like before when he'd told her he'd give her an excuse to sleep with him. He seemed determined that she needed to justify their actions beyond their obvious desire for each other.

"You still haven't told me why you needed the money," she said, trying to slide her hand out from between his.

He didn't release her and kept her hand there,

imprisoned.

"Does it matter why I needed it?"

"No," she replied because in truth, it didn't. It was his money, owed to him. It was right he received it. "But it's the lie. You're asking me to trust you with a part of my past, a part of Tag's past too, and you won't even tell me the truth about what happened today."

"The truth?" he said. "I don't let anyone screw me over. Would set bad precedent. I get paid for every job I do. Every. Job. That was my money, and I would've done whatever it took to get it. It belonged to me. But, yeah, it was important that I get it. Course it was. I support me. I support my mom. Life these days is expensive."

A thought she'd previously dismissed came back. "You don't…" she trailed off. "You don't… I'm not saying it would matter, I mean I've been with guys who've had their issues. But I would like to know up front…"

"What?" he asked when she trailed away again. "What would you like to know, Squirm? Never underestimate the power of just asking a question. You never know what you'll find out."

His pet name for her was apt; discomfort shifted her in her seat. "You don't have a habit, do you?" she asked. "Drugs, gambling, sex…"

"Not one I pay for." Huh, what did that mean? "I don't like debts. I don't like to owe people. So if you're worried I had some bill I had to sell my soul to cover, don't. I needed the money to pay the bills. That's it. There's no big secret."

"Why didn't you just tell me that? If there's no big secret, you could've been honest."

"Yeah," he said. "Right then in the car, in the dark with you, it felt pathetic to tell the truth. After what just happened, you needed a reason, wanted to sympathize with me, so I gave you a reason. It just came out. I didn't plan on bullshitting you… I never lie, normally. The truth always comes out. You can't avoid it. People try to all the time, I know, I'm usually the one they're looking at when they lie. But I can see it. I can tell. I've always been able to do it… might say I can smell bullshit."

Whether or not he made a habit of lying, she'd need time to figure that out. Though in other areas, he seemed to be honest to the point of brutal.

"And that's how you got into this line of work?" she asked. "You were just good at it?"

"Kind of," he said. "I grew up with gangs and rough crowds and got myself into some trouble pretty young. One of my mom's many boyfriends took pity on me, tried to straighten me out. He showed me how to defend myself, how to talk to people, how to win their confidence. I learned I could approach people, get them to tell me things. As a kid it worked because they thought I was innocent. As I got older, harder, people didn't trust me so easily. That was when Derren taught me about knives. I loved it. I loved everything about them, the blade, the feel in my hand, the weight, the smooth texture of the metal, the comfort of the grip. I loved the way the light caught the metallic surface and glinted that blinding beam. The angles, the sheath, the sound of it slicing through flesh, I loved it all. I guess you could say that was my first love."

Listening to him talk about his life, being open about where he came from, erased some of the mystery. It didn't lessen his allure. She was fascinated as he carried on.

"Derren took me hunting, taught me how to take an animal apart."

Her lip curled. She didn't mean to look disgusted, but he stopped talking, not because he was worried about offending her, he smiled.

"Sorry," she said. "I just… I can't imagine doing that."

"Course not, Vegetarian," he said. "I'm sure you get a lot of pleasure ripping those carrots up out the ground and slicing those bastards up good."

She laughed. "That's not the same thing."

"No," he said, appreciating her amusement with his own, "it's not. But you wanted the truth and that's where it came from."

"What happened to Derren? Is he still with your

mom?"

"Fuck, God, no," he said with a slight shake of his head as his eyes fell. Stretching, he slid his hand from her elbow down to rest on her wrist. "No, my mom never keeps a guy for more than a few weeks at a time. She's always been that way. I don't know why Derren stuck around with me, but he did. I didn't appreciate it at first, kept telling him to get lost. Kept thinking he wanted something. I still don't understand why he took pity on me. I owe him a lot and I'll never forget what he did for me. If it wasn't for him, I'd be dead now. Or in jail, doing life."

"Wow," she said. He seemed so sure this guy saved him. "You were lucky to have him."

"He taught me how to read people, how to be careful, how to not leave evidence."

Something about the way Archer talked about this man, beyond the words, betrayed how much he valued the mentor in his youth. Somehow, it was obvious there was more to the story, maybe more to the present or more to the past, he wasn't revealing yet. Not that she could blame him when she'd revealed nothing of herself to him.

"You asked me once," she started, understanding why it was easier to scrutinize their physical interaction than to meet the eye of the person on the cusp of seeing your underbelly. "You asked me once if…"

The words weren't coming to her, and, to her surprise, Archer showed patience. The words kept getting stuck in her throat. It wasn't that she didn't want to be honest. It wasn't that she didn't want to tell him what she'd been through. She just couldn't dislodge the sentences needed to explain.

Part of getting people to tell the truth, to tell him what he wanted to know, included being sympathetic, she'd guess, letting them trip themselves up. Maybe that's what he was doing or maybe he was just being considerate.

After another breath, she turned her hand over so they were palm to palm. "You asked me once if rape was what I feared, and I told you it was," she said. "I didn't tell you why."

SIXTEEN

"SOMEONE HURT YOU," he said in a calm voice with infinite understanding and no judgment, like he'd been trained to be patient.

As if he was a professional. Which he was. Just not in a conventional sense.

The bustle that distracted before faded to nothing.

"Someone tried to," she said. "And it was Tag who got me out."

"When you were fourteen."

Her eyes bounced to his, shocked that he knew. "How do you know that?"

"Because you said he'd been looking out for you since you were fourteen. You said to Gio today that Tag had been butting into your life for fifteen years, the math makes sense."

Amazed he remembered these details, that he'd been listening and paying close attention, was impressive. She sat back in her seat, freeing her hands from his, though they remained on the tabletop.

"Yes."

"What happened?"

The story was so engrained in her identity, such a part of her, it was never far from her thoughts. At the same time, she hadn't said the words to describe events for years.

She avoided telling it, maybe why she was so private. If she'd been more open with people, more willing to tell the truth, and willing to offer information, maybe she would tell this story all the time and it would be easier to get out.

"Tag's a few years older than me," she said. "Him and his brother were friends, good friends, with my brother."

"I didn't know you had a brother."

Archer didn't push, he wasn't probing; he was calm, cool, measured. He'd be assessing her, not only the veracity of what she said, but her mood and how the tale affected her. It was in the nature of him. And he'd want to figure out what impact these people and trials had.

Maybe he wanted to use the information to manipulate her. Or maybe, just maybe, he did genuinely care. It could be he really wanted to know who she was, what made her tick and how she'd come to be her.

"I don't have a brother," she said. Reminded of another story that was difficult to tell, her eyes drifted down to the flatware. "He's… no longer with us."

"Dead?" he asked. "When you were fourteen?"

"No, what happened with him… it didn't happen on the same night Tag saved me. They're two separate stories." Forcing a smile, believing it might alleviate some of the tension, she sat up straight to rest her elbows on the table, accentuating her cleavage as a sort of playful interlude, meant to distract from the serious conversation. "One dramatic story a night. Take your pick. Do you want to know what happened to Ryan or do you want to know how Tag and I got close?"

"One story?" he said, mirroring her position with his elbows on the table. Leaning over, he wrapped both hands around the fist of her two joined hands. "That's not usually how I work. Usually I'm told everything I want to know. Since you sucked my cock today, I'll make an exception. Let's go with Tag."

"Thank you, Fella," she said, bowing over the table to kiss his hands still wrapping hers. "Tag it is." The obvious choice. "I was fourteen. Tag was at my house with his brother and mine, partying in the garage; I wasn't a part of it. It was just them, my dad wasn't home, he never was. If he ever stumbled back, it was just to pass out drunk.

"Ryan was gone, out of it, I mean, drunk and high. I don't know what drugs they were taking, the music was loud, and… I was in the house by myself. I'd learned long before to leave them alone. I never went out there. The garage was Ryan's jurisdiction, he had his stuff out there. I knew what the drugs, the music, the shouting, I knew what it all meant. I went to the kitchen, I can't remember why, maybe for a drink or to answer the phone, or maybe I just left something down there. I can't remember. It was late. Very late.

The first part of the story was easier to tell. Setting the scene rolled off her tongue. As soon as her memory caught up with the monologue, it slowed to replay each second.

"I remember turning around and he was there, just standing there in the middle of the kitchen."

"Tag?"

"No," she said, shaking her head. "His brother. He started making these comments. His eyes were all crazy and his breath smelled of liquor. I remember he grabbed me and I tried to get away, I was screaming, but nobody came. He hit me, hard, I landed on the floor and couldn't see straight, but I couldn't move, I was… I knew what he was going to do and I was terrified, crying, begging him… and that was when Tag came in. Tag was the eldest, he had his own shithole studio apartment that he shared with two other guys." She drifted deeper into the memory; it was hard not to be affected by the terror, even this far away from it. "Anyway, Tag came in, pulled his brother off, beat him half to death… They had this massive brawl through the whole house, they smashed it all up, the kitchen, the living room, they ended up on the porch, out in the yard… I remember running to get Ryan, but he was lying on the couch in the garage, staring at the ceiling, slurring, blubbing, he wasn't even with it enough to open his eyes more than a millimeter.

"My nightdress was torn and I was crying and… Tag took me out of there… that night he took me away from that place and I never went back. I was so scared of my father, I knew… I knew when he saw the mess of the house, all the broken stuff, I knew he would go insane. You could never tell who he'd focus on, who he was going to blame and beat."

His expression didn't betray much. "You lived with Tag from when you were fourteen?"

"Yes, well, kind of," she said, shaking her head. "He let me stay with him for a few months. The other guys didn't get it, they complained. I bounced around with friends. Avoided my brother and Tag's, and my father too. Less than a year later, my dad died. Drove himself into a tree blind drunk; he deserved exactly what he got. After that, I fell into the care of my brother. We lived in a shitty trailer most of the time. He was no better than my dad; he became the same man. He didn't even notice when I wasn't there. I stayed with friends; sometimes their parents took pity on me and kept me a few months. Then, I went to stay with boyfriends. As soon as I was old enough and I could scrape the cash together, I got my own place. But Tag…"

The memory of that night still traumatized her until she would shake. Oddly, there was something heartwarming about remembering Tag caring for her. How he calmed and soothed her. How he fed her and made her laugh.

"After that," she said, "he always kept tabs on me, always knew where I was. He gave me money if I needed it, a place to stay, somewhere to work. He's always been in my life. Even when other people walked away, any time I was hurt, I could always call him. Any time I was in trouble, I would go to him. He's kind of a surrogate big brother, yet he's nothing like my brother at all."

Hazarding a glance at Archer, she read darkness in his eyes and the crease between his brows furrowed deep. The server came over to put their food on the table, braking the intensity of their stare.

"So that's my story."

Twirling pasta around his fork, he lifted it from the plate. "Helps me make sense of things. Guess Tag has some good qualities."

Telling the story might have the unexpected side-effect of resolving the conflict between the men. Maybe if Archer cared about her, he would give Tag a break.

"Good," she said. "I'm glad you feel that way. He's

not such a bad guy." The night had been filled with too much melancholy. Hoping to move things on and shake the discomfort from her bones, she smiled. "Now, tell me how you found out this place existed."

***

THE REST OF THE meal was pleasant. He was funny, she hadn't expected he'd be capable of making her laugh after the story she'd told. Archer pointed out people at the bar, giving her an insight into what he did by sharing his observations. Some of the patrons he knew, some he didn't. Something about each one intrigued him enough to monitor them.

He told her what he liked about what he did and what he didn't. She told him more about how she'd ended up in Sizzle working under Tag and with Jamie. Archer's comfort in the familiar restaurant loosened him up. He ordered dessert, ordered more drinks, and was happy to sit drinking and talking, sharing stories. It didn't seem he was in any hurry to leave or run away, despite her revelations.

Archer paid the bill, then took her hand as they walked out and down the block to his parked car. When he unlocked the door, she stepped back, dropping his hand.

"I'm only a couple of blocks from here," she said. "I can walk to my place. I had a really good night."

Back to the car, he frowned at her. "I can take you home. The car's right here. I won't leave you in the middle of the street."

Sweet he was worried, though his scowl sort of offset the sentiment. "I'll be fine."

Already shaking his head, he wasn't giving up. "I don't leave my dates on shady street corners. I walk you to your door, put you inside, and if you choose to go out again after, that's on you. But we'll stand on this street all night before I'll let you take one step by yourself."

Protective instinct? Or was he taking a chance at a happy ending?

"We did this backwards," she said, walking into his arms, forcing him to hold her by the way she tucked herself in close to his body. "Sex first, dinner after, that's the wrong way around."

"I'm happy for a replay," he said. "At your place or mine."

"I'm sure you are. I… I just don't know if it's a good idea. We're rushing into this because we shared an intense experience. The sex was amazing and… I'm just worried if we keep going at this speed, we'll burn out too fast."

"Hey," he said, resting a hand on the back of her head, closing his fist to gather her hair and pull her head back so she'd look at him. "If you want to go home alone tonight, you go home alone. I won't give you many free passes, but I'll give you this one, this night. Doesn't change the fact I'll be walking you to your door and listening to you lock it before I walk away."

"Are you that protective?" she asked. "Or that much of a control freak?"

He tilted his head and his lower lip slipped out a fraction. "Both."

Guess he'd been honest about the not lying.

Honesty was refreshing. She stretched her hands up to comb her fingers through his hair above his ears.

"Sometimes I want to kiss you, but I can't reach."

"You pout those pretty lips and I'll deliver," he said and bowed, sliding his hands to her ass to boost her up and unite their mouths.

Kissing on street corners wasn't something she'd done for years, probably not since she was a kid. She kissed on doorsteps and sometimes in alleyways or in a club, but on a normal, well-lit street at what could be one or two o'clock in the morning? No, she hadn't done that in years. Damn, it felt good.

Usually, she was aware of everything, she had to be, she'd conditioned herself that way, to be aware of footsteps on the asphalt, car engines, groups of men jeering or shouting or drinking too much. Any whiff of alcohol in the air when she was alone in the street heightened her anxiety. A barking dog would prick her ears, because if that dog was angry and afraid, she should be too.

It came with being a woman used to walking around in rough neighborhoods. She was aware of corners, of alleys, of shadows, of which streetlights worked and which ones didn't. She'd learned how to walk nearer the curb to avoid being snatched from an alley. How to hurry beneath the broken lights to get into the next pool of illumination quickly. How to use the environment to create a barrier between herself and passing cars.

But there, in his arms, with Archer's mouth devoting itself to hers, all that fear melted away. She wasn't worried about anything. A dozen cars could have driven by. An angry mob of Viagra-high louts with alcohol, cocaine, and no-good-sense in their systems could've trundled past. She was aware of none of it because for the first time in her life, she didn't have to be.

For the first time in her life, she was with a man capable of protecting her from every threat. Archer wouldn't just pull her out and run to pick up the pieces after, as Tag would. Archer would memorize every face and make every man who scared her pay, bleeding every drop from them. For her, he'd deprive them of blessed oxygen until she granted their reprieve.

Somehow, she knew it, was sure of it, though they'd never discussed any future together. He'd promised to help her find Jamie's attackers, said he never forgot a debt, and he promised payback on Tag. Archer had integrity. A warped kind of integrity, because although it was absolute, his morals were shaded. He had his own special code that allowed him to do some despicable, horrific things, but for reasons he believed were right, whether they were or not.

Rolling her lips into her mouth, she leaned back, breaking the kiss. "You know, if you park your car on my block, I can't guarantee it'll be there in the morning," she said, slipping her hands around under his arms to slide them into his back pockets, holding herself even closer.

"Oh…" Satisfaction spread a sneer onto his face. "I would love for someone to steal from me."

"If you're willing to take the risk. Maybe you could give me a *ride*," she said, accentuating that last word.

He guided her to the car without releasing her from his arms until the last possible second. He went around the hood to get in and drove back to her place.

The comment about her street wasn't a joke. Her apartment was a shithole; no other word for it. A studio little more than a box without windows. It had a living area to the left, kitchen to the right, and the bedroom was in the back left of the space with the small shower room opposite.

The only natural light came from a long, narrow skylight that ran the width of the apartment above the bedroom and bathroom in the slanted ceiling. The stars shone over her at night and the sun irritated her in the morning.

Usually, she could tell a lot about a guy from the way he reacted to her place. Archer had been there before and hadn't batted an eye. Some were disgusted and struggled to conceal it. Others saw her place as heaven in comparison to where they stayed. It was clean and it was quiet, at least this building was. Sometimes there were shouts on the street that indicated trouble, but she couldn't see out because the skylight was too high. Even if Archer's car was stolen, they'd never witness the act.

He came in and took his jacket and boots off while she locked the door. Talk about making himself at home, this seduction wasn't subtle. While removing her own jacket, he left her kitchen table to go check the locks she'd just secured.

"I've lived here for a long time," she said. "I know how the locks work."

"I know," he said. "It's habit."

"You never seem bothered at your place."

"I lock my door."

Putting her purse on the table, she sat down to slip off her shoes and wiggle her toes. "Yeah, but you answer it without checking who's on the other side."

"Anyone stupid enough to knock if they want to kill me, I can take down."

"Stupid enough?" she asked.

"Sure, my place isn't that big and there's only one way in, one way out. If they wanted to kill me, they'd stand opposite the door and wait until I opened it to take out my trash or something."

"You do have experience," she said, rising up to slip off more than her jacket.

Her top went next, her skirt, she enjoyed how he studied every inch of skin she revealed. Stopping when her bra and panties were the only things left, she turned in a slow half circle to slink toward the bed.

"Come on then, Fella," she murmured, glancing over her shoulder, doing her best to showcase her bedroom eyes. Begging him to follow, she sashayed through the thin curtains that acted as her bedroom walls. "I'm waiting for my goodnight kiss."

SEVENTEEN

SOMETHING ABOUT THE warmth of his body easing away stirred her out of slumber. She moaned and stretched an arm across his chest to squeeze herself close again.

"Not yet," she sighed, "don't leave."

Light streamed in from the skylight above. Which she only knew because of the glow on the other side of her eyelids. She didn't want to open them, she wanted to stay there, nestled in the corner with the wall at her back and her man propped against her chest.

Her man. Solid, stable, a shield between her and the rest of the apartment. Although a studio, she'd separated this space from the rest with two dark gauze curtains pinned to the ceiling and walls. The blurred lines of the furniture were visible through them, but this could still be their private cocoon.

"It's morning," he said.

His hand skimmed up and down her arm until it came to rest on her hip. He buried his mouth and nose in her hair, so she draped a leg over his to nestle her knee between his thighs.

"That doesn't mean we have to get up," she murmured, pointing her tongue to lick the muscle her cheek rested on. "Just stay here."

"You like to lie around in the morning? For how long?"

She shrugged and still hadn't opened her eyes, relishing this chance to get closer to him and squeeze the unyielding muscles that endured through their sessions last night.

"You like to get up?" she asked. "You're a morning person?"

"I'm a breakfast person." The heat of his palm glided up her body and curled around her shoulder. The strength of his arm crushed her chest against his ribs. Mmm, did that signal his surrender to her request? "I prefer the night. It's easier to get my work done."

"Me too."

Most of her jobs were night jobs, had been all her life. Whether it was serving in a restaurant, working a bar, or throwing herself around a pole. For a long time, she'd been nocturnal. It suited her.

"I don't even know what time it is."

His face left her hair, presumably to search for a clock. He'd be searching a while, there wasn't one.

"I use my phone if I need an alarm," she said, unaware of where her purse even was, probably scattered somewhere on the floor with their clothes. "Other than that, I don't need to be anywhere until it gets dark. Let's stay here until we need to move."

"We do need to move," he said, his voice laced with a subtle innuendo.

Exhilarated by what might come, the unspoken promise enticed her.

"We do?"

Easing her knee from between his legs, she lifted it over the other side of his thighs in an indirect invitation. Didn't take him long to accept. Rocking her onto her back, he held both her arms in a stretch high above her head and linked their fingers. He liked to stretch her body as far as it could go and she liked being at his mercy, under the mass of him.

Angling her hips, she coiled her lower limbs around

his and still hadn't opened her eyes. He licked her lips, kissed her chin, rubbed his nose over hers.

"Are you awake?" he asked.

Unable to stop herself from wriggling and writhing, she moved against the thick column of his erection tantalizingly close to slipping inside her. All he needed to do was lift, she could tilt, and then their bodies would dock. Except he kept her there, pinned down, giving her just enough room to squirm beneath in a constant motion fueled by his need bleeding into her.

"I'm talking to you. I'm awake."

"Yeah, but you haven't opened your eyes," he said. "How do I know you're not talking in your sleep? That this isn't a dream, and you won't freak at me when you wake up with my cock rammed in your pussy?"

Nice that he was considerate, though she sensed the teasing, how genuine was the concern? Which words were his way of elongating the seduction, of tormenting her. It was working. He'd get his answer in the slickness of her body as it prepared to accept his. She wanted him, just as she'd wanted him every time they'd come together last night.

Being with him was new and exciting, yet he felt stable, like a relentless force she could get used to having in her life. Although it was too soon, she pried her eyelids apart until she could blink him into focus. Took her a minute while keeping her gaze narrow. This kind of bliss deserved to be memorized. She needed her eyes closed to heighten her other senses, to smell him, to hear him breathe, to feel his chest move against hers and every point of skin contact.

His muscles imprinted themselves on her soft, pliable form ready to be owned and dominated.

"I'm awake," she said again and angled her chin, trying to tempt his mouth.

They only made feather-light contact before he stole himself from her reach. "I thought you had places to be today and things to do."

He hadn't been supposed to spend the night. She'd tried to walk away from him in the street, that turned out to be a joke. Their afternoon sex had been too amazing, their date brought them closer… Had she thought she'd be able to walk away from this man? Impossible.

"You'll need to do something to wake me up then." If she wasn't given a boost of energy, she'd be happy to laze there all day. "To remind me of my responsibilities."

"You're not getting out of this bed until I'm through with you. That might take a very long time."

There was that promise again. Something he didn't say was somehow conveyed in the way he gazed at her.

"I might be able to live with that."

"Good, because what I tasted last night only made me hungry for more."

"More?" she said, too caught up in the intoxication of hormones to remember the aches in her muscles. "Fella, you about squeezed me dry. You fuck me like no other man ever has."

"And I'll keep fucking you like that," he said. "I'll fuck you any damn way I like. I'll fuck you here, at my place, in my car, in your club, any fucking place I choose." And he meant it, he couldn't speak like that, with such conviction, such certainty, without meaning every single word. "I'll guarantee no other man will ever touch you 'cause you'll be touched by me every damn minute of every damn day. They won't have a chance to hurt you, to seduce you, 'cause I'll be there to watch you. I'll learn everything about you, Squirm, everything there is to know. I'll make damn sure you never feel unsafe again. You'll never be vulnerable again. I've got you. Anyone wants to hurt you, they answer to me. I'll always get to them before they get to you."

"Archer," she purred, aroused by his words, his body, his gaze. "I'll never betray you either."

She was sticking around, just like Derren had. Archer might not understand why the man had taken an interest in him, but she did, and it was beyond sexual. There was a power within him, a light dimmed by darkness.

Circumstance made him hard and unforgiving, but she'd looked into the man who rescued her from Sizzle, who couldn't put her to work, who'd freed her from his captivity. She saw a fierce man with his own morality dowsed in integrity. He might cut corners, might do wicked things for money for other people, but he deserved more than the hand he'd been dealt.

He deserved her patience, her loyalty. In a way, they'd been blessed by the need to stay together; their agreement gave them time, and the excuse, to be together for as long as it took. In other circumstances, they might have pushed each other away. She'd been guilty of doing that with men in her past, usually after Tag voiced disapproval of their character.

Not this time. Archer was there, telling her he wouldn't let her get away.

As her pelvis was freed by his, she prepared to accept his kiss, except it didn't come. Archer rose to his knees and got to his feet. Despite his proud erection jutting toward her, he only looked down at her and yawned as he scratched the top of his head.

Then he turned around and separated the drapes of gauze, tossing one over the back of the couch to leave space for her to view him lumbering to the kitchen, on the hunt, opening cabinets and drawers.

"What are you looking for?" she asked when he closed one cabinet to open another.

"Food."

She could understand his need for nourishment, he was a big guy who had to work out to have muscles like he did. He probably needed a lot of energy and he'd expended a lot last night, he'd need to replenish his stores.

"What kind of food?"

"Something decent," he muttered.

Sitting up in the middle of the bed, she held the blanket to her chest and drew up her knees. "I have something you can eat over here."

Only when he twisted away from his search to look at her did she let her raised knees part in sync with the elevation of her brow.

"Horny in the morning, aren't you?" he said and went back to his rifling. When he didn't find anything more exciting, he returned to one of the early cabinets to pull out a box of cereal. "Cheerios. That's all you've got for me?"

She shook her head when he dug his hand in the box to pull out a fistful of cereal. "I told you, there's a feast over here."

Stuffing the cereal into his mouth, he went for another handful as he moseyed back to the bedroom. He guzzled a third lot, discarded the box to the bedside, and picked up the water bottle she'd filled last night to gulp down what remained in it.

After he was done and the bottle was back on its spot, he dropped to his knees at the side of the bed.

"Bring it," he said, patting the mattress in front of him.

Was he actually…? He certainly didn't seem hesitant. He scrubbed the back of his hand over his mouth, cleared his throat, then threw the covers away from where he kneeled, from her, sending them right off the end of the bed.

The position was just fine, so she scooted over. He caught the leg she threw over his head before it landed and hooked it around the back of his shoulder. With his palms on the front of her thighs, he gave her a harsh yank until she was right at the very edge. His head went lower and… yes, the tease of his breath roused her hormones.

But it was his fingers that met flesh first. They spread between each of her creases. He parted her and rubbed the pads of his thumbs back and forth, plumping her clit. The heat of his mouth still warming her.

"Better than Cheerios," he hummed and then his tongue slid inside.

She hadn't been prepared for how close she was or how inspiring the girth of his tongue pushing into her would be. Desire writhed in her bones. Climax tickled the edges of her consciousness; yes, right there, like that. His tongue went deep, deeper than before and his thumbs continued to work. The rhythm was good, building the pressure inside her until… Yeah, it was right there… his tongue slid out slowly before working its way back in, sending her closer to the craved crescendo.

When his hands slid away, disappointment whimpered from her lips and she arched her pelvis, begging a return. They only slid down her thighs, over her knees to direct both legs tighter around his head. Massaging her own breasts, she pinched her nipples, and ran her hands up her shoulders, over her neck to her face and into her hair.

His tongue was still there doing its work. It slid out and upwards, right through the seam of her body. Her enlivened slit quaked, ready to accept him, ready to take what he wanted to give. The very tip of his tongue slithered over her clit. It went up and down to stimulate then pressed it close, covering the entire sensitized nub with the heat of his rough, wet muscle.

His hands slid under her ass, switching the position to allow him to taste her deeper, to suck her harder, to stimulate her clit between his lips. As they eased back and forth, his tongue just met the most alive point on her body. Massaging it with his lips, he kissed her and slid his tongue back down through her. Gentle suction form between his mouth and her body's threshold.

"Archer," she breathed, stuttering his name.

Her hands were on her breasts again, but they didn't stay still for long. They glided over her abdomen. Every tiny touch of his, and of hers, fired endorphins, orgasm was her only option, she wouldn't live without it, wouldn't live without him.

His kiss left. For the briefest moment, she feared that was it. That he planned to abandon her right when she was so close, nearly there, teetering on that precipice… Then like a pro he rubbed her clit with his tongue again, faster this time, and his thumbs were back, beneath her now, coming from below, they rubbed up and down from his mouth to her pussy, up and down. Mmm, a sharp inhale and… When his lips closed on one hard suck, he pushed her over the cliff and she descended into the oblivion of ecstasy.

Without a chance to put her thoughts back in order, or to form words let alone sentences, she was shoved back by his large hands on her ass until her head was flush against the opposite wall.

Then he was there, above her, on her. The consuming nature of his next kiss jolted her equilibrium. The taste of her own body merged on their tongues, unleashing a second wave of climax. Smack, bang, in the middle of this rapture, he pushed his cock into her.

They'd done it so many times that she was becoming accustomed to his size. But she felt every inch of his engorged shaft and every microsecond of his invasion. Yes, she would be sore later when the thrill was gone, but she didn't care. All she cared about was him fucking her, kissing her. Except the kiss didn't last.

"You are horny," he growled. "You're starved. I don't deprive you; I give you every inch of cock you need." She couldn't deny her yearning. "You're gobbling me deep. You want it bad."

Yes, her hips moved fast, but they were racing his. In fact, even though she was beneath, she was almost setting the pace. Her pelvis rose and fell, rose and fell; his was forced to work in opposition, to maximize the sensations driven by this joining.

Their unions had become instinctive. They'd slipped into easy sync. She knew how he wanted her to move, when she should squeeze him inside, when she should let him go. She knew how to run her hands over his chest, how he liked the way she scratched her nails on the side of his neck. He always growled when her fingers combed up into his hair behind his ears and dragged back down to crunch and tug.

She knew how to tempt his mouth to hers, though he would resist her kiss as it was part of the game. Except she triumphed in that moment. She got what she wanted as he was distracted by their hips.

Managing to coil her tongue around his, their intimacy was heightened by the sweetness of the cereal lingering in his mouth, merged with the taste of her. Fused, their tongues and bodies warred for completion. He took her back to the place he'd taught her was her new home.

When he stole dominance of the kiss, she didn't fight to get it back. Tipping her head, she screamed loud, something she would never normally do, something she would ordinarily be self-conscious of. She liked to be private, to keep to herself, to never let others know what she was doing. But with Archer, she was loud, loud enough that she made her own ears ring.

She screamed, she shrieked, she gasped and moaned. Sometimes she said his name, sometimes she said her own. Sometimes she was just screaming, "Yes!" Sometimes she was screaming, "More!"

Every time she opened her eyes, she read his satisfaction, he wore a determination to please her, and a determination to bring himself to that same mindless oblivious insanity she dwelled in when he was inside her.

The sheer force of this scream unleashed what she needed to rid herself of. The passion, the frustration, the anger, the upset, everything she'd been through came out in that scream. Something about the vulnerability, about showing such bare, raw emotion made him retort with a similar growling call. He swore and fired hard into her, his hips shunting hers with such force that her head hit the wall.

Panting, he was done. She was spent too but couldn't stop shivering through the aftershocks.

"Oh, baby," he half whispered in a tone she couldn't decipher, probably because she still couldn't hear right or see straight.

In a subconscious move, she lifted her head and he kissed her before trying to roll away. But just as she had when they woke up, she clamped herself tight, locking her legs around his pelvis and her arms around his neck.

Despite their union being over, she didn't want him to ever leave her body. "Stay."

"Right here?" he asked like he didn't understand what she was getting at, or what this was supposed to achieve.

"Yes, just for a minute."

And he did. He didn't move. He stayed there, braced on his forearms, their sticky bodies glued together. Regardless of their uneven breaths, their lack of cohesive thought… Had she ever been this content in a single moment with a man in her life?

"What's going on?" His forehead bumped hers. "In there."

Her eyes closed again, trying to recapture the sleep he'd forced her from earlier. Not that she was complaining, given how that ended for her.

"Come on," he said, resting his forehead on hers and moving his head side to side as if he could encourage release of the thoughts by agitating her brain inside her skull.

"Nothing bad," she whispered, trying to beg for his kiss, but he didn't give it.

"You tell me what I want to know before you get a treat."

Punishment and reward, if she told him what he wanted to know, he'd kiss her. He'd give her everything. Until she did, she was in the naughty corner and wouldn't be gratified by him.

"It's just…" She didn't want to remind him of how they'd started, how they'd met, but it was relevant to answering the question. "With everything that's happened in these past days, this week, with you at yours and Tag, Bryant, and Jonno, and everyone else, I just… feel like I haven't stopped, feel like I haven't been able to breathe and relax and exist. But with you here, it just… I don't have to worry about any of that. We can just be us. Be happy and chill. And it's been a long time since I've been able to say that. I wish…"

"What do you wish?" he asked when she didn't continue.

It seemed so ridiculous, childish almost, that she didn't want to say it.

"I wish we could shut the world outside for a while," she said. "Stay here and spend this time screwing and getting to know each other. Just being human beings going about their lives without the drama and upset that's waiting for us out there."

"Why don't we?" he asked. Her eyes opened again to find his. "Why don't we stay here for a few days? There's nothing we need to do out there that won't still be there. Jonno's buddies will wait, we'll find them, they're not going anywhere. Tag, if he's really your buddy and you're as close as you say, he'll understand you need some time to yourself."

"And if anyone comes looking for us?"

"Squirm, you've gotta learn. When I'm around, there's nothing that can hurt you. Nothing in this fucking world I'd let touch you."

"I don't know," she said. "I'm not sure."

"Listen, what's the worst that can happen? We stay here as long as we need to, could be a day, could be a week, could be a month. As soon as you're ready to go out and face the world again, we'll do it. We'll go back to the fight. You'll make up with Tag and we'll find the bastards you want hunted down. We'll take it one day at a time. Right now, you want to stay here, you want to screw. I can get on board with that."

And he was right, there was nothing stopping them from doing just that. She could text Tag and tell him she was alive, tell him she would explain everything, that she needed space to regroup. It would give her time to breathe and refocus.

"Okay," she said. "Just a few days."

"However long you need."

EIGHTEEN

FOUR DAYS. Turned out that was how long she needed. They spent four days in her apartment. The only time they went out was to do a grocery run because her cabinets were bare. Archer wasn't one for a vegetarian diet, and most of the food in her fridge spoiled while she was… away.

It was four wonderful days; she probably could've stayed four more, or forty, but she'd achieved her goal. Relaxed and sated, she feared falling in love.

When that thought struck her in the shower on the morning of the fifth day, she had to get out of their bubble. Locking themselves inside was a great plan, but one day reality would break through. That could be catastrophic for them, the relationship, and their deal… unless she controlled the explosion.

Tag was still out there and had been playing on her mind. She hadn't turned her back on him and wanted him to know that. She hadn't used him or meant to hurt him. Explanations were due.

Although with regards to her relationship with Archer, she didn't know where to begin.

The last thing she wanted was for her friend to think she'd been sleeping with Archer all along. That, somehow, she'd played him by staying with him just long enough to steal the money and return it to her lover, which, of course, Archer hadn't been at that time.

The only way to convey that was to look Tag in the eye and tell him the truth. Some version of the truth anyway. Archer said the truth always came out. Yep, she'd agree with that. Except if she told Tag the truth, the whole truth, he wouldn't understand.

Saying goodbye to Archer was strangely difficult. She'd never been particularly needy when it came to men. She'd always been able to give them a kiss and a "See ya later." She never believed the "I'll call you," they tended to toss back.

This time she did.

Archer insisted on driving her to Tag's. He'd taken some convincing, but she'd talked him into letting her go up alone. Archer had his own life to deal with. Four days locked in her apartment must've set his plans back.

So he stopped the car around the corner from the main entrance of Tag's apartment block, out of view of any of Tag's colleagues who may be going in or out. She'd kissed him, more thoroughly than he'd kissed her, then waited because he had to come around and let her out. Stupidly, she'd expected another kiss on the sidewalk but didn't get one. He scooped her chin, locked their eyes, and she was disappointed at the lack of a final kiss.

But, big but, she'd learned something about him and his view of the world: someone was always watching.

Standing on the sidewalk alone, she'd waited for him to drive off. The car didn't move, and he gestured toward the corner, he wasn't going anywhere until she went inside.

Swinging her hips as she sashayed down the sidewalk, she went to the corner. Archer rolled the car forward until he had a clear view down the block to the apartment entrance. He was still there when she went in the revolving door.

Putting Archer out of her mind, she strode into the elevator, rode up and went over to knock on Tag's door. Waiting for a response seemed to take hours. It didn't. It only took a few seconds for the chain on the other side of the door to rattle and the handle to turn. She held her breath, waiting to see who'd answer.

She expected it to be Gio, would he be smiling or frowning? Although the latter was so unlike him, she wouldn't know how to address him if he was. But it wasn't Gio. She kind of recognized the guy who answered the door from when she'd stayed before but didn't know him as a friend.

Tag had mixed up his ranks, something he hadn't done for a long time. Perplexing. So many of his recent behaviors were senseless, like being in that apartment, and the people he surrounded himself with. The fact he was staying inside was weird too, as was his refusal to fight his own battles. It wasn't typical for him to ignore debts either. But, yeah, they had enough friendship issues without her storming in and demanding answers.

Although she didn't recognize the man who let her in, he must've recognized her. He stepped back and allowed her inside. He pointed to the top door to the living area and proceeded to close the front door, fastening the locks in turn. And there were a couple of new chains.

She'd never been nervous facing Tag before. Yet, for some reason, she was now and couldn't put her finger on why. As much as she didn't know what was on the other side of the door, that shouldn't make her nervous, not with this being Tag's domain. He would never let anything bad happen to her.

Tag wouldn't be expecting her. Texting or phoning in advance had been an option, but she hadn't done either. Mostly because there was so much to address. She didn't want to have half a conversation before seeing him face to face. He'd never had a problem with her just dropping by in the past.

So she carried on through into the living space. Tag and Gio were seated at the kitchen table and there were a couple of guys on the couch at the end of the room watching TV. Everyone looked at her, but Tag was the only person she focused on.

"Hey," she said, clutching the strap of her purse that hung across her body.

Tag was calm and didn't look angry, but he didn't look overjoyed either.

"I figured you'd show up," her friend said, pushing back in his seat.

Out of curiosity more than anything else, she glanced at Gio. In all the years she'd known him, he'd always greeted her with a smile.

He wasn't smiling today.

"Where's your boyfriend?"

So it was going to be one of those. Gio was going to be snide and she was supposed to react. What reaction did he want? If he wanted a denial, or wanted her to argue or cry or beg forgiveness, he'd be disappointed.

Usually, Tag would leap in to defend her. This time, he said nothing.

"Not here," she said to Gio because it was the truth.

Archer wasn't there.

"So it's true," Tag said. "You are with him?"

"I told you," Gio said to him. "I didn't want to believe it either. I didn't think she'd be that dumb."

Her patience snapped. "Just what is your problem with him?" she asked unsure exactly who to address, the snide Gio or the aloof Tag.

Both of them had an issue they weren't disguising in their manner.

"We're worried about you," Tag said.

She'd heard the words from him so many times before that she believed them. "Why should you be worried?" she asked. "You have nothing to worry about."

Tag made a whistling sound and sent the other boys out with a wave of his hand. She went toward the kitchen to give the men space to exit. Gio stayed put, unusual, they must've discussed a game plan. Her arrival had been anticipated and this was their orchestrated response.

"Are you pissed about the money?" she asked Tag. "Is that what this is about? Because you can make fifty, sixty grand a month with what you do. You wouldn't miss it. You know I wouldn't have taken it if—"

"This has nothing to do with the money," Tag said. "It's to do with you. You don't understand who he is, what he does, or what he's capable of."

"I understand," she said. Archer could be dangerous, she didn't need anyone to explain that. A wave of defensiveness overcame her. "I understand what he does, why he does it, and who he does it for. I understand."

Curious concern swept over Tag. "You can't possibly," he said, opening his fingers on the glass tabletop. "I don't believe you would know who he is and want to be with him like…" Tag and Gio shared a look. "Like you have been."

"Why not?" she asked. "I've seen what men can do, what people are capable of doing to each other. You know that. You know me better than anyone. You know I don't judge people."

"He's too hard for you," Tag said. "He's too dangerous. You'll get caught up in—"

"What?" she asked, in no mood for hypocrisy. Striding to the table, she rested her hands on the back of the chair at the foot of the table. "I've been a part of your life for fifteen years. I know what you do. I don't ask questions. I keep my nose out and you've never gotten me dirty."

Until now.

"Because I don't want you dirty," Tag said. "Do you know how hard I work to keep you clean? To keep you out of this? To keep you safe?"

"I don't need to be wrapped up and kept safe," she replied. "And Archer would never let anything happen to me."

Tag's anger snapped. "What is it about him? Hmm? What's so damn appealing? Is it the danger? Is it the whole bad boy thing? You're turned on by his evil? His anger?"

"He's not evil," she said, trying not to restrain her temper, which in itself was an achievement for her.

In all the time they'd spent at the restaurant and over the last four days, she'd talked about Tag with Archer a few times. Not so much around her current situation, but he'd come up in talk of previous stories. Tag had always been a big part of her life. One thing she'd failed to ask about was Archer's previous dealings with Tag and their history beyond the one event Tag mentioned.

Did they have a relationship? A solid relationship? She made a mental note to ask Archer later. Given Tag was right there, she'd get his side now.

"What is your problem with him? I've been out with guys before, plenty of them, guys with no job, no money, no prospects, I've been out with guys who've slapped me stupid—"

"Yeah, and how many times have I taken them down?" Tag asked. "And I'll keep doing it. Just because this guy's tougher than the rest doesn't mean I won't start a war for you."

Peace was what she wanted. "That's not what I want," she said. "I want you to get along. I want you to understand. I want you to give him a chance."

"Why would I do that?" Tag asked. "I don't trust him. I don't like him."

She didn't fail to see the irony. Just as she'd convinced Archer to give Tag a chance, there Tag was putting up a brick wall and refusing to do the same, declaring he would never trust the man.

"What do you want me to do?" she asked. "You want me just to dump him and walk away because you say I should? I don't think he'll give me up that easily."

"There," Tag said, slapping a hand on the table as he stood. "That right there, is the reason I don't like him. Because you're right, Archer gets what he wants, and he does whatever it takes to get it. He wanted that money, and I don't know how, but he manipulated you into getting it for him."

"I thought you said this wasn't about the money."

"It's not."

Gio's head moved as his attention bobbed back and forth between the speakers. Why was he even there? Eavesdropping on their conversation that would normally be private, pissing her off just by being present.

"Why is he here?" she asked, pointing at Gio. "Why do you need a witness?"

"I don't need a witness," Tag said and nodded at Gio, indicating him to head to the door.

Gio got out of his chair but was hesitant to leave. "Boss, I can—"

"Go," Tag said, cutting him off. That word, spoken

with authority, was the most like himself she'd seen in a while. "We'll finish later."

Gio's scowl touched her again, offending and hurting her. Forgetting all the years they'd been friends, all the good times and commiserations, he turned fast. All because he didn't like the man she shared her bed with.

After Gio was gone, she took her purse off over her head, put it on the table and went closer to Tag. It didn't feel right for them to be standing at opposite ends of the table when she was so used to being at his side.

"What's going on?" She couldn't believe his strop was all down to her choice of boyfriend. She'd been out with plenty of guys Tag didn't like, he'd never reacted this way. "Talk to me." Taking one of his hands in both of hers, she sat perpendicular to him. "Why are you in this apartment? In this neighborhood? Why are you shut up inside, never going out, never coming to me? Never taking me out. Why did you shut Archer down when you owed him money? Why are you dealing with guys I've never seen before? None of this makes sense."

"Don't worry about it."

The way he sank in his chair, slouching with his back hunched and his arms sagging at his sides, whatever was going on was taking its toll. Dark shadows under his eyes revealed he was exhausted. His hair was a mess, he just didn't look like him.

"I'm still your friend," she said. "Whatever shit's going on between us or however much you want to hate me, you know I've stuck by you through everything. I will always be here for you. Please tell me. Show me you still trust me."

Maybe he was at the end of his rope, maybe he had no fight left, or maybe she just knew how to work him because this was the way it always happened. Tag would tell her not to worry, tell her he was fine, put her off, make excuses. As long as she kept poking and prodding, inching her way closer, he would always eventually tell her the truth.

He rubbed a hand across his forehead and let it fall to the table. "The day I lost three guys." In the trap he'd accused Archer of setting. "I told you I lost three guys?"

"Yes."

"What I didn't tell you…" He stopped to breathe. Guilt over the deaths? Worry she might judge him? What was he feeling? "Four other guys died that day, guys from the other side… See we knew there was a shipment coming into a warehouse. We knew there was money in the merchandise, and I had to have it. I thought it would be a quick job with a big payoff. In and out. Easy. What I didn't know was at the last moment the guy we thought we were ripping off was bought out by a bigger fish. A guy known as Hexam. Nobody messes with Brett Hexam."

"It was his guys in that warehouse?"

He nodded. "And the shipment was bigger than we thought. My guys didn't know who they were dealing with. They didn't know to back off. I wasn't there. I would've told them to split if I'd known. They had their orders and they went in. There was a gunfight; three of my men went down, four of his. The guys I had left grabbed part of the shipment, not all of it, but a decent amount that was already loaded up."

At last, some honesty. No judgment, she felt lighter now he'd confessed.

"Is that why you think Archer led you into a trap? You think he would've known the shipment changed hands before you got there?"

Tag got tense again. "He did know. He had to. He would never have been able to trace that shipment unless he knew who it belonged to."

Okay, she could understand why Tag was pissed off he didn't get that information. And she could already hear Archer arguing that Tag hadn't paid him for those details. Tag had paid for the location and Archer handed it over. He hadn't paid for confirmation on the owner of said merchandise. The deal was muddy, on both sides. Everyone's hands were dirty, and seven men were dead.

"And now Hexam's not happy?" she asked, assuming if he'd lost four men and a chunk of his product, the guy could be baying for blood.

"No, he's not."

"So you're hiding?"

This wasn't like Tag, but then she'd never known him to do something so stupid. He'd ripped people off before, stolen from people, but he always went for those with lesser means. He'd always been smart enough not to get himself caught in the net of a bigger fish with greater resources.

"Hexam's an enigma. He has the tightest inner circle anyone's ever known. No one knows what's happening or what he's planning. I guarantee he'll want payback, but I have no idea what that means. I don't know if he'll hurt me, hurt my men, whether he'll try to ruin the business, whether he'll bide his time and come at me slowly or hit me all at once. I have no idea and it's driving me insane. The waiting, it's making me crazy."

"You have to find out," she said because this could go on forever otherwise. Whatever kind of man Hexam was, if he was the type to want payback, Tag had to find out how the man would go about it. How he felt about Tag was crucial to figuring out his next move. How did Hexam plan to exact his revenge? "You need more information. You can't sit here forever in this shitty apartment, in this crappy neighborhood. Your men will drift off, looking for better things. You'll lose the business—"

"Don't you think I know that?" he snapped and banged his hand on the table again. "Don't you think I know everything is falling apart? I don't want to be here, stuck inside, afraid to walk down the street. I don't know who to trust. I've lost my men, and I've got bastards like Archer chasing after me for pocket change."

Twenty grand wasn't pocket change to Archer, or indeed to her, but she could understand how he'd slid down the priority list given what else her friend had going on. Tag was scared for his life and the lives of his men. His livelihood, his home, his possessions, all of it was at risk.

She'd heard stories of some of the dealers in town, the kingpins, who would do the most horrific things to men and their families if they felt disrespected. Some did it quick, with a bullet in the back of the head when their victim was least expecting it. Others would take men and torture them for days. Some stole their families away and held them for ransom. Some blackmailed, some bribed, some ratted out their adversaries to the authorities.

There were plenty of ways to ruin a man. It was hard to develop a strategy to combat that if they didn't know how someone was going to come at them.

"You need information."

"Yes, I do. I'm up the creek, Yorkie, who can I trust? As soon as I put word out on the street it will lead him back to me. He'll come for me, and I won't know what he wants. I won't know how to stop him."

So they needed to know what Hexam planned to do. And how Tag might be able to mend the rift and erase the slight without losing his life.

"Information," she murmured to herself, linking her fingers through Tag's. "I know who to ask."

NINETEEN

"PLEASE," she whined, feeling like she'd been on his case all night.

"No," Archer said, sticking with the same response he'd been giving her since she first brought it up.

Sitting on his couch, in his apartment, her feet lay in his lap. Because he was watching a news channel on mute with the subtitles streaming along the bottom, his hands were idle. She gave them something to do. He wasn't so much massaging them with conscious thought, but he rubbed her toes and his hands felt good. Every once in a while, he stopped indulging her feet to stroke her bare legs, sending tingles of awareness shooting up to her pelvis.

Shame she had to work on getting him to help Tag, her thoughts were slipping into the inappropriate.

News and sports, that seemed to be all he watched. Maybe he liked to stay in touch with current events, stay privy to what was going on in the world. Just like his need for information in their city, he needed information from across the globe too.

As to why he watched on mute? She'd never asked. Maybe it was something to do with being ready, being aware, listening to what was going on outside the apartment and inside while entertaining himself with the screen.

Given what he did, Archer must have enemies. He gave out information, he sold information, and it would be a tough balancing act to make sure he didn't piss off the wrong people. Though maybe he worked on tit-for-tat, could be after he targeted someone, he then used his skills to benefit them, thus erasing any debt they felt was owed.

Then again, when someone was screwed over, they probably cared more about the person doing the screwing than the person who'd revealed a possible secret. Archer could only get those secrets from a member of the victim's crew, so the betrayer would be more likely to receive retribution. Shooting the messenger was probably low on the priority list.

Right, but no, focus, damn, she had to break the soothing motions of his hands on her responsive skin or they'd never get anywhere. So she sat up in the center seat and crossed her legs to face him while considering how to persuade him to help.

"Come on," she said. "Please. I cooked for you."

His eyes rolled toward her for a second. "I don't know what you put on my plate, but that wasn't food."

In mock offense, she scratched an inch of his forearm back and forth. "It was broccoli and quinoa casserole," she said. "It was food. It just wasn't the hunks of animal you're used to devouring."

He hadn't stopped eating since they'd left the dinner table. First there was dessert, then there was a power bar, and he'd just polished off the fruit salad she whipped up for him.

Going to the store on her way over was intended to stock her arsenal to soften him up. Bringing up Tag's dilemma with Archer wouldn't exactly win her points. As expected, she'd been shut down a few words into her speech with a single clear, and now often repeated, "No."

"But it's what you do," she said.

"No."

Taking his bowl from the far arm of the couch to put it on the coffee table, she wanted his complete concentration. It would be his urge to get up and clean the plate straight away, he was weird about keeping the place neat. She couldn't let that happen or his interest would go elsewhere. Climbing into his lap, she cut off his chance of escape.

"Please," she murmured, allowing a seductive lilt to warm her voice. Rubbing her hands up and down his chest, she kissed his lips, but got no response. Kissing his cheek, then his jaw, she let her lips drift to his ear. "Do this for me and I'll swallow your meat."

Resting his hands on her hips, he stroked them around to her ass, probably because her butt had taken the place of her feet more than because he wanted to get physical.

"You think I work for blowjobs?"

Only half invested in the conversation, he was still watching the television over her shoulder. Massaging his torso, enamored by the muscles he cultivated in the gym and had nurtured that day, his chest was hard, his shoulders broad and solid. Early memories drifted through her mind, like the first time she'd seen him, and noted how formidable he would be in a fight.

"I gave you twenty grand not long ago," she said, arching her back to present her breasts, but his view was stuck on the television. "Won't that cover it?"

"That was money owed to me," he said and squeezed her ass. "Twenty grand for the last job, what would you give me for the next one?"

Oh, hope!

Haggling over price was an improvement over a flat no.

Brushing her lips on his again, she blocked his view, forcing him to switch his focus. "What do you want?"

"What are you offering?"

"Is this how you work?" she asked. "You negotiate maybe based on circumstance? How do you feel about barter?"

"Everybody's price is different," he said. "Depends how tough the job is, how difficult or dangerous it'll be. Depends how much I like the client too."

Had to be great working for himself, making his own rules, changing them up any time he chose. She could completely believe he meant what he said. If he despised the person asking for help, he would probably jack up the price. Wouldn't everyone? What it meant right then? She had an advantage.

"That's good," she said. "Because I know for a fact you like me a lot."

"Oh yeah?" he said, slipping to vague amusement. "What makes you think that?"

"Oh, I don't know…" Rolling her eyes to the ceiling, she pretended to mull over her explanation. "Maybe the fact that you jump my bones every chance you get or the fact that you can't keep your hands off my body. The fact that you gaze at me across the room when you think I'm not paying attention."

"You're the one wriggling all over me. You never keep still, woman," he said, but didn't seem to be complaining. His hands ran up her back then descended to her ass again. "I like it."

"I'm trying to talk to you. I really need you to do this and I wouldn't ask if it wasn't important. Can't you do this one thing for me?"

"Except it's not for you," Archer said, putting her in his spotlight. What did that mean? "This information isn't for you. It's not to make your life better; it won't save you from anything. This information is for your buddy."

Oh, so that was his problem? Okay, she got it. She hadn't understood why he'd put up such resistance when this was how he made his living.

"That's it?" she asked. "You won't help me because this information might help Tag? I thought we were over that, I thought you were giving him a chance. I thought you saw he isn't a bad person."

"I'm grateful he did what he did for you when you were a kid," Archer said. "I hope he tore the guy to shreds. If it had been me, the guy would never have walked again, and wouldn't have had the ability to harm any woman 'cause I'd have ripped his balls from his body. But Tag took care of business in his own way."

"Okay," she said. "So what's the problem?"

Archer hesitated when he contemplated what to say.

She could see irritation blooming in his gaze. Throughout the night, she'd assumed his resistance was part of a game. That maybe he wanted her to offer him something, probably something sex related. That, like he'd said before, she could pretend to be opposed to, but this would give her the excuse to do it.

She'd expected a sexual demand and had every intention of complying. Not only because she wanted the information for Tag, but because she was learning to love their intimacy.

"What he said about me sending his guys into a trap, it pissed me off," Archer said. "I do what I do, and I do it well. I don't screw people over for fun."

This path led to a conversation she hadn't planned to have with him.

Faced with it, she seized the opportunity. "Tag said the shipment you located changed hands at the last minute."

"It wasn't the last minute," Archer said. "It was a couple of days before. But, yeah, it did."

"See, you knew that," she said, splaying her fingers on his upper chest. "That's why Tag is pissed off; you didn't tell him."

"He didn't ask, it's not my job to keep track of what he knows and what he doesn't," Archer said. "How could I know he didn't already know? Hex could've been his intended target. I don't give a fuck about his business. I don't guess what clients want to know, I get specific instructions and they get specific information."

"But you knew. You're not denying it. And this guy, this Hexam guy, he's a big deal. Tag seems really worried about what he'll do."

Archer grumbled. "Maybe your boyfriend should've thought about that before he started ripping people off."

His irritation increased, but so did hers. "Is that what this is about?" she asked. "You judge him for what he does? You don't think it's right that—"

"Drug dealers are scum," Archer said. "It's as simple as that. They do what they do for money, and they don't care whose lives they screw."

To have such a strong, immediate reaction, there could be only one explanation.

"You know someone with a problem," she said. "Someone you care about was hurt by drugs?"

Understandable, she'd seen it herself. She'd lost friends and family members to various substances; every time the grief fractured a piece of her soul. No one liked seeing people they cared about become shadows of themselves, but, maybe harshly, she did believe in taking ownership.

These people made the decision to do what they did, nobody made them do it. They chose to pick up the needle or the pipe or the glass, whatever it was. As far as she was concerned, they screwed themselves.

"I know plenty of people with problems," he said. "Most times I don't judge. I do work for dealers all the time. Live and let live."

"So what's the—"

"Your friend doesn't work on his own supply and distribution network. He doesn't produce what he sells, he screws people over. He steals and then he sells, and he benefits while everyone else falls apart."

Tag did have his own supply chain, it just wasn't as lucrative as he'd like. So it wasn't unheard of for him to swoop in on a shipment last minute. And given his resources, his manpower, most of his victims never fought back. Now, in a way, he was getting a taste of his own medicine. That didn't mean he deserved to pay for his mistakes with his life.

"It all balances out," she said. "I'm not a big fan of what he does, but it's his business as far as I'm concerned. He's my friend and I care about him. I don't want to see him get hurt. He's scared and doesn't know who to trust. We need to help him."

Archer's exhale was frustrated and impatient. "What does he know?" he asked, giving nothing away in his flat tone.

Hope infused her; this could be him letting her in. Was he softening to her cause and planning to help?

"Very little," she said. "Tag just told me Hexam knows it was his men and that he wasn't happy. Four of Hexam's men died and Tag got part of the shipment. He doesn't know enough about what kind of man Hexam is to know how he'll get revenge. Tag's heard he can be a scary sonofabitch, but that's about as far as—"

"Scary is an understatement." His arms wound further around her, pulling her tighter to his torso. "Hexam never lets anything go. He can be reasoned with, but his price is always high. I wouldn't guarantee on Tag getting out of this unless he has something that Hexam wants."

She had no intention of giving up so easily. "Like what?"

"I don't know what he wants. Like most guys in his line of work, he wants respect, power, he wants territory. Your boy Tag can't give him any of those things. Tag doesn't have a patch he can give up, he's already disrespected Hexam. Money won't do it because Hexam has a regular income and can squeeze any guy he wants. Hexam won't be bought."

"Okay," she said, nodding. Hope might be the only thing to get them through this. Although this felt like they were developing a plan, the information wasn't encouraging. Pulling Tag out of a tough spot would help her feel better about all the times he'd done it for her. "So we need to find out what Hexam wants and then we need to get it for him."

"We?" he asked, so incredulous that his brows angled.

"Yeah."

"No," he said, shaking his head. "*We* don't need to do anything. I'm not the take action guy."

That couldn't be completely true. "You agreed to take action with me," she said and read his mind. "About Jamie, not about sex."

Bringing one of his hands from her ass, he laid it on her upper chest, slid it down over her breast then brought it up to curl around the side of her neck.

"In rare circumstances, very rare circumstances," he said, slowing each word to enunciate it for emphasis. "I have been known to get involved."

"Can't this be one of those times?" she asked, optimistic he would agree to help.

Doing it alone wasn't an option, she needed support.

Yeah, okay, maybe she could try, but how would the role of intimidating aggressor fit her? Ha, not so good. On top of that, she didn't know a thing about extracting information from people who didn't want to give it out.

"Why should I take on his cause? He's got plenty of guys on payroll who can go hit Hexam hard. I'm not getting my hands dirty attacking a guy who's done nothing to me. That's the kind of stain that sticks. Messing with Hexam could get you killed. Tag might be a hero in your eyes, but he's not worth either of us dying for."

Okay, so Archer had a point. Tag did have resources of his own, did have men working for him, loyal supporters. Only… none of the men he employed had the network or skills Archer did to get them over the first hurdle.

"You can still help me find out what I need to know though, right? To find out how pissed Hexam is, find out what he plans, find out if there's anything he needs or wants that Tag can use to get himself out of this."

"I could," he said, watching his hands slide over her breasts, up to her neck and down her shoulder.

His rough, stimulating palm was warm. Although the action itself wasn't sexual, the intimacy of it stirred her arousal.

"Will you?" she asked. "You must know who we have to talk to, who we can snatch off the street and tie to your pipe."

He actually smiled and his hand slid up the column of her throat to cup her chin.

"That's not always the first step," he said. "Sometimes all it takes is a conversation. You have to find the right pressure points and then you squeeze, exerting just the right amount of force. Sometimes you have to be nice or offer something in return. Sometimes asking is all it takes."

"I had no idea," she said, thinking about how deep his skills ran.

He didn't just need to know how to imprison and torture people, he had to know how to manipulate them to the highest level, how to identify weak links, and how to target those who might have a bone to pick and therefore be open to defection.

"It's only if things get messy, tricky… dirty… then we start to think about taking it up a level. And that's when the chains and knives come into play."

Ha, subtle. Hmm. Interesting way to play it, and one she hadn't considered. Most of the people they'd come across smiled, and greeted him as a friend, so he couldn't be scary in every quarter.

Gio said he knew everyone. If everyone knew him and wanted to kill him, he wouldn't last long. If Gio was right, Archer could go to his contacts, ask around, and learn what they needed to know without causing anyone harm.

"Will you do it?" she asked. "Will you help me?"

"Understand what you're asking," he said. "A conversation is one thing, but if it progresses and I unwrap the blades, I need to know you can live with it. 'Cause if you're consumed by guilt, that's it, we're over, now. We'll never get past it."

Of course he was right, if she couldn't handle what he did to other people on her instruction, the relationship would never last. She'd see a monster in him. Hating what he did could lead her to hating him. Except it was necessary and she wasn't as soft as he thought. Life on the streets hardened her, and as much as she tried not to grow cynical, she'd seen horrors.

Working in clubs and bars, she'd seen plenty of brawls, seen people OD. Seen blood and fights and even death. He thought he knew so much about her, and she had revealed herself to him. Some of herself. Her experience went beyond what he knew.

"I can live with it," she said. "And maybe this is what we need. Because no matter what you say, one day, I'm gonna walk in that front door and you'll have someone at that table. I will have to make a decision."

"I can protect you from it."

"I know, but you shouldn't have to put up that barrier. What you do is part of who you are, and I want to embrace that. There are times I maybe won't see your reasons, but I have to trust you, have faith you only do these things to people who deserve it, for good reasons. It's why you couldn't hurt me, why you couldn't break my bones and send me out to work off the debt, because you knew I didn't deserve it.

"So when I walk in that door and I see some sniveling lowlife, crying and begging for mercy, yeah, it might shock me, but I will stand behind you. It's not about what you do. If I start to doubt you then our trust is gone. Without trust, I can't be with you, Archer."

"You sound sure," he said. "That just leaves one detail to clear up."

"What's that?"

"Payment."

So he was going to help her. They just had to agree on what it would cost. When his hands settled over her breasts and his thumbs swept back and forth across her nipples, his request spoke for itself. Or so she thought.

"Sex on demand?" she offered herself to him.

To her surprise, he shrugged and didn't seem tempted. "I get that anyway. You haven't said no to me, not since the first time I asked."

The first time they'd had sex he hadn't asked. But there had been a buildup that gave her a window to change her mind.

She couldn't threaten the opposite, to withhold sex unless he did the job. That would be a dangerous power play, a precedent that tapered into a type of manipulation she didn't want to be their foundation. Trust didn't go hand-in-hand with blackmail.

"What do you want then?" she asked, trying to figure out what he may be angling for. Her body was the only thing she had to give. What else could he want? "I don't have money. You've seen my place. Don't you think if I was sitting on a secret hoard of cash, I would have a better apartment?"

"Like I said before, each job is different," he said. "Sometimes I work for a couple of hundred bucks, sometimes it's a couple of grand. Sometimes it's as simple as a free-forever bar tab or car repairs. Hell, there are times I've worked for game tickets or free cable."

So he didn't always work for money, barter worked for him. That was something, given she didn't have many material possessions.

"Free drinks at Sizzle?"

When she ever went back to work there.

Confident as always, he squeezed her breast. "I'd get those anyway."

"I'll cook for you; I make mean cauliflower and chickpea tacos."

One of his eyes narrowed. "Is that a threat?"

Giving his shoulder a shove, Sizzle stayed on her mind. She hadn't been back since the night Jamie died. The place had been shut up for a while, but Tag told her re-opening night was the previous night. And that her job was waiting for her when she was ready.

"Tell me what you want then," she said, running both hands into his hair. He pondered and she sweated. Could be she had nothing to offer, except maybe an open favor for him to call in when he came up with something. "Can't think of anything? There's nothing in the world I have that you want?"

Still, he took his time examining her figure. "You share with me the things I want most. Your body, your mind, your mouth."

She didn't know if the mouth comment was about her words or his meat, but he was right either way.

"There must be something I can do to tempt you into helping me. You want to tie me up? I bet you have the best restraints."

"Nah, I told you, I'm not into the S&M thing."

Elevating her wrist, she displayed her brand. "Want to burn me again?"

Not an experience she'd relish, sure, but she'd endure it for Tag, and sure didn't mind wearing Archer's mark.

"No," he said.

Grasping her wrist, he brought it to his mouth. God, she loved it when he kissed her there, and he wasn't averse to it either. Maybe it was making it up to her, or the reminder it was there, that she was his. Could be he liked permanently marking her. The imprint would always be there, whether they kept their sexual relationship going or not.

"I must have something you want," she said. When

his lips curled slowly, dread made her wary. "What? What did you decide on?"

"No makeup for a week."

She faltered. Uh, what?

That was so not in the ballpark of any demand she expected to come from his lips.

"Excuse me?" she asked, taken aback.

"I've seen you without it, you don't need it. I've watched you dress yourself up in the morning, watched you take your time putting it on so careful. All you're doing is covering up what I want to see. You have a pretty face, Squirm, you don't need to fancy it up. You sure don't need to do it for guys 'cause your cans is all they see."

"That all you see?"

Cupping her bosom, he rubbed his face against her décolletage. "Up close," he said. "I prefer that bare too, like I want your face."

Wow. Makeup was something she'd used since childhood. She didn't go overboard, using only eyeliner, shadow, and mascara. Once in a while maybe a bit of blush, but she didn't go in for all the contouring stuff. Lip gloss was as glam as she got.

She'd always thought her makeup was subtle, not subtle enough for him apparently.

"If I don't wear makeup for a week, you'll find out what Hexam plans to do to Tag? And if there's anything we can do to pay him off?" Archer nodded. "Really? That's all?"

"What do you want me to ask for? Your asshole? The cooking thing is out for sure."

He complained about the food she made during the process. He'd pick up the vegetables, sniff the herbs and the spices and peer over her shoulder as she stirred, as she seasoned and grated and sliced. The man wasn't short on questions about what she was doing, what they were having, what it would taste like and his most frequent one: was it edible?

Yet whenever she put a plate in front of him, he cleared it, he ate everything she made. May not be much of a reflection of her skill, the guy ate all the time. She hadn't come across a food yet that he'd turned his nose up at. If it could be fitted into one of the food groups, even loosely, he would eat it.

"No makeup for a week," she agreed.

Without the routine of putting on her slap, she'd have extra time. Maybe that was his secondary motive—increasing their sex time. Sometimes, she almost didn't recognize herself without makeup on. But it was a low price for what she was asking because there was a serious risk involved. Even just asking questions about a man like Hexam could get Archer into serious trouble.

"That's it?" she said. "Nothing else. You're sure?"

He patted her ass. "I've always had a thing for redheads."

"I'm not dying my hair," she said and laughed.

Her dark brown hair had natural threads of red through it anyway, although they only ever caught in the sunlight. If he pushed, she would dye it, she'd done it before. Her hair had been every color of the rainbow at some point in her life.

"Then it's definitely no deal, the hair was the clincher."

Joking or sincere? Either way a box of hair dye would be on her next shopping list.

"I'll think about it," she said, teasing like she didn't want to surrender at his first request. "No makeup for a week and you'll find out what we need to know about Hexam?"

"I still expect sex on demand."

Leaning in, she joined their mouths to whisper against him. "So do I."

TWENTY

"YOU HAVE TO TELL me what's next," she said.

Archer's bedside clock betrayed it was after four a.m. They really should get some sleep. After sex she was too energized to think about slumber.

"Next what?" he grumbled, tone implying he wasn't eager to chat.

"How does it work? What's your process? You have to find out where Hexam and his people hang out, right?"

"I know where to find them," he mumbled into his pillow.

Good. Encouraging. That would speed things along. She'd go to Tag's tomorrow to tell him Archer was taking up the cause in the hope it would bolster her friend's spirits.

"When should we go over there? Can we do it during the day or should we wait until tonight?"

Rolling onto his back, he lifted one arm around her, coaxing her to lie down in the nook of his body. "You've got big ideas for a little thing."

He didn't sound like he was teasing, but she didn't understand. "You said we were going to do this. I figure we'll have to—"

"There you go with that 'we' shit again," he said,

drumming his fingers on her flesh. "*We* ain't doing a damn thing, baby. I told you I'd do my thing for you and I will. I'll deal with it. Me. You're not going anywhere near it."

The whole thing was her idea, she'd be devastated to be cut out. "You're benching me? I haven't had a chance to fuck up. Why would you—"

"I know you think you're a lioness, Squirm, but you're a cub. Let me worry about the work; you concentrate on the play."

She pinched him. "Don't do your patronizing thing on me, Fella. If you piss me off, I'll be out of this bed like it's on fire."

"Don't do that," he groaned and squeezed her. "Then I'd have to get up and follow you home."

That's right, he didn't let his dates go home without seeing them through their door. They hadn't been on a formal date that night, but she'd cooked for him. They'd hung out and had plenty of sex, so the night probably fell under his definition of a date.

Finding her way in this relationship would involve asserting herself.

Archer was a powerful guy who'd take over if she didn't fight her corner.

"I am plenty capable of helping you. You don't even know what skills I have, you just assume I'm a feeble woman."

His eyes drifted closed again and his arm loosened. "You think you can start a war with the world and win. You can't. I've known you a couple of weeks and question if you know what the hell you're doing half the time. You have no strategy and a lousy game face."

Granted, she didn't have his range. That didn't mean she was useless. The last couple of weeks was hardly a fair gauge to judge her whole personality by. Reducing her volume, she found his lips to speak against, reminding him of their intimacy.

"Hasn't stopped you from taking up with me."

From nowhere, he became more awake, not all the way awake, just enough to startle her.

"Yeah, since we're talking about it," he said, "there's

one thing I wanna get straight if we're gonna do this, if we're gonna be a thing."

Apparently, she wasn't the only one with something on her mind. "Okay," she said, rising to her elbow to look down at him. "What?"

His drowsy eyes and bass tone didn't contradict the certainty of his words. "Second thing I learned about you is proving your loyalty is a major deal, you take it seriously. Third thing was you're stubborn as all hell."

Both true, but it left her to ask. "What was the first thing?"

"Stupid question, Squirm," he said, snagging her wrist to guide her hand beneath the covers to wrap it around his dick.

Her nude body fell onto his. The first thing he'd learned about her was she was attractive? Okay. And he was right, no leap.

She kissed his chest. "What do you want to get straight?"

"If anyone ever asks you where I am, you tell them."

She'd begun stroking his cock in her fist, but his statement stalled that.

"What?" she asked and, this time, sat all the way up. Crossing her legs, she rested her knees on his ribs. "I would never betray you like that."

The only reason anyone would ask about him was if they wanted to hurt him.

Offended by the idea she might give him up, it was concerning he didn't understand what was important to her. The steadfast scowl on his face didn't seem to care about that.

"I'm telling you, if you let yourself be hurt for me, I'll take that as the betrayal."

Spreading her fingers on his torso, she pressed into him, absorbing his strength and relishing their proximity.

"No, I wouldn't give you up. I just wouldn't—"

"I handle pain better than you do, Squirm, and I'm a better fighter. You tell them where I am, then you get yourself set up in bed and wait for me to come to you."

The conversation was supposed to be about Tag and

Hexam. Boy had it taken an enlightening turn.

"Why did you bring this up?" she asked. "Do you think someone wants to get to you?"

"We're lying naked in my apartment," he said. "I've lived here for years. If someone wanted to find me, this is the first place they'd look. I'm saying it 'cause I don't want you thinking you're a hero trying to protect me. That's bullshit. If you're my girl, we do things my way, and that means I protect you, not the other way around."

Another man who expected her to live by his double standards. Typical.

"So what if someone asks you about me?" she asked. "Are you going to give up my location?"

Shifting away, he tipped his body to an angle to examine her face. "Who would be looking for you?"

"No one," she said, exasperated he'd interpret her question as impending trouble. "You brought up this hypothetical villain tailing us."

Her bewilderment didn't affect him one iota, he relaxed onto his back again.

"Once word gets out we're together, no one would be dumb enough to ask me about you," he said, settling back to sleep. "They wouldn't draw breath to ask a follow-up question."

Okay, did he have to talk like that? Shit, it shouldn't turn her on that he spoke of using violence so freely to protect her, but it did.

"Archer," she murmured, climbing onto his body with her forearms squashed between their chests. She kissed him. "I have something better than Cheerios. Are you hungry?"

A gruff laugh vibrated behind his sealed lips. "I'm going to sleep now, horny one."

Kissing him again, she spread her fingers on his chest. "I'll swallow your meat first," she whispered. He wasn't so quick to refuse that prospect, in fact, although his eyes stayed closed, he crooked a brow. "Does that sound like a good deal?"

The head of his cock was already prodding her thigh;

his subconscious sure wasn't averse to the suggestion.

"Good deal," he mumbled and snatched a handful of her hair to speed her way down his body.

Archer didn't want a slow seduction or teasing build-up. All he wanted was release and she was eager to give it. In return for her own, of course.

TWENTY-ONE

"YOU LEFT ME hanging," she mumbled into her cellphone.

Archer was moving too. Wind traveled down the phone line and the hitch in his breathing signaled he had to be walking fast.

"You got yours in bed when we woke up, and in the shower," he said. "Stop bitching."

"I'm just saying, if in future we're doing oral tit-for-tat, I'm going first."

Walking down the sidewalk toward Tag's place, it was about time to hang up. Though the signal would drop in the elevator anyway, why cut it short?

"Are you nervous?"

She entered the warm lobby. "Nervous? No," she said, pressing the call button for the elevator. "Why would I be nervous about visiting my oldest, closest friend?"

"I don't know," he responded. His breathing evened out, indicating he'd stopped. "We only left my place an hour ago and you've called me three times."

She couldn't deny that. They'd spent most of the day in bed, only coming out of the bedroom to eat and watch TV. Archer had been transfixed by her feet when she pulled her pedicure kit from her purse to pamper herself while he read his subtitles. A salon was out of the question, but she'd ignored her preening for too long. Giving herself a pedicure also acted as a distraction from the time she should've spent putting on makeup.

Eating together was becoming one of her favorite things. He'd moan about her food and poke at her plate, making fun of her meal before he tasted it and carried on to eat most of it. She played her own role of gagging at the smell of whatever he cooked for himself. While he ate, she'd comment how nice it looked or how much he seemed to enjoy it.

There was something satisfying about watching him re-fuel. Already he ignored her sneaking salad onto his plate and ate it along with the rest of his food. Had to be a definite sign she was wheedling her way into his routine.

"You don't have to pick up the phone," she said, backing away from the elevator when the doors opened.

A group came out, she gave them room to exit. Staring at the open carriage, the doors closed and the lift ascended without her.

"Next time I probably won't," he said. "I'm trying to do a job here. One you put me on, Squirm."

The long narrow mirrors, part of the lobby décor, caught her eye. Glancing at the side view of herself, just like she'd thought, she almost didn't recognize the reflection of her scrubbed-clean face.

"I know you are."

They'd deliberately wasted the day in his apartment because he wanted to speak to his contacts after dark, which drew in early this time of year.

People done with work would be meeting others to socialize. Those with families would be sitting down to eat and find it very inconvenient for a man like Archer to show up.

With confidence in him, she hadn't argued when he'd told her his intention. Coming to see Tag was a necessity as well as a distraction. Informing Tag the situation was in hand, and that she was being proactive about helping him, should alleviate some of his tension. He could trust her, even if he trusted no one else in his life.

This visit was also a distraction. For days she'd been living in Archer's shadow; now the man had to work, he didn't need her at his side anymore. Instead of pacing her apartment like an animal in a cage, she'd chosen to spend some time with her friend. Except, she wasn't finding it easy to let go.

"You were fine when you saw him yesterday," Archer said. "Do you think something is different today? If you're afraid of him, or his men, don't go up alone. You should've fucking told me you were worried about your safety, I never would've let—"

"I'm not worried about my safety around Tag," she said, fed up with having the same conversation with each of these men with regards to the other. "I trust Tag. He would never hurt me, just as I promised him yesterday that you would never hurt me. Both of you have to get used to each other if you're going to be a part of my life."

"If it's not that, what's the deal? Why all the calls? You're not one of those clingy bitches who thinks I'm stepping out every time I'm not in your eye-line, are you?"

Sneering at his attempt to change the tone of the conversation, she leaned on the wall. "No," she said and could relax now that she sensed his tease. "With all the sex we've had in the last week you've probably got friction burns on your cock. I think he needs a breather."

"Don't go thinking you've got a reprieve just 'cause I let you take your pussy on a trip," he said. "I don't plan to take long. You meet me back at my place soon as you're done. Your pussy has an appointment in my bed and she better be hungry."

Archer sure would be, food wasn't the only thing he had an immense appetite for. They'd agreed to meet back at his place after she'd seen Tag and grabbed essentials from her studio. Her guy gave her a key to his apartment on the condition that she go inside, lock the door behind her, and open it for no one. He really did have a thing about keeping her safe.

"I haven't forgotten. I guess having your phone number is a novelty."

Exchanging numbers after all they'd been through, and oh so many nights of intimacy, was overdue. But that wasn't the truth of why she kept calling him.

"You keep this up and I'll be disconnecting the line before the night's through," he said. "Now tell me why you're so scared to go up to Tag's."

"That's not why I keep calling."

"So why do you—"

"I'm worried about you," she said, knowing it wouldn't be a popular statement.

Sending him into the domain of such a dangerous man seemed like a great idea when listening to Tag's problems. Except Archer's impulse was to refuse her request and she'd persuaded him. Now he was over there alone and she didn't know what would happen.

"If anything happens to you because of something I asked you to do—"

"We talked about this." His voice lost its ease. "I told you if you couldn't handle what I did—"

"This isn't about what you do to them," she said. "This is about what they might do to you. I don't care what you have to do. Yeah, we talked about that. But if someone hurts you…"

"Squirm," he sighed. "There are gonna be plenty of times when we're worried about each other. We don't move in safe circles or hang out in safe places. One thing you can be sure of is I won't show my back to anyone I don't trust. I've been watching my own ass all my life, I'm good at it."

Refuting that was impossible because he did have a fine ass. He'd done a very good job in looking after it. She couldn't talk to him on the phone all night. Hanging around in this lobby would eventually become conspicuous and Archer wanted to arrive at his destination at a certain time for a reason. She didn't know what it was, but he had one.

Distracting him was causing a delay. "Okay," she said. "Just remember I'm better than Cheerios and I'm not through with you yet. I still have fantasies you haven't fulfilled for me."

"We'll talk more about that later," he said. "Get your ass up the stairs where there are people."

"How do you know I'm at Tag's?"

He couldn't possibly have eyes everywhere and couldn't even be sure that she'd come to Tag's. It was just as possible she was having an affair of her own.

"I just do."

It would bug her if she didn't find out. "You have to tell me how."

"I activated the GPS in your phone; I can track you wherever you go."

Instead of being creeped out, she was flattered. If she was a passing fad, he wouldn't have gone to the trouble of stealing her phone to set it up.

"Can I track you?" she asked, eager to check the app on her phone when they hung up.

Except he snickered. "Not a chance, horny one. I let you keep tabs on me like that and you'll be chasing my cock all over the city."

With him, she had developed quite an appetite for sex too, and could be, maybe, she was relentless in seducing him when in need of satisfaction.

"Your cock likes being chased."

"Yeah, but the rest of me needs to get shit done."

Sighing, she gave up. "If I'm not allowed secrets, you're not allowed them either."

"I'm better at keeping them than you," he replied. "Now get up those stairs and I'll speak to you later."

Hanging up, she pressed the elevator button again. Archer was right, he would be fine; he'd been doing this a long time and knew the procedure. With positive news to share, she was looking forward to seeing Tag.

TWENTY-TWO

THIS WAS HER LEAST favorite of all Tag's apartments and he'd had several through the years. This time, instead of the living room being filled with people, it was completely empty. As she went to look out the window, the door opened, and Tag came in by himself, wearing nothing but blue sweatpants.

"Yorkie?" he asked. "What's wrong?"

"Nothing. I texted to say I was coming, didn't you get my message?"

"I did. But you didn't say why, and I thought maybe…"

Squinting, she tried to figure what conclusion he'd reached. "What?" she asked. "That something happened with Archer?"

He came into the middle of the room and shrugged before slipping his hands in his pockets. "It crossed my mind."

"No, everything is fine with Archer," she said, crossing to kiss his cheek and rest her hands on his arms.

"What have you changed?" Tag asked, scrutinizing her. "Something is different."

It took her a second to click. "I'm not wearing makeup."

His expression loosened in agreement. "Ah, that's what it is… Why not?"

"Long story," she murmured. There was no need to tell him she was paying Archer for his kindness in any way, not even with a token gesture. "Can we sit down? Talk for a bit? Are you busy?"

"I always have time for you," he said, which didn't really answer her question. If he was conducting business, he wouldn't be half naked. If he was working out or entertaining a woman, she guessed those things could wait. "What do you need to talk about?"

Ushering her over to the couch, he sat down beside her, arm laid along the backrest, just like her, so close their knees touched. It felt nice to be them again. Their friendship didn't feel as damaged that day as it had the previous one. Could that have something to do with Gio's absence? Gio who'd been so quick to judge her relationship with Archer. Had he poisoned Tag against her?

Excited by the notion of hope, and reminding him he wasn't alone, she was ready to reveal all.

"I came to tell you I talked to Archer last night; he's going to help us."

Concern or intrigue made him frown. "With what?" he asked, raising his fist to his temple though his elbow remained on the backrest.

"I told him we have to know what Hexam is planning and what kind of danger you might be in. He'll find out what Hexam wants, so we can buy him off or placate him. Archer says money alone won't do it. I told him we'll do whatever it takes to save your life."

Throughout their years of friendship, she'd gotten to know Tag well. She recognized his moods and his expressions. Right then, he was blank; she couldn't figure him out. Sitting still for a score of seconds, silent, he managed to charge the air around them.

"You," he said, starting slowly, "talked to Archer about what we discussed?"

No one told her what was said was in confidence. It didn't seem logical to refuse proffered help. Archer was the best at extracting information, which was exactly the service they needed.

"I didn't talk to him about it," she said. "We agreed you needed more information, and he can help us get it."

"And you didn't think you should discuss bringing him in the loop with me first?" he asked. Her friend didn't seem angry, frustrated was a better word. Hadn't he been hinting, the previous day, at bringing Archer in? His offense shocked her. "You didn't think you should ask me before you discussed my personal business with a man I don't trust? A man who was threatening me just last week? Would you come in here and tell me Archer's private business?"

Archer didn't have private business. No, he probably did have private business, she just didn't know it. Her guy had secrets; he'd told her about his past. None of that was relevant to keeping anyone alive this minute like Tag's situation though.

"I didn't go shooting my mouth off to earn brownie points, to impress him, or to insult you."

The male ego had a lot to answer for. More than just a dumb airhead, she could recognize the difference between what should be concealed and what shared. As evidenced by the fact she didn't reveal Tag's location to Jonno, his friends, or even to Archer when her own life was at stake. She kept his secret and would've kept it forever had she and Archer not had their breakthrough.

Her guy could probably make a fortune revealing Tag's whereabouts. He hadn't sold it to the highest bidder. Why? Her. Each of these men were an unlit match. Only she had the power to strike them and start a blaze. Choosing the opposite, she did her best to dowse the flame capable of igniting the entire situation… and most of her life.

"I can't see you sitting in this apartment all by yourself forever. Gio obviously hasn't come up with anything, he's known this was going on for months. I found out yesterday and already I'm taking steps to save your ass. You need to move forward. You need—"

"I'm handling it," he snapped.

He twisted away to put his feet on the floor and

folded his arms, closing himself off.

"Obviously not," she said, calling him on his bullshit.

She didn't do it often, only a handful of times over the last decade and a half actually. Nobody else would risk telling him something he didn't want to hear.

"You're hiding, you're not dealing with what's going on. You're sending Gio on errands you should be doing yourself."

His single laugh was snide. "Interesting observation. Can't say I'm sorry I wasn't the one catching you in Archer's bed."

Ignoring his jibe, because it was misdirected, she stayed on track. "The people you care about are at risk."

"No one I care about is at risk."

"Then what the hell happened at Sizzle? You do know that's why those guys went there? The bouncers were killed so they could get in; Jamie was brutalized to scare me. They were looking for you. This wasn't a random attack, and it wasn't payback. The only answer those men asked was where you were."

Whipping around to glare, his panic was obvious. "You didn't tell anyone—"

"I didn't know then," she said. "We hadn't spoken in a few weeks. I knew you had a job on, and I had my hands full at Sizzle. You know how it is."

Sometimes they could go weeks or months without talking to each other. They'd go about their lives and relationships without needing to speak to each other every ten minutes. They didn't live in each other's pockets. In times of crisis, they could talk twenty times a day. More often than not, they only got in touch when they had a reason.

Once every few months, they'd check in and let the other know they were still alive. Sometimes that was the extent of their relationship for a long while.

"They were coming for you," she said. "And instead they got me. You should know I would never give you up. You should *know* that."

"I do," he said, curling his hand around hers on her lap. "I do and I'm sorry, I'm on edge. I'm snapping and you're right, I'm not being rational."

He ran a hand through his hair. The lines on his face seemed deeper, like psychological scars manifesting themselves.

He inhaled. "Where did you get this?" Tag touched the loop on her leather wristband. "You wear it all the time these days, but I've never seen it before."

"Archer gave it to me," she said, withdrawing it from his touch.

"It's not traditional jewelry for a guy to give a woman he's dating."

Maybe because it wasn't that sort of gift. "He's not a traditional kind of guy."

"Is it a sex thing?"

Her and Tag could talk about anything, though… thinking about Archer in that way while in that room made her squirm.

"No. He's not into the S&M thing."

"Didn't think you were either."

He'd misinterpreted her like she'd been tempting Archer into the lifestyle.

"I'm not. It's not like that. It's… it's an inside joke."

Wearing the cuff wasn't so much a joke as it was a disguise. In time, she'd reveal the brand to Tag. He wasn't ready to hear the tale of her and Archer's start. They were dangerously close to the subject… Luckily, Tag gave up questioning her about her new lover and took her hand again.

"They came to Sizzle looking for me, that's what it was about?"

"Yes."

She'd avoided telling him so far; she didn't want to guilt him about the lives lost. It had been easy to protect him when all she was doing was withholding information. But the time for heads in the sand was over. If he kept on, he'd be unprepared if anyone attacked. It was only a matter of time before Hexam got what he wanted and pinpointed Tag's location.

He softened. The warmth of friendship returned to the eyes of a tired man, immersed in his own troubles. It hadn't occurred to her he'd be completely clueless. It should have. She was the only living witness; no one else made it out of the club.

"The cops weren't even sure you were there, neither was I," Tag said. "No one could tell us what happened."

"You never asked," she said, appreciating the way he stroked and squeezed her hands and arms.

"I wasn't sure I wanted to know."

"But you do now?"

Getting closer, he seemed so sure. "You're here and we have time. We're blessedly alone," he said and smiled as his eyes rose to the heavens. "I hadn't realized how much I enjoyed being alone in my own space until I was surrounded by people constantly, every minute of the day. They're in my head, in my hair, in my face. I'm never alone here. I need a minute to just be with you, you know? I want to know what you went through."

He always did, Tag was great at making time for her. He'd been her go-to person whenever she needed to talk something out.

"It was late," she said. "We'd already closed up, most of the staff had gone home. We were doing one last sweep, and they stormed the place. I never heard the shots outside."

"The cops said they had silencers."

She nodded, recalling the gun's suppressor digging into Jamie's temple. "First, there were five of them, all wearing masks. They got Jamie and me into the breakroom, where they tore her apart."

"Did they hurt you?"

Shaking her head, her own assault was fuzzy, unclear in comparison. It could be trauma her mind blocked out, or maybe witnessing Jamie's death was so powerful it eclipsed everything else.

"Not seriously, not like they hurt her. They came to Sizzle looking for me, because I was the way to get to you. That was all they asked about, where you were. I wouldn't tell them a thing."

"All these years I've looked out for you," he said, caressing further up and down her arm. "Don't like this switching places."

"It feels good," she said. "I liked looking out for you, it didn't matter what they said or did. Our friendship means everything to me. I would've let them do anything; I'd never give you up." Before it got too intense or intimate, she moved on with the story. "That's where I met Archer."

Surprise flashed on his features. "He was one of the masked guys?"

"No," she said. "Two other guys with masks came in to tell us the cops were on their way. Not that it slowed down the guys with Jamie. From nowhere, Archer came in, he wasn't wearing a mask, he wasn't with the other guys. He told them to split. He saved me, Tag. I might not have seen it at the time, I was scared, but he saved my life. Yes, he asked me where you were too, but he did save me. If he hadn't come in, I'd have ended up like Jamie."

Tag wasn't convinced. She didn't blame him after only hearing half the story.

"I still don't like him."

"You don't have to. I trust him, Tag. He can help us. If he was going to give up your location, he'd have done it by now, wouldn't he? He hasn't because, believe it or not, he cares about me. Just like you do."

"Nobody cares about you like I do," he said, picking up both of her hands, resting them on his lap when he leaned in. "What we have, Yorkie, it's more than friendship. We're lucky to have this."

That was the truth. It didn't seem to matter how many ups and downs they had in their lives. They could always trust they'd act in the best interests of their friendship.

"We are."

"If you want me to give the guy a chance, I will. I can't trust him. I can't flip a switch to make it happen for you. I can only promise to give him a fair shake."

That was as much as she could hope for; Archer had said the same about Tag. Like magic, she'd managed to broker a tentative peace between them. For now, that would have to do.

Encouraged, she felt optimistic. "You'll see what kind

of a man he is when he fixes this situation with Hexam. He'll find out what you need to know, everything and more. I'll tell you what he finds out and you'll know how to mobilize."

"Yeah?" Tag asked. "How do I know he won't be selective with what he shares like last time?"

His reservations were justified, but she couldn't see Archer conniving with her. And, thinking about it, her guy was looking past his own misgivings. Hadn't Tag tried to stiff him for twenty K not so long ago?

"I'll make sure of it," she said. "We'll know everything."

Apparently satisfied, he moved on. "What's it gonna cost me this time?" he asked. "Or are you here to swipe another twenty grand from my safe?" A moment of worry was extinguished when he smiled and stroked her face. "I'm kidding, relax, I don't give a fuck about that. Though I do need to know what it will cost me."

"I've got that covered."

Horror and anger seized him. "You're paying him in sexual favors?"

"I'm not a whore," she said, then lowered her volume. "And he wouldn't accept payment in sex."

"No, you're not a fucking whore and if he thinks—"

"He doesn't. What happened to you giving him a chance? He's a good man. He's doing this for me, because I asked him to, because I care about you and he accepts that. He doesn't question our friendship."

"Then I'll do the same," Tag said. "Like you said, when he brings us what he knows, we'll find out how good he is and how much we can trust him. I'm still not sure involving him was the right thing, he is dangerous. Don't forget that. I can tell you're infatuated and when you get like this, Yorkie, there's no switching you off."

It was nice he knew her so well and gave her the respect of recognizing her relationship... sort of. Tag had seen her with men in the past and probably knew her signals as well as she knew his. Infatuation was an accurate word; one she preferred to the alternative. Falling in love with Chase Archer could only end badly.

Until there was some guarantee his heart was in play, she couldn't risk her own. Her guy knew how to slice her deep and his brand would never fade. Infatuated, addicted, would she ever be able to let him go?

TWENTY-THREE

GOING BACK TO Sizzle was Tag's suggestion. Although apologetic about not going with her, he encouraged her to return. He didn't think it was a good idea for her to be away too long, and he was probably right. Sooner she could get back on the horse, the sooner they could all move on.

With Archer tied up in his own work, she had time to kill anyway. It would be better to slip into the club with it in full swing rather than go there while it was deserted. Returning to the scene of the crime was therapeutic. At least, that was the idea. Outside, she walked past Archer's approximate parking spot and had no negative reaction. The guys on the door recognized her, so let her in without a hitch. Tag hadn't replaced any staff. In truth, that task should fall to her, and she'd have to deal with it soon. Until they did, Sizzle could only operate to half capacity.

Ignoring her responsibilities, while insisting Tag face up to his, was hypocritical. The club should never have reopened without her. She understood he had to make a show of strength. Tag didn't want any enemies out there to think he was weak, and everyone knew this was his club. She could've tried to blame male ego for his haste, except if her attackers knew she'd been affected by what they'd done, they'd revel in it. She couldn't let that happen; she had her own pride too.

If those guys thought they'd damaged her psyche, they would get off on the power of lording it over her. She didn't want any of them coming back to gloat. Being attacked again would be more than she could handle.

Blue was the predominant light on the dance floor. The bar was busy and her people worked hard. The heat and scent of the space was familiar and memories flickered. In a blink, in her mind's-eye, the club was empty, then the crowd came back. Side-stepping, beginning to sweat, she wasn't ready to face her colleagues or answer their questions. Dealing with their condolences when she wasn't ready to accept and move on from what happened to Jamie wouldn't be right.

Another blink and she was taken to the moment she'd made eye contact with Jamie, when Jonno had the gun to her head. The noise of music pounded through her skull, slamming her back to the present crowded moment.

Claustrophobia clawed. Returning was never going to be easy, she needed to smack herself with reality to flush the trauma from her system. Exposure therapy. That meant one thing: the breakroom.

Rushing in there, she came up short.

New flooring had been installed, dark blue. It did nothing to quash the muted image of Jamie on the floor with those men. Out of body, she saw herself against the wall, pinned by Jonno.

Overwhelmed, therapy didn't fit this, it wasn't the right word. Her chest tightened to a wheeze, her ears rang, heart pounded. Stumbling backwards, she hit the wall by the door and yelped like she'd been snatched by another attacker.

With blurred vision, she fumbled for the door handle and ran toward freedom. She couldn't be there yet, she needed air. With the walls closing in, she couldn't breathe.

She needed to get out, to find support, she couldn't hold herself up, couldn't… Instinct told her where to go.

***

SHE DIDN'T WAIT for him long. At all, actually. When she

unlocked Archer's apartment and saw him standing at the back of his couch eating a Snickers, she couldn't have been more elated.

"Oh, baby," she exhaled and rushed over to him.

Her face was wet, eyes swollen. God, she must look a mess.

She'd run five blocks in the lashing rain before getting it together enough to hail a cab. In the back, she'd sobbed into her hands like a grief-stricken widow until the driver banged on the screen between them and told her they'd arrived.

Throwing both arms around his defined body, she buried her face in Archer's chest. She hadn't cried in years. Years. Even while locked in Archer's bathroom, she hadn't cried for herself. This kind of meltdown dented the shield she built around herself. In her experience, men took advantage of vulnerable women. She'd never sobbed like this, not even with Tag.

On the night of her teenage attack, she'd been too much in shock to cry. Still a teenager when her father died, she was so bitter and angry that she declared her gratitude and relief he was gone.

Losing Jamie hit hard. She couldn't explain why, except to say she'd been Jamie's superior. The woman had been abused, violated, and murdered, on her watch, to protect her and her friend.

"Did someone hurt you?" Archer asked, grabbing her arms to haul her body away and glare down at her.

She read his anger and confusion through her tears. "No," she said. When she shook her head more tears flowed free. "No, I…"

His scowl didn't fade; it grew deeper, becoming pissed and disgusted.

"You're a fucking mess," he said, walking her backwards.

Confusion replaced her grief in increments. "I… I went back to Sizzle. When I walked into that room, I—"

"You've got to calm your shit down."

She was dumbfounded when he reached over her to open his front door. "What are you—"

"Get your crap together," he said. "Then come back when you're fucking reasonable."

Alone in his hallway staring at his closed door, she was speechless. At least the shock of his reaction to her upset had the benefit of throwing her back down to earth with a crash.

Impulse brought her there. They were meant to meet at the apartment anyway. Archer wasn't warm and fuzzy, sure, but she hadn't expected him to kick her to the curb. If this was a test of reliability, he'd just failed. Of course, if it was a test of how she reacted to and coped with stress and trauma, she'd failed too.

***

GOING HOME LEFT her restless. At some point in the wee hours, she got tired of pacing and threw some things into a bag. Tag's was the only place left. Whenever she needed company, his was the best place to go.

It took a while for someone to answer the door, and she was disappointed to see Gio.

"What the fuck are you doing here?" he demanded, hair a mess, yawning.

"I came to see Tag."

She didn't need to ask if he was there, that was obvious, he was in hiding.

"He's in his room," Gio said, reversing to open the door wider.

His welcome wasn't warm and enthusiastic, but his attitude was better than it had been the last time they'd met.

"Thanks."

Gio locked the door and moseyed into his own room. Even if he wasn't her biggest fan right now, he didn't breathe down her neck, so couldn't see her as a threat to Tag.

Gio might be feeling the stretch of loyalty. He was a social guy who probably wouldn't like being stuck there. Closely associated with Tag's business ventures, his link was tighter than even hers would be. Venturing into the world to take care of Tag's business put Gio at risk, yet he did it anyway.

Their ideas of how to support Tag might be different, but she couldn't fault his loyalty.

Heading for Tag's bedroom, she tapped on the door before going inside. That late, he should be asleep. The lights were off, but he was sitting up, watching TV.

"Hey," she said, coming in and closing the door.

"Hi," he said, grabbing the remote to mute the TV. Tag didn't have subtitles on, he watched TV like a regular person. With no other lights, if he turned off the picture, they'd be plunged into darkness. "What's up?"

He pulled back the blanket beside him. Instead of getting in, she slipped off her shoes, dumped her purse and jacket on the floor, then climbed onto the end of the bed to sit cross-legged in the middle.

"I went back to Sizzle."

Not that she wanted to talk about that experience.

"How is everyone doing?" he asked, sitting up straighter.

"I didn't really speak to anyone." She hadn't spoken to anyone at all. Had they noticed? "I was thinking about security."

"What about it?"

While trying not to think about Archer, she'd been thinking about Sizzle and its desperately needed changes.

"I know we'll never be a top-class establishment." That wasn't meant as an insult, the neighborhood was shitty, and she wasn't qualified to manage a high-class place. "But I would like to shake things up."

"And security is where you want to start?" he asked. "I'll increase your budget for staff, how many do you think you'll need?"

"I don't know. I thought I might talk to someone who knows about this stuff and have them set something up for us. We don't have a proper security manager. I'd like to get some more guys, to protect the customers and the staff. Could we look into getting some radios and maybe cameras?"

Scowling, he didn't appear enthusiastic. "Radios we can pick up for sure, but cameras… people come into Sizzle 'cause they know they're not being watched. We provide an environment for folks to do their business."

And pedal Tag's product too.

Drugs weren't the only thing sold on premises. Anything that anyone wanted to get rid of could be sold in the dark corners and booths of the club. Addicts and pushers all felt at home in Sizzle.

"I guess," she said. "I wasn't thinking so much inside, maybe outside. If we'd had cameras outside and someone watching them, maybe our guys wouldn't have died on the street. The cops could've been called—"

"Even if we had the cops on speed dial, they wouldn't prioritize Sizzle."

Probably not. "I'd still like to talk to a professional," she said. "Could I do that and come back to you? I'd feel better to get some input. We need new staff, it won't be easy to hire anyone trustworthy or reliable," anyone decent, "given what happened. Bouncers don't get paid enough to be shot in the street like dogs, and the servers… Live or die, no woman wants to go through what Jamie did."

"If it will make you feel safer, I'll let you do whatever you need to," he said. "I can make a few calls and…"

"What?" she asked when he didn't finish his thought. It couldn't be easy for Tag to be stuck and out of the loop. "I can make the connections, don't worry about it. I have a few ideas of people who may help out. I'm happy to manage the project on my own, I'd like to. I just needed your approval."

Sliding down in the bed, he took his hands over his head to hold onto the top of the headboard. "I told you when you started at Sizzle you should consider it your own."

Tag had other business interests way more lucrative and exciting than running a nightclub. Sizzle was her own, he didn't say no whenever she wanted to make changes. She'd never considered overhauling the place, but Jamie's death was an omen. History couldn't be allowed to repeat itself.

In light of what Tag did, and the patrons of Sizzle too, future invasions were possible. She wouldn't be taken by surprise again. Something of this magnitude hadn't been her thing, until now. Sizzle was her livelihood; she had no choice except to suck it up and go back there. Maybe when hiring new staff and implementing changes advised by her security expert, she'd talk to Tag about a refurbishment.

In the time she'd worked there, the place hadn't seen a lick of paint. Sure, Tag changed the floor in the breakroom, probably to cover the blood stains rather than because he'd developed a sudden love of interior design.

More than a distraction, maybe if she altered the environment, she wouldn't be assaulted by the memories so much.

"Anything you want, Yorkie," he said. "The bastards who hurt you deserve to suffer. I'm sorry I can't make them pay."

Archer was supposed to help her get revenge, "supposed to," yeah, that was in the dirt now. Once Tag was out of the Hexam mess maybe her friend would change his tune about payback. It would depend what agreement was reached to spare Tag's life.

The people Hexam employed couldn't be merciful types. If Tag was taken by those men, the ones who murdered with impunity and tortured Jamie before taking her life, then he'd probably wish for death.

"I know," she said, dropping her hands to his legs when his feet extended beneath the covers to touch her shins. "I just want to move on."

"We will. Soon this'll be a distant memory and we'll never talk about it again." Good, she looked forward to that day. "You didn't come to talk about Sizzle, did you?"

On the ride over, she'd been happy to focus on business. Though, he was right, that wasn't her reason for visiting at that hour of the night.

"I came over because I didn't want to be by myself."

"Archer?"

She'd never been one to share gossip and her need for privacy intensified when it came to relationships. Until she knew what was going on, and why Archer reacted in the way he did, she wouldn't write him off or share their secrets.

"We're having a night off."

"He can't be an easy guy to bond with," Tag said. "He's kinda renowned for not letting people get close. Archer can get you anything you need, he has a wide network, but doesn't show up at birthday parties, you know?"

So he didn't have much of a social life beyond his work. Hanging out with him taught her that. He'd taken her to dinner but didn't suggest partying in bars and clubs. She didn't care about those places, she worked in one and was glad of the break when off shift. The last thing she wanted in her down time was more pounding music and humid, pungent air.

Sticking at home meant proximity to a bedroom too. While they were still in a fervent stage of their relationship, that was a necessity.

"He's more than just some mindless brute."

"Maybe that's why I don't trust him," Tag said. "He's smarter than he lets anyone think he is."

Smart enough to make a living by getting others to reveal their close-held secrets. "He is."

Dropping his arms, he leaned toward her. "If you guys had a fight, you can tell me."

"No," she said. "We didn't."

"Showing up here at this time in the morning when you have a boyfriend's place to go to? Last time you did that…"

"No," she said, desperate to kill that thought before he finished having it. "He's nothing like Damien."

"No, Damien had a job."

Typical that probably the most respectable man she'd ever dated was also the most vicious.

"For all the difference that made," she said, compelling herself to smile. "Can't I just want a night off?"

If this had been a typical day, she'd have just finished her shift at Sizzle about an hour ago. So if she'd been heading over to visit, that would be the time she arrived. Except this wasn't a typical day, and she wasn't back at work yet. Tag told her to go, spend an hour there, and she hadn't managed ten full minutes.

"Sure you can," Tag said, "and you're always welcome."

"I'm going to get a drink, do you want one?"

"No, I have to get some sleep. Come and join me

when you're ready."

She got off the bed and went to kiss his cheek before he turned off the TV. Climbing into Tag's bed would be easy, but she wouldn't sleep. She'd only feel worse about the Archer situation if she lay in the dark, staring at the ceiling, trying not to wake up her friend.

After leaving the bedroom, she wouldn't be going back in, not unless she was really overcome with a desire to sleep. Somehow, she didn't see that happening.

TWENTY-FOUR

THE NEXT DAY came, and she was right, she'd gotten less than an hour of rest. Even that had been when she accidentally nodded off while Tag was in the shower. He didn't ask questions because she told him not to. Ever patient, he accepted her into his home, comforted and cared for her, without any expectation.

Going to Archer's when their relationship was so new, while she was so distraught, had been a mistake. She hadn't thought it through, she'd just reacted. Right up until he pulled her away from his body, it felt like the right thing to do. It only took him a few seconds to kick her out. It happened so fast that she had no time to comprehend what was going on before it was over.

Standing in Tag's bedroom on this new day, looking out the window at the street below, the world seemed far away. What future could there be with Archer, if she could have one at all? Rushing into a sexual relationship had been dumb when he was her only hope for retribution against Jamie's murderers. Without him, she wouldn't be able to see it through, she'd need his help to locate and take them down.

Except hope of that was lost if she'd lost the relationship. Because how could she go and ask him to honor the original deal when she'd made such an idiot of herself? She'd devoted time and energy to proving she was strong and could keep her shit together even in horrific circumstances. She'd undone all her good work in under a minute.

Going back to work at Sizzle was her only option. She needed a job, and Tag relied on her to run the place. She didn't have the luxury of picking and choosing how she made money. Sizzle was her opportunity, without it, stripping was her fallback. Given her experience the previous night, was she ready to do something so sexual in public?

A couple of hours ago, someone poked their head into Tag's bedroom, where she'd spent most of the day, to offer lunch. She'd refused; food would sit like lead in her guts.

There were two bedrooms in this apartment. Tag and Gio stayed there full-time. And Tag paid a guy to stick around as security. Either the guy stayed up all night in the living room or slept on the couch. Though there was a cot set up in the hall closet, only just large enough for it and nothing more. Maybe someone slept in there sometimes too.

Tag had another apartment on this floor, which served as a sort of barracks. At least four of his men stayed there at all times. Small talk with the on-duty security guy filled in some blanks. The guy had been on alert, her showing up freaked everyone out. On reflection, showing up so late to a place waiting to be ambushed may not have been a smart move.

The security guy, Viti, was forthcoming. He explained the second apartment was also a decoy, meant to throw Hexam off the scent. Tag couldn't be renting under his own name, that would be too obvious for a man concealing his location. If, somehow, he was traced to this block, whoever came after him would have to split their resources to raid both apartments if they didn't want to take the risk of losing Tag again. Smart. Archer wasn't the only wise one.

Watching the clouds drift over the sun, shadow curved around her. Tag was smart, maybe he'd been right not to trust Archer. Maybe she should've listened to her friend.

The bedroom door opened and she turned, expecting Tag. Instead, Gio was the one in the doorway.

"He fucking showed up here," Gio said. "Do you see why I get pissed off? This guy knows where we are. You guys have one blowout and he could send a whole army after us. We're not safe here."

"Wait…" she said, about-facing, dropping her folded arms. "He came here? You… you mean Archer?"

"Who else?" Gio asked like he was eager to fight and building up steam to say more.

Forget that. She didn't have time and strode straight past him to head for the living room. Why was Archer there? She had to get there before him and Tag turned on each other.

Tension was palpable in the living room. Archer and Tag stood ten feet apart. Viti and another couple of guys were on their feet near the couches. Everyone fixated on Archer, primed and ready to move against him.

Defuse the situation, that was her job. She wouldn't jump to conclusions, or Archer's rescue. Assumptions she'd made recently complicated the situation, information first, action after.

"What are you doing here?" she asked, walking a few steps closer to Archer. "Are you alone?"

"Yes, I'm fucking alone," Archer said. "If you don't tell these guys to back off, I'll end them."

Tag was the closest to him, security stayed on the periphery. Archer had to feel threatened enough that he was watching them all at the same time. He claimed he'd defend himself, but if he made the first move, he'd be playing offense. She'd seen what he could do with a blade. And this time, he wouldn't miss.

"Do you have information?" she asked.

Could he be there to hold up his end of the bargain about info on Hexam?

"A bunch, but that's not why I'm here and you know it. We need to find us some space."

So he'd come to talk to her. Less than twenty-four hours after kicking her out of his apartment, he was coming to her. Was he doing it to patch things up and apologize? No assumptions. Could be he wanted to draw the final line and confirm he had no intention of helping get justice for Jamie.

"Okay," she said. "Come with me."

Lifting her cuffed arm toward him, she wasn't surprised when he came over and hooked his finger through the metal loop. She didn't have the chance to turn around before Tag spoke.

"No," her friend said.

She tensed. If he put his foot down, Archer would retaliate, and that would end in a brawl.

"No?" Archer asked.

She didn't like the slow awareness that joined the lowering of his chin.

"Take this room," Tag said, glancing around at his guys, which had to include Gio who must've come in at her back. "We'll leave you alone."

Tag kept his eyes fixed on hers while everyone else shuffled out. Moving in at the rear, her friend watched her until the last second forced his gaze away, then he left the room.

What did Archer want? She didn't know and didn't want to look at him for fear of what she'd see. Her chin fell to her chest. Archer had other ideas. With a single deft tug, he pulled her off balance and her body collided with his.

"I fucked up."

Stating the obvious was a good start, but it didn't clarify what brought him there. "Yes, you did," she said. "How can I trust you after the way you—"

"Three things happened when you walked through my door last night," he said. "First thing that hit me was rage. Fuck, I wanted to hurt whatever hurt you. Bad. Hard. In fucking excruciating ways. I've never felt overpowering, uncontrollable anger like that. Never. Never in my life, Squirm. You don't understand… it might seem like I'm an evil sonofabitch sometimes, but I'm always together. In my head, I have a plan. I know what I'm doing; I keep it together. All that went to shit last night."

She couldn't deny that truth, his ability to be calm and collected was enviable. It was one of the first things she noticed about him when he walked into the Sizzle breakroom, so casual, with swagger. Like he was picking a movie instead of witnessing a murder.

"What do you want me to say?" He'd been that angry but hadn't taken it out on her, not with violence. Maybe that's why he'd kicked her out. Maybe he didn't trust himself not to hurt her. "Is that why you threw me out?" she asked. "Because you thought you might beat the shit out of me?"

"No," he said, sure of the fact. Stroking her shoulders, he imparted some of his composure. He scooped her chin with one hand and let the other drop to snag her cuff again, this time to force her hand to his hip. "Second thing, it hit me, only reason I could blow up seeing you that upset was if I was crazy for you. Crazy for you in a serious, long-term kinda way."

And that freaked him out? He'd told her once he was only interested in women who'd stick around. Didn't that mean he had to be a serious relationship kind of guy?

"What's wrong with that?" she asked. "You thought this was temporary? You were using me?"

"No way," he said. "Something I've never told you, something I'm ashamed of…" His volume dropped so much that she had to strain to hear him even though their bodies were flush. "My mom is… she's a mess. She's with a different guy every week, know what I mean?"

He commented on her never keeping a man, told her that he bunked in with his mom to stop other men from climbing into her bed. It was no leap to find out she was promiscuous. He'd talked about supporting his mother too, so mother and son had to be in each other's lives.

At one point, his strong reaction to whores and comments about bitches being all the same led her to believe he'd been hurt by a girlfriend. Now she… A love interest didn't break his heart, his mother did, probably at a very young age.

That might explain why he was only interested in women who stuck around instead of claiming one who'd sleep around. Happy as she was that he was revealing more of himself, she didn't understand why he was doing it now.

"What has that got to do with last night?" she asked. "What has that got to do with you tossing me out on my ass?

Are you telling me you're like her? That you had another woman in your bed?"

"Fuck no!" he exclaimed. Offense almost made him recoil. "I'm telling you because she shows up in a state sometimes. She gets her heart broken, she gets high, and drunk, and shows up telling me to go after the guy who dumped her. Tells me to hurt him. Tells me she's devastated, she cries and drinks and curses all guys. She forgets that last week she was dumping some poor schmuck promising her the world. Usually she ditches the ones there could actually be a future with 'cause they'll put up with her shit.

"She screws around on them, takes them for all she can then dumps them when she gets bored. I get so pissed off, but I'd never hurt her. So I let her cry like a fucking idiot. She gets herself worked up. Ninety percent of the time I can just ignore her. Every time she shows up, it's the same routine, and I fucking hate it. She's been the same since I was a kid."

So her showing up brought back memories? Maybe for a minute, he wondered if he'd fallen for a woman just like his mother. He was pissed someone hurt her, realized he cared far more than he'd admitted, and then got angry with himself for falling for a woman who'd use him like his mother did. One, two, three.

"You didn't even listen to me, you kicked me out. You hurt me, Arch, embarrassed me."

"I know. I fucked up. I know I did. Shit, I was fucking pissed at myself the minute you left. I didn't know what to do, figured you'd be cursing me out."

"I would've been if I wasn't in shock. I got upset and came to you on autopilot. I shouldn't have. I know we haven't been together long and you're not an emotions kind of guy. I felt safe with you, Archer. That was it. I think it's why I came to you, because the memories from Sizzle upset me. I recognize now you pulled me out and protected me from… Jamie's attackers. I came to you because I care about you. I guess I wanted to share my vulnerability with you. I felt comfortable enough to do that, not with anyone else but with you, and you've shot that all to shit now. Guaranteed I'll never do that again."

"I am so fucking pissed you ended up here," he said. "Not pissed at you, at me. I shouldn't have let this happen." His jaw clenched and his grip on her face tightened. "I drove you into another guy's bed; you can't know how that tears me the fuck apart. I'm so fucking pissed at myself for forcing you to—"

"I didn't sleep with him," she said. Although at the time it had been less to do with loyalty and more to do with restlessness. Still, it was the truth. "I went home after I left yours, but I was already upset. I felt alone. You weren't an option, you'd made that clear, so I came here."

"Did you tell him?" Archer asked. "Did you tell him what happened?"

"No," she said. "I couldn't talk about Sizzle. If I did, he'd tell me to never go back and that's where I work. I run that place, and I won't let those assholes beat me. I'll figure it out. I hadn't prepared myself and the club was busy—it doesn't matter, I'll figure it out."

"I'll be there," he said. "If you don't want to go back, we'll figure it out. You don't have to rely on Tag."

The truth ached in her chest. "I can't rely on you."

His agitation provoked a need to soothe, but she had to be honest. Archer had come to apologize, and she would accept that offering. His reaction to seeing her so distraught was understandable. This was a new relationship. They were still figuring things out and had been through a lot together. The previous night was just another step in them finding their way.

But if she ever got that upset again, she would question whether Archer could handle seeing it. Damage had been done. There was a fracture in their relationship, it could heal in a scar and make them tougher, or it would widen into a chasm they'd never cross.

"We rushed into this," she said. "We've been moving so fast. Maybe we should take a step back. You were right to toss me out. We should take a breather and—"

"I don't want to take a breather," he said. "You're coming home with me."

Given how their association started… was that a

threat? The pain of his guilt about the previous night morphed into a determination so intense she shivered. The truth had to out.

"I want to," she said. "I want us to be like we were. I want to hang out and have sex and talk. But I need a man who'll be with me, not a playmate only interested in fun. I'm done with all that crap. I need to know my guy can handle shit."

They'd spent time worrying about her handling what he did. If she would still be able to look him in the eye after he'd hurt the people she'd sent him after. But there was another side to the coin they hadn't considered.

"I can handle it," he said. "I'm here telling you I fucked up. I'm fucking human, sue me. You think your boy Tag is perfect—"

"This is not about Tag. You're not in competition with him. Why can't you see that?"

"I see I did something to hurt you, and this is the first place you came. I see that every time we fight, every time you leave me, this is where you're gonna come. So it doesn't matter about your past with him or ours, or how many times him and me say we'll give each other a break. Every time I fuck up, he's gonna see it. So he's gonna hate me and you're gonna have to live with that. 'Cept you said if I was gonna be in your life, I had to make peace with the guy. That ain't ever gonna happen if this is what happens every time we fight."

Except they hadn't fought, she'd been upset, he'd kicked her out, that was the end of the incident. It was over in a heartbeat.

Still, she could see his point. "You might not believe me, but I don't usually lose control like that. I might be driven by emotion but getting upset like that… it never happens."

"You don't have to make excuses," he said. "It's my fucked-up-ness that caused it. I felt something strong and positive and I reacted by super-imposing something negative onto it. How fucked up is that?"

Their emerging honesty was encouraging and beginning to erase some of last night's doubt. Yeah, they'd had an issue, but they didn't let it fester. They got over their egos and were dealing with it.

"You remember when we were on your kitchen table right before we first had sex? You told me you were fucked up; said I was fucked up too. I guess we'll have to get used to the idea that we're both going to fuck up sometimes."

"I guess," Archer said. "I feel like shit for kicking you out."

"And I feel like an idiot for showing up in a mess."

"If you're sad or hurt or angry, I want you on my doorstep. I want you in my arms. I won't ever compare you to her again, I promise."

Mommy issues, she wouldn't have pegged him to be that type. She had issues of her own, who was she to judge his? He hadn't dumped her, sneered, or humiliated her by ridiculing her emotions. But he had made her question if he could cope with a real, honest relationship.

Tag didn't wait to be told he could come in. Their allotted time for privacy must have expired because the door opened. Tag came back in with Gio not too far behind him.

"You want us to toss him out?" Tag asked her, looking only at her, disregarding Archer's presence.

"No," she said, turning back to Archer. "No, we've figured it out."

"Wonderful," Gio said, his voice thick with sarcasm. "Are you gonna take off?"

She was about to say yes. If they wanted privacy to continue the conversation it was only right they do it in one of their own apartments as opposed to taking up time and space in Tag's.

Archer's words made it out before hers did. "We have business," he said. "I found out some things you'll want to know."

Hexam.

Last night he'd been out talking to Hexam's associates before the whole apartment upset bullshit happened. What had he found out? There hadn't been time to talk. He didn't have to share there in front of Tag, he could've filtered it through her and strung them along, keeping the specifics to himself until their relationship stuff was sorted out. But there he was, being honest and up front, just like he told her he would be.

"What did you find out?" Tag asked. "Who did you speak to?"

"The *who* doesn't matter," Archer said. Like journalists and spies, he probably didn't give up a source. "We should sit down."

TWENTY-FIVE

MUCH TO HER chagrin, Gio stayed. All the while she was in the kitchen making coffee, she kept one eye on the table. The men maintained a distance from each other, and nobody said anything out of line. Out of line? Sorry, nobody said anything period.

Tag, Archer, and Gio spent so much time glaring like lions ready to defend their territory, that no one had the time to make small or trash talk.

Laying everything on the tray, she carried it to the table and stood near the center to pour their drinks. Tag sat at the head of the table, Archer at the opposite end. There were three place settings at each side and Gio sat at the one on Tag's left.

As a neutral party, where should she sit? She really didn't want to sit next to Gio. For the sake of symmetry, after she'd distributed the drinks, she took a seat next to Archer. She wanted him to be comfortable enough to tell the truth. And not to worry he'd been used for his skills without compensation, like last time.

"You're right Hexam's pissed," Archer said. "And he's making a big deal of it in circles that could do you a lot of harm."

His low tone was detached, professional, not apathetic. She was impressed he managed to be concise without being patronizing, which would be very easy given the fizzing hostility.

"That's what you hear?" Gio asked.

Oh, he was desperate to ridicule Archer. Is that what came from being beta all the way?

Archer ignored him. "What you won't hear is that three of the four guys taken down were guys Hexam wanted rid of anyway. Guys he didn't trust. Guys he would've picked off if they hadn't died that day."

"But he's making a big deal of those four?" Gio asked.

Archer nodded. "Sure is, 'cause he got ripped off. It sounds better if that happened after four of his best guys were taken down, guns blazing, than his operation was weak and easily infiltrated."

"Does he plan to hurt Tag?" she asked.

Answering her question, Archer focused on Tag. "All I can tell you is this isn't over. He doesn't have a concrete plan, but he's talking the big talk. Means if you saunter onto his radar, he'll smack you down hard. He'll do it in public to embarrass and humiliate you; I'd guess that's his plan."

"You'd guess?" Tag said, infected by Gio's cynicism. "Nobody's paying you to guess."

Nobody was paying him at all, not in monetary terms. Somehow, Archer kept his cool. Was she part of the reason? She wanted her opinion of him to matter.

"I can tell you there's a way in. He's setting up some big deal with a guy in Mexico, a guy I know, actually," Archer said. "A good guy. I dated his sister." Leaning back, he scratched his ear, relaxed and comfortable. "That's not important. So Hexam's leaving the country soon, for a while. If you don't settle this debt now, soon, it's gonna hang around your neck for a long time. The only way to settle it is direct with Hexam. If Hexam's out of the country and one of his guys finds you, you won't be able to reason with them 'cause their orders are pretty damn clear."

"To kill him?" Gio asked.

Archer shook his head once before taking her hand from the table to his mouth. Talking to the men at the opposite end of the table, he still hadn't looked at her. Claiming her hand seemed an absent gesture, like his subconscious reached for her because his mouth couldn't resist the instinctive urge to taste her.

"Death on the spot would be a gift," Archer said. "Hexam doesn't order assassinations." Continuing to kiss her hand, he tasted her knuckles and her palm while pondering something. Pressing her palm to his chest, he held it in place with both of his flat on top of it. "I'm trying to remember if I've ever heard of Hexam ordering a clean hit. Don't think there's even been a hint of it."

Watching him access information in his memory banks was fascinating. Cool and casual, he searched through his internal directory of fathomless facts and squadrons of secrets to locate what he'd heard about the man who wanted to hurt Tag. He had to have some sort of internal index system given the amount of data he had to have stored. He thought about it for another minute.

"No, even the dealers, the couriers… Anyone who's screwed him over or fucked up and made a mistake, he doesn't order quick deaths for them."

Listening to him talk was kind of a turn on. "You know everything," she murmured, but he didn't seem to hear her.

"Last time Hexam formed a partnership with a guy in Bogota… well, he thought he'd formed a partnership. Turned into one big fucked up mess. He left the country for that too and there was a guy, I can't think of his name…" Archer said, narrowing his gaze at nothing.

She smiled. His heart pumped against her flat hand at a low resting rate. Her guy wasn't worried and in no rush. Even sitting in what could be classed as enemy territory, he wasn't breaking a sweat.

"It was something…" Archer was still thinking. "Ruiz, that was it…Hexam had left this loose end at home. His men weren't ordered to kill the traitor. They kept him hostage in this beautiful house up north, though I guess the captive didn't see much of it. They kept the poor schmuck for months until Hexam got back."

"How do you know so much?" Gio asked.

"And why are you sharing it?" Tag questioned. "I've never heard you talk this much."

This was the time Archer chose to look at her. "Because it's what my lady wants, and I'm in the doghouse," he said. "This is what you want, isn't it, Squirm?"

Whether he meant complete honesty, transparency, or just showing respect for Tag, she wanted it all. He was doing this for her. Damn, she was glad she hadn't put makeup on that morning.

"This is what I want," she said. "Thank you, Fella, you're amazing."

"I'm not done," he said. "I have a couple more guys I'll check in with to find out exactly when he's going and how long he plans to be gone. I'll let you know the best way to get in touch with him 'cause showing up at his place without an invitation isn't a great idea."

"Why are you doing this?" Gio asked. The thread of his suspicion took Archer's concentration away from her. "How can we trust you? How do we know this isn't another trap?"

"Why would I want to hurt either of you? I don't give a fuck."

Vindicated, Gio straightened. "Exactly, so why are you doing this?"

"I've already told you. It's important to Nya. She told me to do it, so I'm doing it."

Gio had some nerve to still be treating Archer like shit.

"Does it matter why?" she asked. Archer had given them so much; her defensive hackles rose. Neither Tag nor Gio had offered so much as a thank you. "Look how much more you know, that you didn't know this morning. You guys have been holed up here for months, doing nothing. Sitting, waiting like pussies to be taken down. Now we know he's leaving the country, now we know what he's capable of. We know we have to reach out to him."

She didn't have Tag's full attention because that was trained on Archer. "You said there was a way," her friend said, linking his hands and leaning on the table. "You said there was a way to fix this."

"There might be," Archer said, kissing the back of her fingers, then locking her hand between both of his. "I'm working on it."

"And what's this solution gonna cost me?" Tag asked. "You give us all this information and withhold the most important detail."

"Listen, I can tell you the way. I can ask the questions. I can find out what you want to know. What you choose to do with the information is your deal."

Her guy was losing his patience, it was the edge in his voice. She could understand why when he was faced with such a lack of gratitude after taking risks to dig these guys out of a hole.

Tag and Gio looked at each other. "He's going out of town," Gio said.

Something went unsaid between the two men at the other end of the table.

The tone made her uneasy.

"Don't even think about doing anything stupid," she said, sure she could hear the cranks and levers in their minds manufacturing a plan. "He might be going out of town, but his men aren't. You'll still be at risk if you don't fix this. Archer just said that."

"But how well will he be guarding his patch?" Gio asked.

All these years she'd thought he was a fun-loving guy, laid back and easy to get along with. Now it seemed the tension was taking its toll because he was talking crazy. The question was one of the stupidest she'd ever heard.

Exasperation warred with disbelief. "This guy wants your blood, he wants to stop you breathing, and you're thinking about ripping him off again?"

Archer stood up in a move she hadn't anticipated. "This is why I don't get involved with guys like you. Why I don't offer all the information up front," her guy said.

"Because even when good sense smacks you between the eyes, greed gives you a hard-on. You get a whiff of power and nothing else matters anymore. I don't give two fucks if you two get yourselves killed, but what you forgot"—he dropped his knuckles to the table to glare ire into Tag—"is when this guy was trying to find you, Nya and her friend paid the price. If you're too much of a chickenshit to face Hexam, you've got no right to poach his patch when he's not in town. You are a pussy. Face him like a man or get the hell out of Dodge. I won't let Nya get hurt 'cause you can't take care of business. You take care of this before Hexam leaves, or I'll take care of it myself."

Archer backed away from the table.

Both Tag and Gio leaped to their feet.

"What does that mean?" Gio asked, frantic. The reality check served him right. "What the fuck does that mean?"

"It means if I have to hand you to Hexam on a plate to protect Nya, that's what I'll do."

These men couldn't get along with each other for more than five minutes at a time. It was like dealing with quarrelsome children.

"You're not gonna do that," she said, getting up to join their hands before she turned to Tag. "He's not gonna do that because you're going to deal with this. We're going to find out what Hexam wants and we're going to find a way for you to give it to him. No more games. No more going after men who might hurt you."

"We do what's right for the business," Gio said.

Tag didn't look convinced. She didn't trust Gio not to get into his head. Leaving Archer's side, she went to the top of the table to link both her hands in Tag's, palm-to-palm.

"I need you to fix this," she said. "Just fix it so we can move on and forget this guy exists. Will you please do that for me? Let's just get this guy out of our lives."

Tag let go of one of her hands to stroke her face. It connected them and calmed him, so she smiled. Archer wouldn't like watching it.

"I'll hear what Archer has to say when he figures it

out," Tag said. "If I have something Hexam wants that I can give to make this go away, I'll do it."

"Wait a minute," Gio butted in.

Tag was still fixated on her.

"That's a promise," she said, grabbing the opportunity. "You promise you'll do this for me? You know how I feel about a person's word."

If he'd learned nothing else about her in all their years as friends, he knew how she valued integrity. If he gave her his word, she would believe it.

"I promise," he said. "If it's in my power to give it, I'll do it. I'll make this go away if it will make you happy."

"You being safe," she said. "That makes me happy. I want this over so we can move on. Give us some time and we'll be in touch when we know what we have to do."

TWENTY-SIX

CLOSING HER EYES, she let her head drop back onto the headrest of the passenger seat of Archer's car.

"You look tired," he said.

Although he was driving, his hand curled around her knee.

She didn't bother to open her eyes. "I am," she said. Her night had been emotional, and she hadn't slept. Fatigue was no surprise. "I think I'll take a nap when I get back to my place. Do you mind dropping me off there?"

"We're not going to your studio."

Relaxing her hand over his, she lifted her head. "I know we have things to fix between us. But I can't come back to yours and fall into bed with you, Archer. For one thing, I'm too tired to think about sex."

"We're not going to my place either."

Now she really was confused. If they weren't going to his or hers, and he'd insisted on taking her away from Tag's… Where could they be headed?

"I'm not hungry," she said, despite not eating a thing all day, she was too tired to consider a meal. She'd probably rather have sex than sit upright in a restaurant for the next few hours being social. "I just need to lie down and close my eyes.

Can we do dinner another night?"

"I'm not taking you to dinner either."

Eliminating destinations didn't help her figure out what was going on. For the first time since they'd got in the car, she took a long look outside. Familiar buildings zipped by. The roads were clear, he'd made good progress in getting away from Tag's.

"Then where are we…"

She trailed off after the next corner. Alarm edged out exhaustion. They drove another three blocks and he turned another corner. Her fear was confirmed. She knew exactly where they were going.

"You can rely on me," he said.

"No." Gripping the door, her nails curled into his palm. "I don't want to do this, Archer. Please don't make me do this."

"You told me you have to go back and that I make you feel safe. I'll put my blade through the throat of any man you nod at. No one can hurt you, Squirm. If you want to keep your job, you have to be able to show up without flipping out."

That might be true, but she wasn't ready. Her mind had shut down after her reaction last night and the mental block wouldn't lower. She couldn't go to Sizzle and walk in there; she just couldn't do it. Archer kept driving until he pulled up right outside the front entrance.

Without pausing to talk or hesitating for a second, he got out, came around and opened her door. When he'd made a decision, he didn't dick around. So he grabbed her arm and hauled her out to slam the door behind her.

"Do you have keys?"

For a moment, she considered saying no because maybe if she could convince him they had no legitimate way to get in, he would give up and take her away. Except, he wouldn't be that easily defeated and no doubt knew exactly how to pick a lock or find a building's weakness. He'd get them inside whether she admitted to having the keys or not.

Digging her hand into her bag, she clutched her keychain, and was extracting it when she stepped forward.

Archer snatched her arm to pull her to a halt. "Don't rush it."

What did that mean?

If they'd come there to go inside, as far as she was concerned, they should get this over with as fast as possible.

"What do you mean?" Following his line of vision to the sidewalk for a brief moment, she looked back at him. "What are you doing?"

"If you're gonna work here, spend nights here, you have to face everything that happened here. This is where it started, right? The bouncers died here on this sidewalk."

That was true. The dark gray asphalt showed no hint of blood. The rain from earlier in the day, stained it dark and wet. She hadn't seen the bodies, or maybe she had but blocked it out.

Screaming and kicking were her priorities when she'd been hauled out of Sizzle, hanging over Archer's shoulder, terrified of what would come next.

Archer was right. The men she'd worked with, trusted, overseen, they died on this street.

Going in and out of Sizzle every night, she'd have to walk over that ground. There were side doors and a back entrance, but usually she entered and exited via the front. Every time she crossed the space, she'd be walking on their final resting place, the spot where these men had taken their last breaths.

Pity and sorrow for their lost lives and mourning loved ones overwhelmed her. They'd died for no good reason as so many people in the deprived area did.

"I want you to stop and think about it," he said.

Taking the keys from her hand to leave her by the car staring at the concrete, he went ahead to unlock the door.

With his back against the door, he held it open for her and waited, giving her the time to breathe and face the trauma at her own gradual pace. Coming to terms with how that fateful night played out could only be done in increments. That's why he'd stopped her there. Exposing her to the timeline, one event at a time, helped her to reflect and accept.

When she was ready, without saying a word, she went

across the pavement and sailed past him, through the entrance, and into the corridor that led to the club. She must have walked this way a thousand times. At this moment, it was dark and though the low ceiling didn't help to quell her fears, the corridor's width staved off the anxiety of claustrophobia.

Immediately to her left were the admission booths where patrons paid. Further along was the now silent cloakroom with its shutter pulled down. Right at the end was the flood of light coming from the club. It wasn't illuminated by its artificial lights, but there were glass panels in the roof letting in some patches of natural light.

Striding up the hallway, she stepped into the main club and stopped to think about Jamie. Only a few feet from there was where she'd been snatched by the men who rushed in, surprising them both.

Even though she'd tried to fight, Jamie hadn't stood a chance. In that initial moment, it had been Jamie against five guys. And two more coming up the rear, she now knew, who'd have jumped in if there was a scuffle.

Those two were probably left with the corpses to act as lookouts, waiting to see if the shots had been heard. Their second task would've been to search the building for Tag, who, of course, hadn't been present.

The bar was on the far side of the room, that's where she'd been standing. Long and straight, it curved at both ends into shorter straight unmanned sections. Large as it was, that wasn't the only bar. There was a small, circular one in the back corner of the dance floor opposite the DJ booth. A VIP area hung over it on a mezzanine floor. With a view over the full dance floor, when it was rented out, it came with its own server.

Three stories above was the roof of the club, leaving plenty of empty space for the lights and speakers to hang far overhead, never intruding on the revelers' space. Sizzle was supposed to be a place of pleasure, a place of happiness and fun. That illusion had been destroyed in the space of just one night.

Behind the bar, in a secret crevice off-limits to customers, was the office where she did the paperwork and where the safe was situated. The raiders hadn't cared about the office or the money, all they'd wanted was Tag.

A presence behind her turned her head, she didn't have to look to know who was there supporting her.

"She was so young, just twenty-two, and always so damn happy and innocent. Not virginal, but you know, not like us."

He laid his hands on her shoulders and skimmed them up to cup the sides of her neck. The physical contact was enough to comfort her. When she blinked, moisture tracked down her face.

"You weren't responsible," he murmured. "It's survivor's guilt that's making you feel like this."

She exhaled because he was right. Relinquishing some of her rigidity, her weight sagged onto his supporting body. Needing more, she guided his hands from her neck to wrap them around her shoulders. Keeping hold of his hands, she forced him to squeeze her tight.

"I was behind the bar when they came in. I sent Jamie to talk to the bouncers, to tell them we were ready to leave. Maybe if I had—"

"What?" he asked. "Gone yourself? Gone with her? It wouldn't have made a difference. Those idiots didn't have a fucking clue what they were doing. They were trigger happy. They took out the bouncers 'cause they were scared pussies. Their fuck-up saved your life."

Like he'd said when he sauntered into the breakroom that night, leaving the bodies on the street drew attention to what they were doing. Archer had said if he was in charge, he'd have brought everyone inside. She wasn't sure if it was intelligence or conniving on his part, but he understood how to handle fraught situations to achieve his goal.

Brushing her lips on his arm, she already knew the answer to her question but asked it anyway.

"Do you ever work with others?" she asked.

"Sometimes. Not like, officially, but yeah, brief alliances can bring mutual benefit."

"Is that how you knew Jonno? Have you worked with him before?"

His chin met her crown. "Sort of," he said, "I guess you could say that."

Twisting around in the constricting circle formed by his arms, which he didn't loosen, she had to look him in the eye.

"Have you…? Have you watched him… hurt women? Like they hurt Jamie?"

Touching her hairline, his fingertips slid around the perimeter of her face until they paused under her chin.

"I figure you'd know by now how I feel about rape," he said. "I'd never let that shit go on in front of me."

Grief weighed on her chest. "She was so scared," she said, hating her uneven voice. "She was terrified. He held that gun to her head and she lost control. I did exactly what they said when they ordered me in there… I don't know what I thought would happen."

"You did the right thing," he said. "The where didn't matter. They'd have done the same thing to her in here as they did in there."

The breakroom door wasn't quite in sight because they weren't far beyond the threshold. But she looked to her right anyway, to the wall it was on. Archer wouldn't let her out of there until she'd faced that demon.

"Do you think if I told them where Tag was, they'd have let her live?" she asked, distant, and unsure which response she wanted.

He dipped his head until his lips moved into her hair. "No," he said, returning his arm to her shoulders. "They'd probably have killed you too."

Would they have raped her first? Would it have mattered? If she'd given Tag up, maybe the guys would've put a bullet in her and one in Jamie, saving them from the horror of violent sexual assault. But if they had been raped, Archer would've had time to get there and might have saved the day.

Except…

"You said Jamie was too far gone when you walked in," she said. "If you'd walked in on them raping me, would you have walked away?"

Back then, she was nothing to him. They didn't have

a relationship. So he'd have had no reason to care any more about her than he cared about Jamie. But she was the link to Tag he needed, maybe he would've stepped in to help her because he needed her alive for the information.

"I've never watched Jonno rape a woman. He's a sick sonofabitch. I've seen him do some shady shit, and I'm not saying what he did was right, but when he does screw women without their permission, it's opportunistic."

"Like? I don't get it."

"He's your classic GHB predator. I think he packs roofies in his wallet next to the condom. Those guys with Jamie wanted her to fight. Like Bryant. Those sick fucks get off on that. Jonno wants a woman helpless. And, Squirm, you ain't nothing close to helpless."

"He had friends," she said. "The one who touched me first and those two who came in after."

"I didn't say you'd have been left alone," he said. "I'm just telling you that Jonno would've been more interested in getting the job done than getting off."

That didn't make her feel better, but she understood his point. Urging her head forward, she laid it on his chest.

"I think about that night. When I was lying on your bathroom floor. All those nights I was at Tag's… I think about it and I can't sleep… I've had nightmares, like I'm a stupid kid. How dumb is that?"

"You have nightmares with me?" he asked, tucking her hair away and she bowed back.

"Not in your bed, no, I… I've never been scared lying beside you."

His open palm pushed her head to its previous place on his torso. "Good."

"I think about what I could've done. Should I have been nicer? Should I have been more cooperative and told them what they needed to know?"

"You acted on instinct and that was to protect Taggert."

Archer's excuses for her actions didn't relieve her guilt.

"Jamie was beautiful. Young and vibrant. She lost her

life. It doesn't seem right."

"It never does," he said. "How many junkies and whores and gangbangers have you known to die for no reason?"

Loads. Most days she heard news of people dying because of ODs, domestic violence, or turf wars.

"But Jamie wasn't like that," she said. "She wasn't one of those people, she had prospects, you know? It just seems so wrong."

"And that's why you're desperate for payback."

Standing in his arms, talking this out, was so much more therapeutic than the terror and panic that ripped through her when she tried to do it alone.

"I don't know what I am. Tag doesn't think it's a good idea. He told me to stay away from it."

"Taggert thought it was a good idea for you to come back here on your own last night when it was packed to the rafters. Tag stiffed me and I have the ability to hurt him. He ripped off Hexam who's one dangerous motherfucker. Your boyfriend doesn't always make the best decisions."

Digging her hands into his back jean's pockets, she leaned away to make eye contact. "I know we're maybe in a gray area now," she said, surprised and pleased her tears were drying. "But when does that become your job?"

"My job?"

"You fucked up last night, we both agree on that. But you're here now proving you care enough to support me even with the not-so-fun stuff."

"Yeah," he said. "And…?"

"And… we've done a lot of fun stuff. You'd think all the times you've put your dick in my pussy might have clued you in that I'm open to being with you. All those times I've asked you to eat me or had your cock in my mouth…"

"What about them?"

"Add those to all the times we've lay around together in our underwear watching TV, sharing meals, talking about our lives and our histories, sharing our secrets… Don't look now, Fella, but I think we're in a relationship."

Tag had referred to Archer as her boyfriend last night.

Although Archer used the word to refer to Tag to get a rise out of her, she wanted him to take ownership of the role, to take ownership of her.

"You think I didn't notice?" he asked.

For a guy who spent his entire life observing everyone around him, scrutinizing their behaviors, monitoring their actions, she'd like to think he'd figured out what was going on in his private bedroom.

"Did you?"

"There's a reason I don't call you my girlfriend."

So it wasn't incidental, it had been a conscious choice?

"What reason?"

"'Cause I have to explain some stuff to you before I make this public."

"We've been out together in public, we had dinner."

"Yeah, once," he said. "And you're hot. That meant squat. Could've been a one-night stand. Soon as you're working again, I'll be spending a lot of time here. I'll be making it clear to every customer that you're my property."

A fist of intrigue clenched inside her core. "How will you do that?"

"I'll kiss you," he said, pressing his lips to her head. "I'll touch you." He bent to squeeze her ass. "And I'll be demanding submission." She gasped as he caught the loop on her cuff and thrust her arm in the air to drape it around his neck. "You need me to own you, and once you're mine, I won't care where we are, I'll do whatever I want with you."

Her heart beat so hard that she felt it in her thighs. "Doing what I'm told gets me hot," she whispered.

Bending to kiss her, he brushed his nose over hers. "I know," he murmured. "It won't take long for word to get out that your pussy has a permanent tenant."

Everybody knew Archer, those words returned to her mind. "So why not call me your girlfriend?"

"I want everyone to know, and they will, damn soon too, 'cause I don't dick around with my lady's status. You're taken. Every cock in the joint will have to sniff for scraps elsewhere. Only a guy seeking suicide would think about hitting on you."

"Is this the part where you tell me that you have enemies and they'll try to get to me to get to you?"

"No," he said. "Fuckers would have to be straight-up looney toon to consider hurting you, they know what I'm capable of."

"What then?"

"No one will hurt you. But they'll assume you know everything I know."

Ah, clarity relaxed her. "Oh," she exhaled. "I'll be inundated with information requests."

"Probably. That and the begging will start. People want to know what I know, and I don't take every job on offer."

Being selective meant he had to turn people down. Those people would be disappointed, maybe desperate.

"So I'll get the sob stories? People assuming I can get you to work for them?"

"Yep. And that's why we need to talk before going public; we need to lay down some rules."

She wasn't worried. Working bar meant she heard a lot of tales from desperate people.

"I can handle people," she said. "I've already talked to Tag about getting more security around here anyway. We don't have to worry about nut-jobs. I'm going to get someone in who knows what they're doing, to install some sort of security system and maybe hire some more guys."

"Good plan," Archer said. "I can hook you up."

Appreciating his show of support, she smiled, but had to assert herself even in a playful way. "I have contacts."

He bumped his forehead on hers. "Not like mine, you don't."

Not having a male ego weighing her down, she could yield. He would know the best and the best was what she needed.

TWENTY-SEVEN

"OKAY, WE'LL TALK about it more when I start making plans," she said, still in his arms, surrounded by the empty club.

"I'll set it up," he said, taking control as was his natural urge. "Run of the mill crazies you can handle. But I need to know you won't manipulate me after you've fallen for the bullshit. You can't ask me to take every job."

Protecting his time and his livelihood was important, the last thing she wanted to be was his weak spot.

"You think I'm a soft touch. You think I'll fall into every pair of batted eyes and believe every tear that falls?"

"I don't know yet," he said. "And you can't know either, 'cause we never know what we'll be faced with or how it will affect us."

"True."

She couldn't argue against that point given where they were standing, and why they were there.

"Seeing you upset last night… I got mad at myself for letting you down," he said. "If you push my buttons just right, I'll give you the whole damn world. I will do whatever you fucking ask me to, I fucking know it."

And she could tell the power of their connection

pissed him off.

"But you have a rep," she said, assuming the male ego was once again in play. "And I can't have you running around after every lost kitten just because it puts a smile on my face."

"We have to be careful about who we give information to. It's not always as simple as somebody asking, handing me money, and me dishing out everything I know. There are times I withhold for good reason. If I tell you that's what I'm doing, I need you to accept that without giving me shit."

"Okay," she said. In the interests of honesty, she made a clarification. "But if I believe something is worthy enough, I will bring it to your attention and if I push you, I will expect more than just a no."

"As long as you're not doing it every day, I think that's okay," he said. "Now, show me around."

It wouldn't surprise her if he knew the layout of the whole building, he'd probably seen the plans. He was the kind of guy who would do reconnaissance before thinking of attempting a raid. But they went through every room and corner anyway. In the cellar where the stock was kept, Archer waited while she counted barrels and took notes. She showed him around the office, around the bar and the dance floor and every secret closet.

They went into the cloakroom, which was a mess, and made further notes to chastise her staff running the club in her absence. When she found money left in the registers of the admission booths, she was ready to issue reprimands.

Ranting on about how irresponsible people could be and Sizzle being vulnerable, she tried to identify the staff members last on shift. Giving him a rundown on their histories, their strengths and flaws, she didn't even notice which door he'd directed her through until she turned around and saw the couch.

Stopping dead. Her words vanished.

Spinning away to try to flee, she came up against his damming body. "Why are we in here?" she asked.

"You have to face it. You have to stand in here and face it."

Her tears came back and this time, she trembled. "No." Her breathing quickened like last time. The constriction in her chest returned. "No, I can't be in here."

"You can. I'm here. What do you think can happen to you while I'm here?" he said, walking her forward. With his strong hands gripping her shoulders, he guided her to the middle of the room. "They had you there." Aiming her body toward the wall she'd been pushed up against, he wouldn't let her shy away. "Were you scared?"

"Yes," she said. "Yes, I was, and I hated them for it. I hated them for coming into my space and making me vulnerable. But I couldn't give in to fear. I focused on Jamie instead of myself."

"And what did you see?" he asked, voice low, even, understanding, yet firm.

Squeezing her eyes closed, she shook her head, and wet globes seeped from her tear ducts. "I told them to stop. I shouted. I screamed. But they wouldn't… I don't think they heard me. Jamie tried to fight but they fought back. He hit her so hard…" Her voice trailed into a sob.

"It's okay," he said, rubbing her arms

When she opened her eyes, he'd turned her around to face the couch and the floor where Jamie had been assaulted and killed.

"She wasn't dead. She wasn't dead when we left. I saw bubbles, in the blood, she was breathing."

"She was unconscious," he said. "And never regained consciousness. They made a mess of her body inside and out. Even if she'd made it to the hospital, they would never have been able to save her. There was swelling in her brain, bleeding, he hit her so hard that he fractured her skull."

Whipping around, she grabbed his tee shirt in both fists. "How do you know that?" she asked in a rush of desperation.

"I've seen the police report, the ME's report."

"You have? When?"

"You told me you wanted to go after these guys. I had to know who we were dealing with. Rapists, like serial killers, quite often have an MO. I figured if I could work out his routine, it would help me figure out who he was.”

"Identify him. You're already trying to identify them?”

"Sure." Putting both arms around her, he gave her something to hold onto. "I knew you weren't ready, that you'd have to deal with coming here first. Coming back was always going to be emotional for you. You need a cool head for revenge; I'd never have let you go after them in anger. If we deal with this, build you back up, and you still want to go after them, I wanted to be ready. The more time I have, the more subtle I can be. It didn't matter if it took six days or six years. As soon as I figure out who these fuckers are, I can monitor them. I'll be ready to hand them to you, baby, with everything you need to take them down. I swear it.”

Lost for words, her jaw loosened. He wasn't just blowing smoke; he was taking action, anticipating her needs before she'd declared having them. Predicting her intentions because he had a clue what they were. If he kept going like this, she'd never be able to stop herself from falling in love with him.

"Jonno," she said. "He'll know who they are. Were they all Hexam's men?”

"No. I know who four of the seven were.”

Disbelief, gratitude, and pride merged in warmth inside of her. "Four of the seven," she exhaled.

"Jonno doesn't work for Hexam. Three of the guys did.”

"Who did Jonno work for? Did the other three work for him?”

"Jonno works for himself, and I'd bet at least one of the other guys was with him. I haven't had a sit-down with Jonno. I won't 'cause I don't want to tip our hand, not when I still have other avenues to work. If we can come at them from behind, it'll be better.”

"The element of surprise.”

"Exactly.”

He kissed her forehead. He had an incredible talent for focusing her mind. It started with a distraction, like surprising her with what he already knew. The distraction cleared her mind of the clawing emotion and helped her concentrate on the practical, until once again her breathing returned to normal and the blur departed her eyes.

"We can get them," she said. "We can pick each one of them off."

"Yeah. I thought Hexam's men wouldn't be so easy 'cause their boss is a bastard. With Hexam leaving the country, a lot of these guys are, I guess you could say, independent contractors."

"So when Hexam takes off," she said. "They'll be unemployed, moving onto other jobs?"

"Probably. It might make it harder to keep an eye on them. But it will make them easier to get to when they don't have Hexam's protection."

"So how did they all end up working together?"

"It's like I said before, mutual benefit. Jonno wanted Taggert. Hexam wanted Taggert. I wanted Taggert. It came out in conversation when we all showed up in the same spot that we were all looking for the same guy. So in a kind of unofficial meeting, we agreed if one found him, we'd notify the others."

"And that's how you ended up in Sizzle?"

"Jonno found you," he said. "I mean, I knew you existed, knew Taggert had a girl he cared about. I figured you guys were screwing. I hadn't invested time to research you 'cause going after a guy's girl is not my style."

No, he would rather go after the guy and just chain him to the bathroom floor until he spilled his guts, resorting to hacking off body parts if the need arose.

"You knew I existed," she said.

Having not known Archer existed, it was weird to think she'd been on the radar of dangerous men while remaining oblivious.

"If I'd had to, I would've come to you," he said like it was nothing, in his usual half-sighing, lazy voice. "Jonno wasn't patient. We weren't working together, so I didn't know what he was doing until I got the call to say he was coming here. He'd called Hexam's guys and they were cooking some plan. I work alone as much as I can, they didn't bother to include me in the details. I nodded along and told them I wasn't interested in being part of his roundup gang. But he was coming for you and I was in the area…"

"You were in the area," she repeated. He told these stories like they were no big deal. Something so incidental had changed the course of her life, saved her life, and to him it had just been a logical convenience to stick his head round the door to see what Jonno had turned up.

"I figured I'd drive by and ask Jonno what you'd said, though I didn't think he'd get anything out of you. Women are loyal to the point of stupid when it comes to men they're in love with."

Back then he'd been sure she was Tag's girl.

"Then you saw the bodies outside?" she asked.

He nodded. "Thought what a fucking mess they'd made. But I was too curious not to look in."

Too curious? Too nosey. The man had to know everything. He'd seen dead bodies and known who'd stolen the lives. Bingo, he had lucrative blackmail to tuck into his back pocket for later.

An idea perked her up. "We can hand them Hexam's men. The cops. What's to stop us trading Tag's freedom for the freedom of Hexam's men? We tell Hexam, if he doesn't forgive Tag then I'll go to the cops and tell them exactly what happened that night."

"We have no evidence," he said. "And you can't testify to a thing 'cause all you saw was a bunch of guys in masks. You don't know anybody's names except Jonno's, which you learned from me. You wouldn't be able to track him down—"

"But you could," she said, inspired with hope.

"And what am I gonna do?" he asked. "Go to the cops and tell them, 'Yeah, I know exactly who Jonno is and I saw the whole thing too.' They'll want to know why I was here. They'll want to know why I wanted to find Taggert and how I knew Jonno and his buddies were there. Soon as they find out I knew what was going on before it went down, boom, I'm in the cell right next to Jonno."

She didn't want him going to jail. "Okay, but we must

be able to build a plan from there somehow."

"It's the worst idea I've ever heard," he said. She'd be offended if brutal honesty wasn't his inherent style. "You're asking Hexam to forgive Taggert by putting yourself in his direct firing line. Do you think you'll last any longer than the guy who's been holed up in an apartment for months, hiding from a guy he knows will delight in torturing him?"

"But—"

"You stand up for Taggert, great, you feel good for twenty minutes, until you find yourself chained to somebody else's wall. I guarantee my brand will be insignificant compared to what those guys will do to you."

"You could protect me," she said, tucking in close in the way she knew he liked.

His body betrayed his enjoyment of her wriggling act when she came into contact with the reaction in his jeans. Perhaps in respect for where they were and what had happened there, he eased his pelvis away a fraction of a second after she felt it.

"I could," he said. "You're damn right I fucking could. But you won't like the way I protect you."

Drawing back an inch to seek an explanation in his expression, she wasn't satisfied. "What does that mean?"

"Because my way of protecting you would involve chaining you to my fucking floor again."

"Your floor?" she asked. "What's wrong with the bed?"

"Not into that S&M shit."

"Still I'd think you'd let your girl have some comfort. How would you earn a living if I was taking up space in the place reserved for your victims?"

"If I was protecting you, it would be my full-time job. 'Cause I know as soon as you got the chance to wriggle out, you would be off. I got a taste of what losing you was like last night and that ain't never gonna happen again."

If her way wouldn't work, they'd rely on whatever Archer was planning.

"You said there might be a way to appease Hexam?"

"There might. I'm still working it out."

Sizzle wasn't open yet and wouldn't be for a couple of hours. There were things she could do, the staff would be coming in soon, and the place needed its manager back. Though, in truth, she was too tired to think about doing a good job.

"I need to rest," she said, blinking to try reawakening her heavy lids. "I just need to close my eyes for a while."

"I have people to talk to tonight. As soon as we can get this Taggert crap sorted out…"

"The sooner we can get back to normal?"

What would normal look like for them?

"And to start thinking about what you want to do next."

Like going after Jamie's killers. They did have a lot to think about. After resting up, she'd have to work out what to do about security at Sizzle. It would have to be concrete before she started thinking about going after gangsters.

If they were part of any kind of network, it wouldn't take them long to figure out what she was doing. She and Archer might be able to take down two or three, and then the others would want to come for her.

She'd be putting herself in a very unsafe position and it wasn't Archer's responsibility to give up his life to protect her. So she'd make sure her club was as safe as it could be before she thought about inviting trouble.

"Take a night off," he said.

"From us?"

"From here."

All this time he'd been holding her, and now he turned her toward the door. He locked both arms around her shoulders to press her back into his chest as they proceeded outside. His physical signals reassured her he was a force who could shield her from harm.

He had let her cry and talk and made up for his negative kneejerk reaction the previous night. Their relationship wasn't perfect, but like he'd said, he was human and made mistakes.

"I'll take you home," he said.

She trusted him to lock up the club while she sat in

the car and waited.

She did need rest, physical and emotional rest, and he did exactly what he said he would. Not only driving her to her apartment but walking her up the stairs and unlocking her door.

Opening it an inch, he handed her the keys. "I'll wait here until I hear you lock it," he said. "I know you're tired, but try to eat something after you've slept, and take your pills if you need them."

Managing a loose nod, she accepted his kiss on the corner of her mouth, then turned to go inside. Her eyes were already closing and her body felt like stone. She was so grateful for the proximity of her bed.

Before she was all the way inside, she stopped. "When you're done with your work tonight…" she started. Turning around, she offered up the metal loop on her cuff. "Will you come over? I'll feel better if you're here."

"Sure," he said, curling his finger around her loop. "But we can take the night off if—"

"We had last night off." She put the keys he'd just handed her back into his palm. "I might be unconscious, but I want to wake up beside you." Because he didn't answer right away, paranoia seeped in. "If you want to spend the night in my bed that is."

"Damn straight," he said and lunged down to kiss her more thoroughly than he had all day, in a kiss more alike the ones they'd shared before.

Too soon he took his tongue from her mouth. Sex now would be half-hearted. She would rather wait until they were both energized and ready to do it properly.

"Get as much rest as you can," he said, kissing his way to her ear. "I'll be depriving you of the luxury of sleep for a while. Won't take me long to exhaust you again."

TWENTY-EIGHT

JUST AS SHE came out of the bathroom the next morning, Archer disconnected her cellphone.

"Taggert called," he said.

Instead of returning the phone to the kitchen table, he focused on it and his thumbs moved across the screen.

"What did he say?" she asked, straightening her towel, waiting for him to put the phone down.

Her cell was all she had, there was no need for a hard line.

"Asked if I spent the night," he muttered, reading her phone. "Does he keep notes on your sex life?"

"Sort of," she said. That admission was enough to raise his head. "Looking for anything special in there?"

Her expectant brow raise was supposed to precede an apology for his snooping.

Instead, he went back to his prying. "Old boyfriends, naked pictures, internet search history."

Honesty, she couldn't fault him for that. "You think about asking?"

"You know what I do," he said. "Don't expect to keep any secrets. Any chance I get to pry into your life, I'll take it."

"Maybe I want to keep secrets," she said, but got no response. Seeking a reaction, she dropped her towel and ran her hands through her damp hair. "Fella, you wanna come over here?"

They hadn't had sex last night. She hadn't heard him come in. By the time she knew he was in her bed, he was already snoring.

"In a minute," he mumbled.

Cupping her breasts, she trailed the tips of her middle fingers to her nipples and circled, stimulating them to taut peaks. Sashaying over to him, she curled her fingers around her phone and tried to take it from him. He didn't let go and tugged it back, forcing her another step toward him.

"You ever play with yourself in front of a guy?"

Shock stole some of her prowess. "Archer," she whispered in a gasp.

"I want to know," he said, tossing the phone to the table.

It skittered across the surface and fell onto the floor.

"You probably just broke that."

He grabbed her other wrist and opened her arms wide, forcing her body to his for a second before whirling her around to walk her toward the bed.

"I'll buy you a new one," he said. "You'll need one anyway. I don't want old boyfriends calling you."

"You've got a real hard-on for my exes."

The open bedroom curtains fluttered over their extended hands.

"Nah, Squirm, that's all for you." Shunting her onto the bed, he stood over her. "Play," he ordered.

"What?" she asked, heat flicking her cheeks.

"I wanna watch you finger yourself."

He had a real thing for watching.

"Why should I do it myself when you can do it for me?"

"Have you done it in front of another guy?" he asked. She shook her head. "How old were you when you started taking the pill?"

"Fifteen," she answered.

"You taken it ever since?" She nodded. "Ever used any other forms of birth control?"

"Condoms," she said, sitting up to unbuckle his belt.

"How many guys have you been with?" he asked, grabbing a handful of her hair to pull her back and look her in the eye.

"None, I'm a virgin," she said. His glare grew cold. Unbuttoning his jeans, she tugged them down to his thighs, hmm, no underwear. That was less interesting than the tempting liquid glistening at the tip of his impressive cock. Extending her tongue to a point, she sampled it. "Is this for me or do the questions turn you on?"

"Both," he said. "I didn't know how hot it would be to learn everything about you. How many, Squirm?"

"Five," she said.

Sass could be fun, but if she wanted arousing, all she had to do was surrender to his command. Her center swelled and tingled, excitement sparked up into her belly and the breasts she'd stimulated earlier sought his attention.

"How old were you when you lost your virginity?"

"Sixteen," she said.

"How long were you with him?"

"Three years."

The quick-fire interrogation was making her pant. Stroking her hands over his hips, she rubbed them around to his ass, down the back of his thighs to the sheath always attached to his belt. She'd forgotten it was there until her fingertips made contact. When they did, the urge to pull out the blade overwhelmed her. Intrigued, she tugged his knife free from its secure lodging.

"You said a boyfriend hit you, who was that?"

Turning the blade in the light, she was transfixed by the beauty. "The worst was Damien."

"What happened to him?"

She shrugged. "I don't know. Tag got me out; I stayed with him for months after. He never told me what happened to Damien and I didn't ask."

Bringing the blade closer, she touched its cool, flat side to her breast.

He seized her wrist to pull it away. "That's sharp."

"I know," she said. It wasn't the same one he'd branded her with, but it was the one he'd used to scar Bryant. "That mark you left on Bryant, you've practiced it?"

"I leave it on everyone I confront with my blade."

"You didn't leave it on me," she said, blinking up at him.

Sinking to his haunches, he closed his fist around hers on the handle of his knife.

He raised it to kiss her branded wrist. "My blades exist to protect you now; they'll never harm you again."

With their hands united around the knife handle, she slanted forward to capture his mouth. Archer was dangerous with a weapon and without. There was something seductive about the power in such a simple object, maybe because he knew how to wield it so well.

Her slim fingers were squashed between the solid shaft of the handle and his broad, proficient digits. Despite her being between him and his weapon of protection, he wasn't fighting her for it.

He'd put the suggestion into her head, so she allowed her fingers to trail from the bed to the apex of her thighs. While his tongue tangled with hers, she spread her legs and pressed a finger to her clit.

The odd sensation of being kissed while massaging her own clit in an act she usually partook in alone, didn't breed embarrassment as she thought it would. Something about enjoying the private intimacy exposed a vulnerability. Being so open and weak in his company took their trust to a level so intense it scared her.

"Wait, stop," she said, thrusting a hand to his shoulder.

They hadn't been doing anything except kissing. She wasn't even sure if he knew she'd been touching herself. Her heart was racing so fast, she couldn't breathe.

"What's the problem?" he asked, tightening his hold to prevent her from letting go of the knife.

"I can't," she whispered, pressing her fingers to his lips to stop his questions. Except he parted them and took her fingers inside his mouth. At, she assumed, the surprise of her taste, passion flamed in his gaze and he exuded a primal growl of satisfaction. "How can I trust you this much?"

The level of desire and emotion this man churned up had the power to consume her. Touching herself in front of any other boyfriend would've turned her off, but Archer wanted the complete package. He wanted to learn about her in every state, even her most private.

He liberated her hand. "Maybe 'cause we both know I had the chance to ruin you and I was too weak to take it.

"Not weak," she said, touching his face. "You still have that power, but it doesn't scare me."

"Then why did you stop?" he asked, directing her hand to her pussy.

"Because I scare myself. It's not like me to be so drawn to a guy, especially one like you… I'm falling hard."

"That's right where I want you," he said and eased her onto her back with one hand.

Loosening her grip on the knife, he directed her hand to her breast then sank back to his crouch, licking her fingertips on the way. He kissed her knee and moved her hand to her pubis.

"Play," he muttered, resting his lips on her knee again.

Sliding her fingers up and down, she found a rhythm that raised her knees. As her toes curled into the blanket, she let her legs fall wide.

"What are you thinking about?" he asked.

His shoulders pressured the inside of her thighs and he directed her fingers down to push them into her opening.

"You," she whispered. "What it feels like when you push your cock into me. Your body, what it does to me when I see your muscles move, when you touch me, when you kiss me…"

"When I do this?" he asked.

His mouth closed around her clit, he sucked hard and flicked it with his tongue.

"Yes," she whimpered then cried out when he did it again. "Yes!"

Her fingers slid free, but he caught her hand and

urged them back inside.

"Keep doing it," he said, working her in and out of herself. "That's hot, Squirm, I like it."

With his hold on her pumping her fingers, he paid her clit special attention until she yelped and reared up.

"Oh, God, Fella, no more!"

Sated and exhausted, her body became boneless. That was when he appeared on top of her, fist around his dick, guiding himself inside. At that first hint of contact, fresh energy infused her, and she hooked her legs around his hips.

Climax had prepared her for him; he slid in deep with one smooth advance.

His hair fell over his brow as he worked his hips faster. She reached for it when he drove a hand under her pelvis, tilting it. At the extreme angle, his head hit her g-spot and she screamed.

No man had ever touched her there and she'd never sought it herself. The intensity of pleasure it delivered tightened her breathing.

"Oh! Arch! Fella! It's… too much! Too much!"

A short reprieve came when he pulled out to roll her to her stomach. Yanking up her hips, he plunged into her from behind. With her ass in the air and her face buried in the bed, she opened her mouth and dug her teeth into the comforter, muffling a scream.

From her hips, his hands leaped to her shoulders, and he propelled himself into her so hard, he hit her limit. Surging onto her hands, she screamed in unison with his guttural growl when they collided in orgasm together.

Still on her hands and knees with him behind her, she was panting and searching for something to say when there was a knock on her front door.

Startled upright, her back bounced on his chest. He threw a strong forearm around her waist to balance them both high on their knees.

"Who the fuck could that be?" she whispered, in case they chose not to answer it.

"Forgot to say, your boyfriend's coming over." He kissed the groove where her neck met her shoulder and jumped off the bed to grab his jeans. "Toss some clothes on, Squirm. Don't want your boyfriend to know I've been handling your goods."

TWENTY-NINE

BARE-CHESTED AND with nothing on his feet, Archer was still buckling his jeans as he hopped across the room to open the front door. She scarcely had the chance to scramble off the bed to snatch his tee shirt before he opened it. In true Archer style, he anticipated her need for time and didn't let their visitors in straight away.

She pulled the tee shirt over her head and leaped to her feet. His seed was still warm and wet inside her. The bed was a mess. The stench of sex permeated the air and she had no way to ventilate the room. There was no denying what they'd just done. The only part of the skylight that opened was in the bathroom and even that had to be done with a long hook-ended pole, hardly subtle.

Hunting in her top drawer for panties, she leaped into the first pair she found and had just pulled them over her knees when Archer opened the door and Tag came in with Gio behind him.

"We've got company, honey!" Archer called out with a hint of condescension in his voice, not aimed at her but at the men he'd just invited inside.

It was ridiculous to presume she wouldn't have known people had arrived when the studio was so tiny. The knock would've been heard in every corner. The fact it had also taken them time to answer indicated they may have had a conversation before Archer got to answering it.

Fumbling her fingers through her hair, she had no hope of taming it. When she bent to straighten out the bed, she nicked her fingertip on the blade lost in the sheets. Hissing at the pain, she pressed the growing bud of blood to her lips.

They'd been lucky the knife hadn't sliced them during their frantic screwing. Grabbing it up, she guessed the sheath was still on his belt, and he didn't like being unarmed. Although Tag would be no threat to their safety, so he shouldn't need a weapon. Still, returning it gave her an excuse to join the men.

Choosing not to leave them alone any longer than necessary, she passed through the bedroom curtains and pulled them down to conceal the bed. Though the attempt to cover up what they'd been doing was pathetic. From Tag's glare, it was clear he knew exactly what had been happening before he knocked on that door.

Gio looked no friendlier. In contrast, Archer seemed relaxed, with a wide stance and his arms folded, there was almost a smile on his face. Whatever he was playing at, it looked like he'd succeeded in his goal. What exactly had been said during his and Tag's phone conversation?

It hadn't slipped his mind that Tag was coming over, he'd chosen not to tell her. She'd guess he orchestrated this to play out exactly as he wanted it to. Which was why she didn't loosen her scowl when he glanced at her.

"Hi," she said, flashing a smile at Tag and Gio as they went into her living room to seat themselves on the couch in front of the curtain that concealed the bedroom.

"What took you so long to answer the door?" Gio barked. "What the fuck were you doing?"

"Enjoying my Cheerios," Archer said.

When Tag and Gio sought out a bowl, or other evidence of cereal, there was none.

Showed what they knew. Even if they had just eaten cereal, the bowl would be gone by now anyway. Archer was too meticulous about tidying up to leave dirty plates lying around.

Still sucking on her finger, she snuck around Archer after he noticed the knife. Without a care or doubt, he trusted her behind him with this slick blade that she could easily slide into his back. Then again, she'd had it in her hand while her face was level with his dick; a guy would probably consider that a greater display of trust.

Grabbing the horizontal sheath attached to his belt, she made sure the blade was in its slot before giving it a hard shove to lodge it in its secure pouch. Archer smiled at her over his shoulder and reached around to grab her hand.

"Thanks, Squirm," he said, elevating her finger to examine her wound.

Suspicious of his motive and his mood, she stayed wary. "Don't mention it."

"You'll think twice before you start the knife play next time," he murmured, kissing her injury then sucking her bleeding fingertip into his mouth, salving it with his tongue.

"You take his knives to bed?" Gio asked. Tag's lips thinned further. "Isn't that all kinds of crazy? Figured he should be smarter than that, thought he was supposed to be some kind of pro."

She popped out from behind Archer; he didn't relinquish his hold.

"If he wasn't, I'd have a lot more wounds," she said. Trying not to share her suspicion with the room, she changed the subject. "Do you guys want a drink?"

"No," Tag said, snapping the word. "Archer told me he'd made progress, I'm here to find out what it is."

"Progress?" she asked.

To get away from the tantalizing motion of her man's tongue running around her finger, she yanked her hand free and went to sit on the coffee table in front of Tag.

Archer took a chair from the kitchen table and turned it around as he brought it over, then dropped down to sit astride it, angled toward the couch. Between her need for sleep and their sex just now, she hadn't had time to find out what had happened last night.

"I may have figured something out that will save your ass," Archer said, tilting his head to scratch his ear before he folded both forearms along the back of the chair. "Hexam doesn't want money and he doesn't need your professional services. He sure doesn't want you involved in his operation… obviously, 'cause you're a fuckwit."

"Ah!" she said, raising a pointed finger to each of the men. "We're on the same side, no jibes, Fella. And Tag, don't forget you need to know what Archer knows."

Though Tag's cheeks puffed a little as he grinded his teeth, he eventually exhaled and forced a smile.

"What does that leave?" he asked. "This is your great plan? How can I pay off a man who has no use for me?"

"He has a use," Archer said. "A personal one."

"Personal?" she asked, not sure she liked the concept of Tag being personally involved with a guy like Hexam.

"He has a personal problem."

Again, Archer wasn't looking at her; he rarely did when business was being discussed. He would answer if she asked a question, it wasn't like he ignored her, but he did have a habit of focusing on the men, rather than addressing her direct.

"What?" Tag asked.

"Hexam has a sister," Archer said. "A beautiful one, young and naïve, but vivacious. He's kept Farrah protected for years. Their parents were killed when they were kids, he's always cared for her."

Relations in the room were already strained; introducing more attitude didn't help.

"What's that got to do with us?" Gio asked.

"It's got fuck all to do with you," Archer said, displaying no patience with Tag's number two. "There's a guy in her life, Hexam doesn't trust him, thinks he's only interested in infiltrating the operation and is bad for his baby sister. Hexam wants rid."

Dread increased. "Rid?" she asked. "I thought you said he didn't order hits."

"He doesn't want him dead," Archer said, then conceded. "No, he probably does, but that's not what he's asking you to do. See, if Farrah knows her brother's involved, she'll rebel. She's got that Modern Woman Syndrome; thinks she knows better than the men in her life."

Her mouth opened to argue, but Archer winked at her and she lost her bluster.

"Hexam doesn't want to be pushed out of Farrah's life," Gio said.

Archer bobbed his head in a loose nod. "Right. He has to be subtle about booting this guy to the curb and that means letting her think it's her idea. Best way to do that is to introduce other options. Scaring him under the radar, you know, bar brawl gone wrong, didn't work. And if any of his own guys make a move on her it will be obvious what they're doing."

These guys were willing to go to any lengths to get what they wanted and seemed to be experts at considering contingencies and outcomes. Manipulation upon manipulation. Annoyance curled her fingers tight around the edge of the coffee table.

She growled out frustration. "This is so typical of men. This girl has made a choice about who she wants to be with, what gives him the right to screw with her relationship?"

"We don't give a fuck," Archer said. "'Cause this is your way out. Your only way. Seduce the sister away from the boyfriend and Hexam will forgive everything. If you fail, it's over."

Tag sat back and raised both hands over his head to drape them over the back of the couch. "I'm supposed to screw his little sister and that will make everything better?"

Archer's slow blink was unimpressed. "I don't think the point is to screw her. I think the point is to seduce her," he said. "There's a difference."

Another frown. Yes, Archer was definitely in condescending mode.

She scoffed. "Not with you there isn't, Fella," she said, only half teasing.

Granting her the steady gift of eye contact, he didn't flinch. "Comes from you being so easy, horny one. You're begging for sex before your eyes open in the morning."

"I'm competing with breakfast," she sneered. "I have to put my order in early."

"Serving you is the highlight of my day. Nothing tastes better in the morning."

Okay, so their conversation might be antagonistic, but she was feeling that rumbling awareness that came with the increase in her pulse rate. This was foreplay. Archer's seductions may not be typical, but that made them no less intense.

"You guys want to put each other down for ten minutes and focus on the actual problem?" Gio snapped.

He was right. Shaking herself from her distraction, she slapped her hands onto Tag's thighs.

"This is a gift," she said. "You have a way with women, you can do this. You can make her think about being with you. Once she realizes she's attracted to you, she'll dump this other guy. We'll figure out how to set up a couple of chance meetings, take her out for a meal. Flirt it up. Kiss her."

"Yeah," Gio said. "Then we get the boyfriend to catch you together, and the relationship will fall apart."

Concern took her attention to Archer. "What do you know about the boyfriend? Is he stable?"

This wouldn't be such a gift if Tag got himself slaughtered for seducing a woman he hadn't even been interested in in the first place.

"The way I see it is this," Archer said. "Your boy here is at risk of harm either way. From what I know about the sister, she's stubborn when it comes to her brother, but flighty and not used to the attention of men. Guys have always been too afraid to make a move. But, for sure, she's a flirt... she wasn't shy about flirting with me."

She was on her feet before she'd even thought to stand. "You were flirting with the gangster's sister? Flirting with another woman?"

His tone and expression stayed level. "She was in the room for about thirty seconds," Archer said. "I was there to talk to Hexam but happy I got a look at her, and a feel for what she's like. It will help. There was nothing to it, Squirm."

Working in a bar, she flirted with men all the time, it meant nothing. "Nothing to it," she said and frowned at the tone of her voice.

It didn't sound like her to be irrationally jealous over a casual flirtation.

Archer was relaxed. "I knew she was interested when I caught her checking me out. Getting a feel for her was important. I'd heard on the street Hexam's only issue was getting his sister away from this guy, I had to know how easy it would be to do that."

"So that's what you meant the other night," Tag said. "When you said you had an idea."

"You can't come at him with business, you'll insult him," Archer said. "He thinks he's the best, better than you, that's for damn sure. He has an ego."

Who didn't? Definitely every man in this room. Every man she'd met was guilty of having one of those.

"This is the only personal problem he has. If you fix it, he'll forgive you," she said. "I'd rather you do this than sell your soul to him forever."

Gio had been quiet for too long. With his next words she figured out what he'd been mulling.

"What if we just got rid of the boyfriend?" Gio asked. "How would Hexam feel about that?"

"He doesn't order hits," Archer said. "Nya reminded you of that like two minutes ago. Are you paying attention, wingman?"

Gio was nodding. "I know he doesn't order it, but it would solve his problem and save Tag from having to catch this girl's eye. What if she's not attracted to him?"

"She's attracted to you," Tag said to Archer.

Oh, God, did—she was horrified to hear her friend make such a suggestion. Archer laughed and leaned back. Clutching the back of the chair, he took it onto its two front legs before dropping it down again.

"Yeah," he said. "You'd like that. I'll solve your little problem by screwing the princess and fuck up my relationship with Nya in the process. Sorry, shithead, that's not gonna happen."

"I agree," she said.

Agreed with the sentiment, not the insult.

Something about their last sex session must have

screwed with her head. She seemed to be reacting and speaking without thinking through the whys and consequences. She'd been willing to give up her life to protect Tag's location, but she wouldn't give up her relationship with Archer when this was something her friend could do himself.

Skirting the coffee table, she went to Archer and put her hands to his bare shoulders. Bending as she slid them around him, she laid her cheek against his.

"You've got me, Squirm, don't worry," he assured her on a murmur. "My cock's going nowhere."

"Archer's gone way beyond what you would've done for him," she said to Tag.

"I have to stay neutral anyway," Archer said after kissing her arm. "I can only broker these deals 'cause I have no investment in the outcome. That's the only reason I can walk into Hexam's place and walk out again with all my limbs. He trusts me. Just as I can be paid to give out information I extract, I can be paid for my silence too… If I screwed the princess, Hexam would know I did it to protect you and would want to know why. I'm not opening myself to that kind of scrutiny."

Reading between the lines, he meant he wasn't opening *her* to that kind of scrutiny. Archer was only involved in this because of her and her connection to Tag. It wouldn't take long for someone like Hexam to figure that out.

"It's your call," Archer said. "I can tell Hexam you'll do it and he'll set it up for you to meet his sister. It will have to look random, and you can't tell her what's going on."

Gio straightened up. "All you have to do is kiss her, we'll make sure the boyfriend sees it."

Something so simple. She stood up, sliding her hands to the sides of Archer's neck and down his shoulders again.

Hexam's sister must mean the world to him and protecting her was his priority. Neither she nor Tag could argue with that level of allegiance. Although they weren't blood, they had a similar relationship; she'd proved that by watching Jamie die instead of giving up her friend.

When her absent stroking took her hand into Archer's hair, he caught it and brought it around to kiss her brand. Immediately, she tensed. Shit. The brand. Archer's tee shirt was huge on her, but the sleeves were nowhere near long enough to cover her wrists. Her cuff was in the bathroom.

"Uh, excuse me," she said, side-stepping to hurry away.

Except before she could get too far, Archer caught her hand.

His brows clamped together. "What's wrong?" he asked, probably sensing her anxiety.

"Nothing," she said. The word was too hurried for him to believe it. Mr. Human Lie Detector knew there was something up. "I'm going to the bathroom."

Clutching her branded wrist to her chest, she widened her eyes at him. Her need to cradle her limb betrayed her secret and he let her go. Hurrying to the bathroom, she found her cuff, and strapped it on fast. When she came back out, she swiped up the towel she'd dropped when trying to get Archer's attention.

She folded it as she went back to the men. All three were on their feet.

"That cuff again," Tag said. "It's so important to you."

Moving in at Archer's side when he extended his arm around her shoulders, she hooked her thumb in his belt loop.

"Yeah," she said, wearing a smile, praying he wouldn't ask any more about it. Because Gio was on his way to the door, she guessed they were making their exit. "You guys just got here; you're leaving already?"

"We have some stuff to work out," Tag said. "I'll call you later."

She showed them to the door and Tag kissed her cheek before disappearing down the hallway. Closing the door, she leaned against it. Archer reached past her to secure the locks.

"You have a lot to answer for," she said, prodding a finger into his chest. "You set that up so we'd be having sex when they got here."

"Yeah," he said, not bothering to deny it. "His attitude on the phone pissed me off. He's got no fucking right to ask what we do with each other. This is our business, not his."

From a man who needed to always know everything about everyone, that seemed like a ridiculous thing for him to get his back up about. That said, privacy was important to her, so she appreciated him defending theirs.

"Okay," she said, "but what would you have done if we hadn't finished?"

He didn't answer her question, just did the locks, then pressed his palms to the door on either side of her head, pinning her in. "And what about you?"

"What about me?"

"Didn't have you pegged as the jealous sort."

Her inhale was joined by an eye roll. "You declared in front of a room full of guys that you were flirting it up with some young, gorgeous, probably dangerous woman."

"I didn't say gorgeous."

"You said she was beautiful," she said. The difference between the two words was so negligible that semantics weren't going to change anything. "It doesn't matter. As soon as I opened my mouth I felt like an idiot. You can flirt with whoever you want, just don't touch."

"Okay, good deal. So long as you know you've nothing to be jealous of."

"I do. What are we going to do for the rest of the day while Tag makes his decision?"

He put an arm around her again to lead her away from the door. "I'm in the mood for Cheerios," he said, burying his face in her hair.

Smiling, she turned her face toward his chest. "Then Cheerios it is."

THIRTY

"THIS ISN'T RIGHT," she said, looking into the plate of sumptuous food just put down in front of her.

"What's wrong with it," Archer asked, leaning over the table to peer at her plate as he gnawed on a meatball. "Looks fine. You haven't tasted it."

"Not the food."

They'd come back to Louie's and had the same reception. The atmosphere was cozy, it wasn't quite as busy that night and they'd received such an enthusiastic welcome that she got a free bottle of wine into the bargain. Archer must've done some recent work for someone associated with this place.

"Then what?" he asked, scooping up more food. "The wine?"

"No, it feels wrong to be sitting here safe and happy when Tag could be in danger."

It had taken another ten days to work out the details between the parties and set up the con for Hexam's unsuspecting sister. None of the men had a problem with what they were going to do to Farrah Hexam. She voiced her unhappiness several times but was ignored until she just gave up arguing.

It didn't matter how many times Archer tried to explain that this was business, and it would bail Tag out, it didn't feel right to play with a woman's emotions. Though he also pointed out, if Farrah was that into her current boyfriend, Tag wouldn't turn her head. So they'd just have to wait and see how everything played out.

"In danger on a date?" he asked, not sharing her apprehension. "Her sexual tastes are vanilla; you have nothing to worry about."

It was her turn to be unimpressed. "I don't want to know how you know that."

He smiled. "No, you probably don't."

She refrained from making a sound of disgust. "What if he's in trouble?"

His impatience didn't slow his eating, nothing did. It annoyed her that he could be so loose about Tag making a move on Hexam's sister with only Gio nearby for support. Though it probably served her better that Archer was focused on his food rather than turning his irritation into anger.

"The whole reason you made us come out was so we were ready and could move fast if we had to."

Eating at Louie's hadn't been her original request, it had been a compromise. "We could help quicker if we'd gone to the club they're at."

"She's seen my face," he said. "I can't be too close. And your boyfriend has his own reinforcements hanging nearby. He doesn't need you."

"I'd feel better if I knew he was safe. What if—"

Archer's fork clattered to his plate, startling her into silence. In the same move, he sat straight, slamming both palms to the table.

"This has to stop."

Surprised by his abrupt action, she took a few seconds to stutter. "Wha… what?"

"I love you, baby, you gotta know that, but your obsession with Taggert is a buzz kill."

Offended, his outburst didn't ease her anxiety, in fact it made her madder. "I'm not obsessed with him," she said. "He's my friend. You might enjoy going through life without anyone to worry about except yourself, but the rest of us need to connect with other humans."

"I got plenty of human connections," he said, bowing over the table. "Wait 'til we get home and my cock will spend the night connecting with your throat, will that be human enough for you?"

Maybe he was insecure, but she'd never given him any reason to think there was anything beyond friendship between her and Tag.

"He's like my brother, would you be this pissed if I was worried about my brother?"

"Like a brother is not the same as a brother," he said. "And he doesn't think of you as a sibling, you heard his dig about setting me up with Hexam's sister. He wants us apart."

"Hexam wants his sister away from her boyfriend and they are siblings. What Tag is doing is the same thing. He's trying to protect me 'cause he thinks you're bad for me."

"Why?" Archer demanded. "I challenge him to compare the limit of what he'll do for you to what I would."

Stabbing at her plate, she tried her food. "I've told you before, it's not a competition."

"Listening to you talk about him makes me think it is. Would you be this worried about me?"

"You wouldn't be on a date with a gangster's sister," she said, forcing the pasta down her throat. "You should be supportive. You should realize he's important to me."

His shoulders went up. "What the fuck else could I do but eat the girl's pussy for him! I saved his ass and got nothing but shit from him. Where's the gratitude?"

"Is that what this is about?" she asked. "God, men are such—"Although it wasn't the relevant point, her concentration glued on something she'd missed that now smacked her in the chest. "Wait, you… you said you love me."

"So what?" he grumbled, hunching over his plate and forking up some spaghetti.

"So what?" she asked, unable to believe he'd be that clueless. "You fucking love me and you say, 'so what?' Like it's no big deal."

"If you hadn't figured it out already you need your

head checked," he said, swiping his beer bottle from the table to glug half of it down.

Being with him was like nothing she'd experienced. Her own feelings ran deep, but it hadn't occurred to her he might be ready to declare his own. And, bam, it was out in the open without awkwardness or hesitation.

Anger was gone and she was almost breathless. "Fella," she whispered, resenting the table between them.

Sliding out of her seat, she swept around to his side of the booth and had just sunk down beside him when he slammed the bottle onto the table. His eyes moved over her body, watching her actions like he wasn't sure what she might do next.

"What are you doing over here?" he asked. "Go back to your own side."

He could see over her head, so it wasn't like she was blocking his view of anything interesting going on in the restaurant. She stroked her hands up his jacket, under his collar, then over it to clasp his jaw.

"I love you too, Archer. You infuriate me and I never know what you're thinking but… I love you."

"Then you'll have to get over the obsession."

He wasn't asking her to choose, just to talk about Tag less. And that night, after what he'd revealed, she was okay with that.

"I guess I'll have to find something else to obsess over then."

"I'll help you out with that," he said, wrapping his fingers in her hair at the back of her head, he pulled it back to drop his mouth to hers.

Archer loved her and she'd admitted to feeling the same. Neither of them was running for the hills, not yet. Tag was out with the girl who was going to save his life. If her friend succeeded, they'd never have to worry about Hexam ever again.

"Archer," she said, easing away from their kiss.

"What?" he asked, seeking her kiss again.

She resisted because she had something to say. Over the last ten days they'd been focused on solving Tag's problem. With that out of the way, she could think about her own mission. It was time.

"I'm ready."

"Ready for what?" he asked, keeping one hand at the back of her head while the other snagged her chin, forcing their kiss.

"To take them down."

Kissing was forgotten when he became serious and frowned at her. "You're sure?"

She nodded. "We had a deal and I'm calling it in."

TO BE CONTINUED...

Thank you for reading this tale!
If you can, please take the time to review.

~

Ask your local library for more Scarlett Finn
novels!

~

For all things Scarlett Finn
check out:

www.scarlettfinn.com

BOOK TWO

scarred

scarlett finn

OUT NOW!

www.ingramcontent.com/pod-product-compliance
Lightning Source LLC
Chambersburg PA
CBHW051255210726

48287CB00002B/521